Totally Bou

The Words to Bind

The Playgrounds

THE WORDS TO BIND

P. STORMCROW

THANKS FOR READING!

The Words to Bind
ISBN # 978-1-83943-891-2
©Copyright P. Stormcrow 2020
Cover Art by Louisa Maggio ©Copyright May 2020
Interior text design by Claire Siemaszkiewicz
Totally Bound Publishing

Published in 2020 by Totally Bound Publishing, United Kingdom.

THE WORDS
TO BIND

Dedication

To my families, on and offline, without whom
none of this would be possible.

Chapter One

What the hell am I doing here?

Luna Weir stared at the mirror above the sink, tapping the porcelain rim as she bit her lower lip, studying herself. The woman in the mirror looked almost sickly, her features lost in the pale complexion framed by almost-silver hair. The only spots of color were the startling blue of her eyes and the red lips that were bruised from being chewed raw. Nervousness was making her twitch this way and that.

She was in no shape to meet new people.

Outside the public washroom she was in was a group of pure strangers sitting down to have a nice Sunday brunch together. If it were any other networking event, Luna would stride out there with all the confidence of an ambitious newbie in the industry.

But this was not a professional meetup — and the topic at hand wasn't what she would call work-safe.

Eating with strangers... Talking about kinks and fetishes...

Why am I doing this again? Right... She'd said she would give this one last shot.

'We're done, Luna. I get you want my opinion, but stop making me make all the decisions. It's exhausting. You're just too intense. Look... I wish you luck, but I'm not the guy for you.'

She winced at the memory. He'd also expressed other choice words, like what he thought about her lack of enthusiasm in bed. It was true. She had a low libido. And yet, she couldn't reconcile the earlier memories of how turned on she'd been by even the faintest idea of something kinky. *That's why I'm here, right?*

Luna startled as the toilet flushed behind her. A woman emerged from the stall, a bounce of impossible red curls matched with impossible stilettos. She was stunning, with brilliant hazel eyes lighting up at the sight of...something.

Wait... She can't be looking at me, can she?

"Hello, sweetie. Luna, right?"

Oh God. Oh God. Oh God.

Luna mustered a smile, watching as the woman walked up to the sink next to her with a sway of hips and washed her hands. A pang of envy stabbed through her. The woman oozed confidence and swagger in a way she only wished she could emulate.

"I'm Lani, the hostess for the munch this month." She smiled, glowing with warmth, and Luna could not help but relax just a smidgen.

"Yeah, I'm Luna. Nice to meet you." *Always be nice to the hostess.*

"Let me guess... You've come up with a case of nerves and that's why you're hiding in here?" Lani leaned forward, but before Luna could protest, she added with a lowered whisper, "It's okay. My first time, I hid in here most of the munch and kept peeking out until the last person had left." She winked and tilted her head toward Luna, as if sharing a conspiracy.

She couldn't imagine the self-assured woman in front of her afraid of anything, but somehow, it made her feel better.

"Now, if you're feeling lost, why don't you come sit with me? I can point out who's who."

Luna stared at the offered arm, beginning to wonder why she had been so scared before. They were just people—people like her. Okay, she was nothing like Lani, the indomitable force, but Luna found her easy manner hard to resist. She looped her arm around the other woman's and nodded. "All right, I can do this. Lead the way!"

Lani tossed her head back and laughed. "That's the spirit!"

The waiter was just arriving to take people's orders just as they made their way to the long table in an alcove at the back of the restaurant. As Luna sat, the waiter came around with a friendly smile.

"And what can I get for you today?"

It was an easy decision for a sugar fiend like her. "French toast, please, with the whipped cream and strawberries."

"Sure."

Surprise made her turn with as much discretion as possible to study Lani as she ordered the same. The woman flashed her a quick grin and nodded toward the rest of the table, an invitation to look.

Luna ventured to observe the people around the group. Seven, including herself, rounded the table— three on each side with Lani at the head. She was seated to Lani's left, while to her own right was a lanky man with a mop of light brown hair and rimmed glasses. Across from her was another woman about her age, a slim Asian who was built like a ballerina. A couple sat farther down the table across from her, but she could only catch an occasional glimpse of the last person on her side. From what Luna could tell, the three at the other end of the table were deep in discussion about the best flogging techniques. She bit her lower lip, memories surfacing before she clamped down hard on them. A distant echo of a sensation — the pain — and the sheer lack of pleasure.

"Luna, I'd like you to meet Cassandra and August."

Thankful for the distraction, Luna gave a little awkward wave.

"Oo-o, fresh meat," the girl across from her squealed.

"Cassie, stop trying to scare her off. Not everyone's competition," August cut right in.

"Was not!" she protested in return.

The man ignored her and turned toward Luna instead with a cordial incline of his head. "So, Luna, what brings you to the munch?"

Although she appreciated the save, *wow...biting*. To the question he'd directed at her, she answered without hesitation. "Curiosity." It was the answer she'd prepared before she'd left her apartment.

Lani's eyes sharpened with interest and Luna braced herself for more questions. Instead, Lani grinned and clapped her hands together. "Excellent answer." She lifted a long-stemmed glass of orange liquid to her lips and Luna wished she had ordered a mimosa too. She could use some liquid courage.

"So, has anyone heard about the private play party Erica and Dominique are throwing in a few weeks?" Lani was quick to open the topic.

She had heard about these play parties before in her chat room.

"I heard it was invitation only?" August asked with a lift of his brow.

Cassandra—or Cassie, as everyone else seemed to call her—grinned like a cat with a large bowl of milk. "Guess who already got an invitation?"

August ignored her again and instead turned to Lani. "Ma'am, would you happen to know who would be attending?"

Ma'am. Things snapped into focus. Lani was a Dominant and August was likely submissive. Or did their relationship go deeper than that? *Wait...* Did they have a relationship of any sort?

"Well, Jacob and Darryl are both going to be there, I believe, though I think Jacob may be working as a dungeon monitor. Erica mentioned she also invited a shibari master to come to demonstrate."

Dungeon monitor, shibari... These were all terms Luna knew, in theory. A voice in her head suggested that she should make a hasty exit right about now. It was one thing to keep things online. Words were easy, sexy. The one time it had spilled to real life... Luna opened her mouth to make her excuse to leave.

"French toast for the ladies." The waiter set the plates down and Luna snapped her mouth shut, lest drool escape. *Okay, maybe after the food.*

Decadent pieces of brioche, dipped and fried in batter, were layered on top of each other, with bright red syrup drizzled over them. Slices of fresh strawberries spilled from the top, held in place by a generous mound of whipped cream, which was topped by a single large strawberry. A light dusting of powdered sugar provided the finishing touch to the delectable dish.

Heaven on a plate.

Luna licked her lips, beholding the indulgence set before her. Given the choice of food or sex, she would pick food...every time. Tempted to dig right in but aware that manners dictated that she should wait, she reached for her glass instead, to take a sip of water.

"Is it just me or does that look like a boob with a red nipple?"

Oh God. Luna's eyes watered and she started coughing as liquid went down the wrong way. She turned from the table and bent over, struggling for breath as her face was likely turning red as a tomato, or in this case, the strawberry in the discussion.

"Cassie!" Lani exclaimed, though she was stifling a giggle. She turned to Luna after realizing she was choking on the comment and the hostess patted her back. "Oh dear. Here. Breathe, sweetie. Drink more water."

"What? It's true!"

Recovering, Luna sat back up in her chair and eyed her plate. Now she couldn't unsee it. Her gaze traveled to Cassie, who gave her a quick wink, and she wondered if the woman had made the crass comment on purpose in an attempt to help ease her nerves. Well, that would be what Luna chose to believe.

As the food arrived for everyone else, Luna took her fork and knife in each hand. Inhaling to summon her humor, she grinned, mischief tugging the corner of her lips upward. "Well then, let's deconstruct this boob!"

It earned her a round of laughter and helped silence her nagging doubts for a moment.

Over the meal, chatter ranged from the mundane to the kinky. Content to just listen, Luna adopted the strategic approach of pacing her eating so that there were no expectations for her to join in on the conversation. Even when Lani moved to the other end of the table as part of her hostess duties to mix, Cassie and August kept her entertained with their antics.

Before long, people were settling their bills and saying their goodbyes. Satisfied that she had done what she had set out to do, Luna did the same and attempted an inconspicuous exit.

"Luna!"

She paused and turned, one hand already at the door. Lani approached, a light coat in one hand, a handbag in the other. "Got any plans after this? Wanna grab a coffee?"

Coffee? But didn't we just…? She blinked and tilted her head, only to realize the woman took it as assent.

"Oh goodie. Come on!" Lani guided Luna outside.

Coffee turned out to be two tall iced teas and a meander through a nearby park. The early summer sun had warmed the day and sounds of kids laughing as they ran, conversations from couples lounging on the grass and yips and barks from puppies playing all blended together into pleasant background noise.

"So, what did you think?"

Oh, so here comes the grilling. But somehow, from Lani, Luna didn't mind so much. "It was less scary than I imagined," she admitted.

"Good." Lani stopped and settled on a park bench, patting the spot next to her. When Luna sat, she shifted her body to face her. "Are you fairly new to the scene then?"

Luna took a sip of her tea to buy herself time to formulate the reply. That they had just met and Lani was not far from a stranger hovered on the edge of her consciousness, so Luna took a more conservative route. "Why do you ask?" It came out harsher than she'd intended. She added in a rush. "I mean no disrespect. It's just—"

A hand waved her excuses away. Lani's smile lit up her eyes in amusement. "No, it's a fair question. We're a small community here. Most of us know each other — or at least faces are familiar. When a new person shows up at a munch, not just at the club, I always like to do a little debrief and get to know them."

"You mean The Playgrounds?" It was the only fetish club close by, complete with a public dungeon and private rooms.

"Yeah. We get quite a few tourists there — people just out for thrills or couples wanting to spice things up. The munches are where we know someone is more serious about the lifestyle — and we don't often get new faces."

Oh. She had gone to The Playgrounds a few times by herself but it hadn't given her much to go on. It had been more like a kind of teasing taste without substance. Not that it was a bad place... The music was great, the dancing was hot and people were friendly, but she had felt like another faceless entity in a sea of people. In other words, she'd had no idea what she was doing there.

After a while, Luna realized that there was only silence and she turned toward Lani. The other woman still had on an indulging smile and was waiting, composed with patience.

"I...have some experience." The words came, pauses between each one as she tried to sum it up without going into details. "Most of it was online but I've scened a few times, in private, as a bottom."

"Ah-h." Lani bobbed her head in understanding. "So what aspects are you curious about?"

"The community," Luna blurted out, maybe a little too fast. She wasn't outright lying, but she knew inside that what she'd said wasn't the most foremost reason.

Something in her didn't want to lie to Lani. *Is that my inner submissiveness responding to the presence of a Dom?*

She bowed her head and fiddled with the hem of her T-shirt. "I've tried more 'normal' relationships but the dynamic just never sat right with me. I guess I just want to explore what other possibilities are out there."

"Well, then…"

When Luna looked up, she saw Lani's eyes were sparkling and she swallowed hard. Apprehension mingled with an odd sense of excitement.

"Why don't you come to the private party as my plus one?"

"What" Luna's eyes widened at the unexpected invitation.

"Come on. It'd be fun. It'll be mostly experienced people, so you'll be perfectly safe, and there won't be any pressure. You can observe, look at what appeals to you."

Luna's jaw dropped a little, and she blushed at the idea. "But you hardly know me and —"

For a second time, Lani waved her protests away. "We have time. The party's a few weeks away. I can drill you on the rules to make sure you're ready beforehand and won't get culture-shocked or worry about making a mis-step." The woman beamed and reached out to take her hand. "This is not me hitting on you, in case you're wondering. I just remember how scary and lonely it can be when you're starting out. Many subs get taken advantage of when they first dip their toes into this world, then they never come back. It's sad. You seem nice and I don't want to see you hurt, so I'd be happy to be your guide."

Luna was finding it harder and harder to say no to Lani. Something in her, though, fluttered against the bars of its cage. It was that something that made her nod in agreement.

Memorizing the rules was not a problem — *be respectful, don't interrupt a scene, no touching unless invited, expect the same respect from others and ask if I have any questions*. They were easy, basic and simple rules.

The shopping Lani suggested, however, was a whole new level of exhaustion. Her new guide seemed to have an unending source of energy for hitting up all manners of stores. Luna had no idea that there were so many fetish-wear, goth-wear and lingerie stores in town. Then there were the shoes. *Oh dear God, the shoes.*

By the end, she had begged off, only buying a few outfits, including a corset and two sets of lingerie, on the excuse that she had a limited budget. Lani had been skeptical at first, but Luna had distracted her by pointing out a pair of boots with beautiful tattooed roses across the sides. From there on, she was more of a shopping-assistant-slash-fashion-consultant than anything else. And if she were hard-pressed, she would have to admit that it was fun too.

There was one more thing, an idea of her own. The last thing she wanted was to gawk like a tourist at the more intimate play party, so perhaps some real-life desensitization was in order.

It couldn't hurt, right?

Chapter Two

"You can stop looking so bored any time now," Darryl strolled over to whisper to Jacob, elbowing him after his third yawn.

It was quiet at The Playgrounds, and Jacob almost felt bad for the money Erica and Dominique were paying him for the hours he was going to clock in as a dungeon monitor. He scanned the floor, which consisted mostly of regulars. An older couple was starting a scene by one of the sawhorse play benches, the top just strapping the bottom, accompanying the action with a low murmuring of words. Another woman, sporting only a thong, was bent over and locked in what looked like a medieval stockade. She squealed from time to time as her partner would press a low voltage Taser to one of her rear cheeks. Normally, that kind of play would draw closer attention from the dungeon monitors, but the top had a reputation for his knowledge of how to handle this special brand of kink and the bottom was squirming with a little too much eagerness for any concerns.

Then, *she* walked in.

He'd caught a few glimpses of her at The Playgrounds before but never up here where the public dungeon spanned the second floor. Her pale hair with a paler complexion, combined with her sharp features, reminded him of a delicate fairy. The way she watched everything with an almost childlike curiosity that was reflected in those large baby blue eyes showed that she was likely a tourist, curious after reading *Fifty Shades of Grey*.

And judging by how she pressed herself against a wall, hovering close to the stairs, looking as if she would flee at any minute, it looked like his guess wasn't far off.

Which didn't explain why one look at the little mouse and everything in him had sharpened with interest.

He kept an eye on the ongoing scenes but, to be honest, it was much more interesting to watch her reaction, a blend of apprehension and fascination. Every time the sub squealed from a shock, she jumped. Every time she moaned, the mouse would swallow. At some point, she began to chew her lower lip and Jacob felt an urge to command her to stop. And when her tongue peeked out to wet her lips, he felt a stirring in his groin.

What the hell is wrong with me?

"Looks like we have a newbie voyeur." Darryl kept his voice low, nodding toward Jacob's little mouse.

All of a sudden, Darryl seemed more like competition than a friend. His comment scraped against Jacob's nerves and he had to rein in his temper. In the back of his mind, he could hear Lani's mock-clinical voice asling just how long it had been since he'd played, much less taken on a sub. She had hinted at it before, though not in so many words, during one of their previous sessions. Few would advise to blow off some steam as a solution, but Lani was a pro-kink counselor.

Still, so not my style.

But why did the little mouse intrigue him?

"Interested?"

Startled, Jacob came to realize he'd never replied to Darryl. When he managed to tear his eyes away from the girl, his gaze met his friend's knowing one, complete with a smug smirk. *The prick.* Refusing to dignify that with an answer, he shrugged and turned to the couple on the bench, where the top had begun to employ a paddle. From the corner of his eye, he saw the mouse flinch. *Ah, not into pain play. Good.* Darryl wouldn't be interested as much then, as the bigger man had a sadistic streak in him.

"Well, if you're not, I'm going over for a chat."

Darryl must have missed that flinch, though Jacob didn't blame him, for it was so very subtle. She'd hidden it well. Still, he could feel a growl growing from the back of his throat. The more primal part of him shouted at him, urged him to stake his claim. *Mine.*

Okay, this is getting out of hand. Maybe there was some merit to imaginary-Lani's advice.

A sudden loud clattering jolted him out of his thoughts. All play came to a halt. He turned to see his little mouse flushed bright red, frantic in her attempt to replace the spreader bars back onto their hooks that she had somehow knocked off.

With a growl released for a very different reason, he pushed his way past Darryl to approach the flustered girl.

Something in him softened when he saw how panicked and embarrassed she was. Crouching down, he helped her pick up and remount the bars without a word.

Once they had set everything right again, she turned to him and ducked her head, her eyes not quite meeting his. "I'm really sorry," she murmured beneath her breath.

The submissiveness of her posture tightened his jeans with a shot of lust, and an image of her with her ankles strapped to one of those spreader bars popped in his head. The more logical part of his brain told his libido to take a hike.

"Please refrain from touching the equipment if you are not using it for play." He kept his voice soft but stern. It was his job as a dungeon monitor. In the background, he registered activities beginning to resume once more.

"I'm really sorry," she mumbled again, still staring at the floor.

He stared at her, resisting the urge to tilt her chin up, all too aware of how intimidating he could be, towering over her. No, he didn't want her to be scared of him — quite the opposite. So instead, as if he were consoling her — but, in truth, to soothe the urge in him — he placed a hand on her shoulder and ducked a little to catch her gaze.

Her peasant blouse underneath a mock cincher had left her shoulders bare and her skin cool to touch, and it soothed the heat that radiated from him. When she looked up, his breathing hitched. Up close, her eyes were stunning, the color of serene waters. The earlier turmoil in him calmed.

He opened his mouth to speak, to tell her it was okay.

"Jacob, Erica would like to speak with you," Dominique called out as she walked toward them. At five-foot-nine plus heels, the Amazonian brunette looked over most women's and some men's heads.

Worst timing ever. Jacob snapped his mouth shut and straightened to look up at Dominique, who only inclined her head. As Erica's submissive, she was deferential to many of the regular Dominants at or involved with The Playgrounds. However, none of them were ever under the illusion that Dominique wasn't also an authority herself within these premises. After all, she did have a share in the club's ownership.

"I'll be right there." With a sigh, he flashed the little mouse what he hoped was a warmer smile and dropped his hand from her shoulder to follow Dominique up the stairs.

She took him to the third and top floor of the building, past the long hall with doors leading to the private rooms—some more functional, others more themed, but all catering to different tastes. Toward the end of the hall, the rooms ceded territory to the offices required to run the place.

Arriving at the very last closed door, Dominique rapped her knuckles on the panel of wood then waited for a "Come in" before opening it. "Jacob, as requested, Ma'am." She stepped aside to allow Jacob to precede her.

Erica sat behind her desk, reading glasses perched on her nose as she scanned through the papers in her hand, her legs crossed in composure. Since the woman was blonde and petite, the inexperienced might mistake her at first glance for a submissive, but it would be hard to miss the air of authority that clung to her.

"Good evening, Erica," Jacob greeted, with wariness reflected in every move. Although he had known the majority owner of the club for over a year now as an employee, and longer as a club patron, he was still trying to settle into the right dynamic with her as a fellow Dominant. It didn't help that everyone else had nicknamed her and Dominique 'the two goddesses of The Playgrounds'.

"Good evening, Jacob. Please have a seat." Erica gestured to the chair across from her.

A younger version of him would have stood, just to spite her, but he was past that time of having something to prove. He eased himself into the chair, curiosity keeping him from reclining.

"I wanted to check in with you regarding the party this weekend." Erica pulled the glasses from her face, folded them and placed them on the desk. "Are you sure you don't need me to arrange for someone to relieve you for a shift or two so you have some time to enjoy too?"

Had Lani said something to Erica? *That pest.*

"No, I'm fine with the schedule."

He sat still, aware of Erica's scrutiny. Minutes ticked by before she nodded, as if to herself. "Very well. In that case, I'd like you to keep an eye on someone."

Now that he did not expect. Everyone on the guest list he had seen were people who were well known within their small community. He raised a brow in question.

"Lani asked me for permission to bring a new one to the community, as her personal guest. From what I gathered, this one made an impression when she showed up at the last munch. It also appears that she's likely a sub but is exploring what that means for her. I'd like for you to keep an eye on her."

While he had no problem acting as a dungeon monitor, babysitting was a different matter. He tensed, ready with protests.

"I understand you are quite skilled as a trainer. While I have no expectation for you to do any training at the party, I believe you are in a unique position to answer any questions and ensure that she follows the proper etiquette while she's there."

Damn that woman. When put that way, it was hard to argue with her.

"Are we expecting any trouble?"

"No, Lani has assured me that she has been training this one in the proper protocols of a play party and feels she is ready." Erica's eyes hardened. "And while I trust my guest, I also want to ensure that the new person does not feel pressured into anything before she's ready."

And Jacob understood. It was an unspoken pact for the Dominants in the community to ensure that the subs were protected, especially the new ones, who were the most vulnerable. With a sigh of resignation, he brushed his bangs back. "All right... What's her name?"

"Luna."

Chapter Three

Luna couldn't get him out of her mind. It wasn't even the fact that he fit her type — tall, a bit on the lanky side, dark hair and gorgeous warm brown eyes — or that every single gesture, every word, along with the way he held himself, spoke of dominance. No, it was that damn smile he'd given her, despite her embarrassing klutziness, that had melted her insides. It said to her, "Hello, I'm a Dom, but I know how to have fun and be gentle too."

Okay, she had been building up the guy way too much in her mind the whole week.

Jacob… His name is Jacob. That was what the tall woman had called him when she'd come to fetch him on behalf of another.

She was so out of her depth.

She stared at the little clock on the lower right corner of her computer screen. There were thirty minutes until quitting time. Next, her gaze traveled to the rest of the screen, which showcased the world's most boring document that she should be editing. With a loud groan, she let her head fall to her desk, her forehead landing on it with a dull thud. The play party was the next day and already she had too much nervous energy to focus on work.

Her longtime friend and cubicle neighbor, Ted, popped his head over the wall, peering down at her with curiosity. "What's up, Luna?

She turned her face toward him but kept her head down, her cheek now pressed against the cool surface. Grumbling, she closed her eyes.

"That bad?" Ted rested his chin against the wall, his tone sympathetic. "Chin up. It's minion duties now, but you'll work your way to more advanced stuff soon."

Ted meant well. A few years her senior, he was already leading his own projects. Career-wise, she aspired to be like him. But all she could manage was a grunt in assent.

"Tell you what. I'm meeting Brandon and a few of his friends for drinks. Why don't you come along?"

That caught her attention. Luna opened her eyes and pushed herself upright. "Are you guys introducing each other to friends now?" She already knew Brandon, as he was her sensei from the dojo, and she might have been the one who had introduced the two of them in the first place, but they had yet to all hang out together as a group. Luna remained hands off, letting them develop their relationship at their own pace after her initial push.

The sheepish smile on Ted's face told her everything she needed to know and her heart sang with gladness for her friend. He deserved to have someone good in his life. Things hadn't been easy since he'd come out of the closet.

Which was why, despite the nerves and the fact that she just wanted to sleep until it was time tomorrow, Luna nodded in agreement. "Sure, I'll come."

She began regretting her decision about an hour later when she occupied one of the four seats around a small table at the pub close to work. To her left was Ted. To her right, a 'friend' of Brandon's. He had introduced himself as Dylan. Never mind that Dylan was super cute with his dimpled smile, hippie vibe and climber build. It was a setup and a sneak attack. She didn't dare be mad at her sensei, but Luna vowed to never be supportive of Ted ever again.

Still fuming, she lifted her pint of craft cider to her lips, trying to give herself time to get rid of the scowl that was threatening to break across her face. Dylan didn't deserve that. He looked just as uncomfortable as she did.

"So, Luna, any plans this weekend?" Ted asked, with an innocent smile plastered on his face.

Oh yes, now would be a great time to tell everyone at the table about the play party she was going to. She swallowed and shook her head. "Not particularly," she mumbled. At least she hadn't choked on her drink.

"How about you, Dylan?"

"Well, I was thinking about a climb this weekend. The weather is supposed to be good. Gotta take advantage of that before fall and rain hits."

Well, that confirmed her guess about him being a climber. It was time to be polite and salvage the situation at hand however she could. "What kind of climbing do you do?"

"Nothing too crazy, just top rope and sport climbing. I do some bouldering too but usually more in a gym in the winter." He shifted in his seat, excitement lighting up in his eyes. It was clear as day where the man's passion lay. "Do you climb?"

"Nah." Luna set her drink down. "But I always wanted to try. I've always thought it's a neat challenge, engaging the whole body physically and the mind at the same time."

"Exactly! Lots of people don't get the mental aspect, but it's totally true. It takes careful planning and consideration to figure out the right path up, where the hands and feet should go, given the limitations of your own body and abilities."

Okay, he was adorable. Perhaps she could forgive Ted — a little bit.

"So what happens if you're halfway up and you're stuck?" That had always been a fear of hers and what held her back from trying.

"Well, that's why the ropes. For beginners, we'd more likely start them out at an indoor gym where, if all else fails, they can let go. The rope will keep them up and there are big cushy mats to prevent any injuries." Dylan's voice softened, a shyness creeping in that only endeared him to her. "Would you like to try sometime? I'd be happy to show you the ropes, so to speak."

A pun. It was a pun. He was making a corny climber pun. All Luna could think of, though, was bondage and the shibari master Lani had said would be at the party tomorrow. *Oh dear God.* Her face heated.

"Climbing is also an excellent supplement to your training at the dojo, Luna," Brandon cut in. He sounded so much like a father that it worked to deter her from inappropriate thoughts. "It promotes awareness of your own body and helps develop your sense of balance. I think it'd be worth giving it a shot."

Trapped! But, in this case, she didn't mind. And why the hell not? She was single, and he was cute. The worst that could happen was that she made a new friend instead. That wasn't a a a bad deal. "Sure, I'll take you up on the offer."

"Awesome! This weekend?"

Oh crap. She had just said she wasn't up to anything this weekend, so being busy as an excuse was out. *Something else, quick.* "I don't want to interrupt your outdoor climb. Why don't we book for the following Saturday, if you're free?"

He beamed, his smile reaching from ear to ear. "Sounds good to me. What's your number? I'll text you mine."

Smooth. But she didn't mind smooth. After exchanging numbers, they lapsed back into small talk and Luna felt a smidge more comfortable about the whole thing.

"So, what did you think of Dylan?" Ted insisted on walking Luna to the bus stop. That was sweet but she still glared at him. His knowing smugness only annoyed her further.

"The next time you and Brandon want to set me up with some guy, warn me beforehand, 'kay?"

"Hey, maybe there won't be a next time! You two seemed to hit it off."

"Yeah, yeah, you got lucky. And it's too soon to really tell, Ted, too soon. I don't even know the guy yet."

They came to the bus stop just as Ted chuckled. "Well, let's see how climbing goes then. Text me when you get home, Luna."

"Yes, Dad!" She stuck her tongue out at him as he turned and walked away with a wave.

Between fixing a late dinner, a re-run of the first *Iron Man* — still the best one, in her opinion — and cleaning her apartment the next day, it was time to get ready for the play party before she knew it.

As she stood in front of the bathroom vanity, she struggled with the makeup. Mascara, eye shadow, eyeliner, a dab of lipstick… That was as far as she was willing to go. The makeup was much more subdued than she imagined was appropriate for the event, but she had always been a natural kind of girl. Then she got dressed.

She wasn't sure if there was enough material to call the dress Lani had chosen for her a dress, but it was certainly nothing like she had ever worn in her life. Made of faux leather, the deep V of the garment dipped so low that it almost reached her navel, strings crisscrossing across the peekaboo glimpses of her cleavage. The back was bare, for the most part, save for the strip of material across her upper back to keep the top half of the dress up. The fabric of the bottom half began at about the hip and ended just below the rear. Luna wondered if she was flashing people more with the top of her butt crack or the bottom of her cheeks.

She had promised Lani fishnet stockings and heels to complete the look, so she put them on, but part of her was afraid to look in the mirror. Luckily, her phone went off with a message from Lani saying she was downstairs. Soon there was no time to doubt anymore. She shrugged on a large jacket to cover herself, despite the summer heat, then grabbed a large bag with a change of clothing. After that, she was off.

Lani pouted when she saw Luna approach the car but gestured her inside, nonetheless. When Luna settled, the Domme gave a small chuckle. "Afraid you may run into a neighbor?" The teasing had begun.

"Something like that," Luna mumbled, blushing as she sank lower into the seat.

Instead, she got a sting from a slap to her thigh from Lani. "Ow!"

"Sit up straight. Be proud. Confidence is sexy."

The tone brooked no nonsense and Luna recognized the command in her mentor's voice. She obeyed without another thought, pushing herself up and straightening.

"Good, dolly."

The tone of approval warmed Luna. She recognized that it was what Lani liked to call subs.

"Now, let's go over the rules one more time."

Luna began, "Be respectful. No touching unless invited. Don't interrupt a scene. No recording of any kind. If I have any questions, see a dungeon monitor. Safe, sane and consensual." Luna repeated for the nth time. She didn't mind, though. She understood these rules' importance.

"Good. Don't forget, too, that the touching goes both ways. No one should be touching you if you didn't invite them. If you feel pressured or uncomfortable with something happening, come find me or a dungeon monitor. They'll be wearing a green ribbon around their arm.

Luna nodded once more. "Got it."

"Good. Jacob is the main dungeon monitor tonight. The others are on rotation. So if anything, I'll make sure you get introduced to him right away."

Jacob. Oh God. That *Jacob?* As the memory of the conversation at the munch surfaced in her mind, all the pieces fell into place. *Well, crap.*

What was Mr. Tall, Dark and Dominant going to think of her outfit? Was she going to be able to string a sentence together to save her life? Did he only think of her as the klutz from The Playgrounds?

"Luna?" Lani's hand on her knee jolted her from her panic. Luckily, the Domme's eyes were on the road, so she couldn't have seen the color of her heated cheeks.

"Are you okay?"

"Yeah, just nervous." Luna let out a shaky laugh.

"Relax. You don't have to do anything you don't want to do, okay? Just think of it as research."

Then there was no more time to reply as the car pulled into the driveway of a gorgeous two-story white house that had lights twinkling in the fading sun of a late summer's day. Out here in the suburbs, she was sure few could imagine the perfectly maintained house with the modern architecture behind a fancy black steel gate and tall hedges would be a site of the kinds of debauchery promised tonight. Luna tried her best not to let her jaw drop.

"Well, here we are. Are you ready, sweetie?" Lani asked, grabbing her own bag.

Confidence was sexy. Luna slipped out of the car and shrugged off her coat, slinging it over her arm before retrieving her bag.

"Yeah, as ready as I'll ever be. Let's do this."

Chapter Four

When the same drop-dead gorgeous Amazon of a woman who had called Jacob away at The Playgrounds opened the door, clad in nothing but a lace bodysuit and five-inch stilettos, a sense of awe and intimidation threatened to overwhelm Luna. As she stood three steps behind Lani, she hunched over and shifted her weight from one foot to another, like a child caught playing dress-up among adults.

She kept her eyes downcast as Lani hugged the woman before she entered. Trailing behind, Luna rummaged in her bag to pull out yet another bag, a tall gift one containing a bottle of Zinfandel, and she offered it to the hostess. "Please, Ma'am, accept this gift as a token of gratitude for allowing me to join." Inside, she cringed at how awkward and formal she sounded.

The woman smiled, warmth lighting up her face as she accepted the bag. "Please, simply Dominique is fine. I'm more like you. Thank you. I'll make sure my Mistress receives this." With that, the woman ushered her inside.

Luna blushed in embarrassment for assuming the other was a Dominant. *Great, not even inside yet and already I've blundered.* But then there was no time to berate herself when she stood stunned by the decor of the place.

Every line was clean, sleek and modern. A small stone fountain stood by one side, water gurgling to provide a subtle ambience. Beyond the foyer, light hardwood flooring stretched into a semi-open concept to meet with large windows that let the light of the setting sun bathe the place in warm oranges and reds. The living room was immaculate, like something out of a showcase spread in an interior decorating magazine.

To her left, she heard laughter drifting from what must be the kitchen. Still following Lani's lead, Luna stepped inside.

A small crowd had gathered around the massive kitchen island, onto which was placed a large charcuterie platter in the middle and punch, coffees and teas to one side. There was no alcohol. For a minute, the mundaneness caught Luna by surprise, but she kicked herself for it. She had been so focused on the play element that she had forgotten about the party part.

Her gaze followed Dominique, who had approached and remained behind a small blonde in a golden corset. She noted that the sub waited until a break in the conversation between the blonde and someone else before leaning down to whisper in her ear. Already, her own nature was taking mental notes of what they deemed appropriate behavior.

The woman, whom she assumed was Dominique's Mistress, smiled at the gift and looked their way before she sauntered over in confident strides.

"Lani!" The two greeted each other with a hug before Lani took a step back. "Erica, may I introduce my friend Luna."

Luna had the strongest urge to curtsey, not that she knew how. Instead, she inclined her head. "Good evening, Mistress Erica. Thank you for having me at this party."

"Heavens, are you sure the girl is new at this?" Erica asked Lani.

"Nah, just a natural," her friend replied, and Luna wasn't sure if she should be proud or not. Actually, with the bundle of nerves she was, she wasn't sure what else she should be feeling.

Erica eyed Luna before turning to address her. "You are welcome, little one—and my thanks for the gift. Please relax and enjoy yourself."

Something must have drawn Erica's attention, as she looked up and over Luna's shoulder, and Luna had to resist the urge to look with her. Erica gave a wave to whoever it was that must have just entered the kitchen then gave them both a polite smile. "Please excuse me for a moment."

As Erica and Dominique walked off, Luna swallowed hard, only to feel Lani's hand on her with an encouraging smile. "You're doing great. You even impressed Erica—and that's no small feat."

"Oh." Luna sucked in a breath. "She was a bit...intimidating," she admitted.

Lani laughed, keeping her voice soft. "Of course. Those are the two goddesses of The Playgrounds." At Luna's blank stare, Lani giggled harder. "The owners."

"Oh!"

"Lani, may I speak with you for a minute?" someone called out from behind them, although Luna wasn't sure who it was. Panic welled in her at the thought of being left alone. She didn't want to be that clingy friend at a party, and she knew that at some point Lani would leave to scene, but she couldn't hold back her fears.

Something must have shown on her face. Lani reached out to take her hand and gave it a reassuring squeeze. "I won't be long. Go eat something and I'll be back before you know it."

Luna smiled gratefully and nodded. She squared her shoulders in an attempt to recover that bravado from earlier and threaded her way to the kitchen island.

The various cheeses and meats had her mouth watering and, bit by bit, her nerves calmed. A rather succulent-looking prosciutto next to the most beautiful wheel of brie she'd ever seen caught her eye. She grabbed a plate and made a beeline for it, only for her hand to be brushed by someone else's. Startled, she looked up to stare into the dark chocolate brown eyes from the other night.

Her mind blanked.

Surprise made the man's eyes widen before one brow arched. How the hell could a man have such long lashes and perfectly shaped brows? It was a crime against all women.

No, the smile that came next was the crime against all women.

"Go ahead."

Crap...his voice. Low and smooth. Luna swallowed and thought she may have found her voice. "Thank you, Master." She drew another blank at his name. "Sir..." Her voice was squeaking and she kicked herself. He was just a guy.

"Jacob. Here..." He chuckled and turned, taking a small cheese knife to cut a piece of brie, then placed it on her plate. Next, he took a small fork and speared a piece of the prosciutto, dropping that onto her plate as well.

Dear God, the 'just-a-guy' is feeding me.

"Thank... Thank you, Master Jacob." Inside, she willed herself to stop stammering.

"Jacob!" Lani's voice rang out from behind, causing both of them to turn. *Lani to the rescue!* As she approached, she placed a reassuring hand on Luna's back and pivoted them both to face Jacob once more. "I see you've met Luna. She's here as a guest of mine."

"Luna." There was that surprise in his eyes again. "I see. Well, welcome to the party."

"Luna, remember that Jacob is the main dungeon monitor tonight, so if you have questions, you can go to him."

She nodded a little, though she wondered if she could even formulate a sentence around the man. She had never been so flustered around anyone in her life. Well, one. Sorta.

Jacob's eyes captured hers, reminiscent of that night at The Playgrounds, and, with that, she was barely aware of anyone else being around.

"Yes. And if there's something you're uncomfortable with any time, please come to me right away. I'll be on the floor," he offered.

The floor?

"Ah, Jacob, why don't you take Luna and show her around the main areas. I think Erica and Dominique are going to be busy for a while playing hostesses."

"Sure."

Luna half expected to be scrambling after him — or at least following behind. Instead, Jacob gestured for her to go ahead. She cast a last glance back at Lani, only to see her give a wide grin and a wink. It was so reminiscent of Ted that the realization whacked her over the head. Lani was matchmaking.

And was that such a bad thing?

Her stomach did a little flip at the unbidden question in her head. It was just a tour of the place. She didn't have to answer any complicated questions or decide yet. He. Was. Just. A. Guy.

She flashed Jacob a small smile of gratitude in an attempt at recovery, then started walking in the direction he'd indicated to leave the kitchen. Once out, Jacob stepped forward to lead the way.

"The kitchen will have snacks and water laid out at all times. If you need, there'll also be Gatorade and juice in the fridge. Help yourself to any of the food you find." They walked toward the living room, Luna falling in place just to the right of him, three steps behind.

"The living room on this floor will be for relaxing and chit-chatting. There won't be any play here." That was a bit of relief to know. If her senses got a bit overloaded, she could just curl up on one of those couches or beanbag chairs.

"Let's go upstairs." Jacob led the way once more, though he kept his pace slow and paused to ensure Luna was following. Luckily, he stopped doing that as they climbed up the stairs, or else he would have caught her staring at his butt — firm, round and like the rest of his body, speaking of powerful muscles beneath the black bondage pants he wore. Was it wrong, she wondered, to want to see what he looked like underneath?

Where is that lust coming from? It was *so* not her.

"Any open door means it's a private guest room available for use. You're welcome also to use any towels you find in there. The rooms are just for rest, not play. The party tonight is public play only, just to let you know, so you don't have to worry about running into something you didn't want to see up here. Most of the rooms have private bathrooms as well, if you need to clean up."

Was Jacob expecting she was going to play? "Um... that's good to know, but I'm not planning on doing anything beyond observing."

"Good." He smiled at that, a genuine smile that made her wonder what she'd said to deserve it. His compliment made her straighten, but she tilted her head to one side, a question on her lips.

Jacob turned toward her, approval clear in his voice, even as he explained. "It's good to observe for a while, figure out what you like and don't like before diving in. The worst mistake someone new to the scene can make is to jump right in without thinking things through first. It's how people get hurt."

Luna suppressed the urge to find a pen and paper to take notes, so she nodded instead. It was reassuring to hear that she was on the right path. "So, what did you mean when you said 'floor' earlier?" After a split second, she realized she had forgotten the honorific. "Master Jacob—or do you prefer Sir? I'm always confused with which I should use."

He chuckled and she couldn't help but blush. "Relax, just Jacob is fine. We're not scening, and as much as I appreciate the respect, you're also just exploring right now." His lips quirked into a crooked grin. "Besides, even for a scene, I prefer my partner screaming out my name instead of some generic title."

Oh. Dear. God.

She had to be turning as red as a tomato and Luna swallowed as those words, combined with that grin, sent a shot of heat straight to her core. "I...see..."

None of it made sense. She usually had such a low sex drive.

"Come on. You asked me about the floor. Let's head to the basement and I'll show you."

He led the way once more and, after a slight pause, Luna followed, thankful for his lack of comment about how red or flustered she was.

She was still struggling to calm her pounding heart and clamp down on her arousal when they arrived. As she took the last steps down, her eyes widened at the different stations featuring an array of large apparatuses along the perimeter of the room. In a lot of ways, the setup was like a kinky version of a gym. But it was the center that drew her attention, a small stage with spotlights set up on the ground. The stage was empty for now, but Luna could see hooks installed above and strong ropes dangling from them. There was no doubt that their hosts had prepped for the shibari demonstration.

It was not much different from The Playgrounds' dungeon. At least, that's what Luna kept trying to tell herself. But standing in the empty dungeon, aware of it being on personal property and alone with Jacob, a Dom she found immensely attractive, made it feel much more private, intimate. Luna flushed and tugged at her dress, finding it warmer and warmer. Everything was surreal, almost like she was having an out-of-body experience.

"Luna?" Jacob's voice was a little distant and she struggled to focus. Why did the man look worried? "Luna!" His voice was louder, more demanding of her attention. She blinked at him, trying to clear the fog in her head. He waved his hand in front of her and her gaze followed it.

"Shit," Jacob said.

She couldn't help but wonder... *Why is Jacob swearing?*

Chapter Five

"Shit."

Jacob looked around but it was just the two of them. He had only ever heard of someone entering into subspace by only psychological triggers but he had never seen it himself, nor would he have expected for anyone to dive so deep, so quickly.

"Luna," he tried again but when his little mouse only stared at him with a blank unfocused look, he sighed. There was no helping it. With a gentle hand, he guided her to sit on the steps then crouched before her. "Luna, can you hear me?"

"Mm-hm-m."

"Good girl. Now I want you to concentrate on your breathing. In. Out. That's it." He kept his voice soft, as lulling as he could make it. "Now keep going, breathe deep. Good. Now focus on your fingers and your hands. Wiggle them." He kept careful watch as she obeyed with sluggishness. "Focus on how they feel. Focus on what they're touching. That's it."

Bit by bit, Luna began to show signs of returning to herself. When she reached up to rub her eyes, her gaze refocusing, Jacob allowed himself to slump to the ground next to her at last, one leg tucked under the other, bent at the knee to brace his arm against it

"Um...Jacob?"

"Yeah, sweetheart?" The endearment came easy, way too easy. It had just kind of slipped out by accident, but it was too late to take it back.

Out of the corner of his eye, he saw her face redden and he scolded himself. He didn't want her to feel awkward, but another part of him couldn't help but wonder whether the rest of her body turned red the same way.

"Ah... Um... What happened? I mean, I know you were talking me through breathing, but everything felt far away, floaty..."

His curiosity piqued now, Jacob shifted so he could study her more closely. "Has this happened to you before?"

"Sometimes, but never this intensely."

"Tell me what was going through your mind when things began to feel unfocused."

There was a pause and he read hesitation in every line of her body. But it was important. If she entered into subspace so easily, he needed to understand the triggers, so he could train her to protect herself. If the same thing ever happened in front of another Dom, there were no guarantees that they might not take advantage of her in that state, talk her into doing something she didn't want. Damn it, she was even more vulnerable than he'd thought at first.

"I..." She faltered then straightened to start again. "I was thinking about this place, how it was like the dungeon at The Playgrounds but that it felt more personal. Then I was thinking about" — she swallowed, as if to steel herself — "about you. And that it was just the two of us here. Then it just felt kind of hot and overwhelming." Her last words came tumbling out so fast that they almost slurred together.

She was hot, thinking about the two of them alone. She'd gone into subspace just thinking about it.

His cock hardened. *Shit.*

It didn't help that the confession was a sign of submission that appealed to every dominant instinct in him, admitting her attraction to him at his command, despite her reluctance. *God, she is a treasure.*

He breathed and shifted to hide his arousal. The last thing he wanted was to scare off his little mouse or to pressure her in any way. He was still of the firm opinion that she should be observing tonight, and he stuck to that belief, regardless of his own urges. Somehow he felt responsible for her, not because Lani had put her in his hands or because Erica had asked him to keep watch. No, it was because his mere presence had a hand in bringing her to subspace and he was the one who had managed to ground her.

"Okay. All right." He gave her a gentle pat on the knee. It was nothing sexual, just something meant to be reassuring. "What happened was that you slipped into subspace. It's a feeling of detachment, kind of like a high that can be caused by both physiological and psychological triggers. It usually happens because of endorphins, but it seems like you go into it more easily than most. It can get dangerous. You're highly susceptible to suggestions in that state. So, the next time you feel it starting to happen, I want you to remember the exercise I just led you through. Focus on your breathing and slowly increase awareness of your own body. It'll ground you and help you come back. Okay?"

His little mouse looked startled at first, then pensive, considering his words. "Can you recommend any site or book on the topic? I'd like to read up more on it."

Ah-ha! As he suspected, there was a large brain behind that submissive nature. It was damn sexy. "Yeah, sure." He pulled out his phone and handed it to her. "Give me your email and I'll send you some links."

Once they'd exchanged contact information, he got up and offered his hand. "Come on. The party'll probably move down here soon. Do you want to stay upstairs for the rest of the night?"

"No, I'll come down later." She slipped her hand into his, hers cool to touch compared to his heat. "Even if I end up in subspace again, it'll be a chance to practice. Better here than The Playgrounds, right?" She didn't wait for him to answer her rhetorical question. "Besides, I have you here to keep me safe."

The trust she'd placed in him was incredible. In part, it was because he was the main dungeon monitor tonight, but somehow, her comment had felt more private, like it was something only they shared. He liked that.

With a small tug, he helped her to her feet and wondered if it was obvious that he couldn't quite stop grinning.

They had just gotten to the top of the stairs when a squeal made them both jump. But it was Luna who nearly got tackled. Jacob took a step back.

"Oh my God, I can't believe you're here!" Cassie beamed as she pulled back to regard Luna, who was once more blushing in embarrassment.

"Yeah, Mistress Lani invited me." She was back to being that little shy mouse again and somehow, Jacob didn't mind. He shifted, positioning himself to stand behind her, even before he realized what he was doing. Cassie was a switch, and bi, and Jacob had to wonder if Luna was bi as well. Again the Neanderthal urge to stake his claim rose once more and he had to shake his head at himself.

"What?" Cassie must have caught that small movement then gasped. "Luna, have you already been spoken for? Has Jacob claimed you for the night?"

"What?"

Interesting. Luna was turning beet red, even as she looked at Cassie with her jaw dropping.

"What? No, I mean…"

A part of him also wanted to say yes, just to see what Luna's reaction would be like. Instead, he chose the gentlemanly route. "Cassie, I'm full-time monitoring tonight," he chided instead, saving the little mouse from her stammering.

"Oh goodie. Maybe we can play later, Luna." Cassie winked.

If Luna had been flustered before, the ways her eyes widened and her mouth gaped with no words coming out, took her display of embarrassment to a whole new level. Jacob found himself torn between amusement at her reaction and wanting to whisk her away from any other offers she may get that night.

"Cassie, leave the poor girl alone." August approached from behind, as prim and proper as ever.

In return, Cassie pouted. "Well, fine then." She blew a kiss to Luna then bobbed her head toward Jacob. "I'm going to go find Darryl. See you guys later."

August sighed, watching the girl flounce away before rubbing his temple with his index and third fingers, as if trying to stave off a headache. "I'm terribly sorry, Master Jacob, Luna."

Chuckling once more, Jacob shook his head. "No apologies necessary, August. Just because you and Cassie play on a regular basis, it doesn't mean you're responsible for her."

The other man only sighed and eyed him with doubt evident on his face before giving a slight shrug. "Would anyone know by chance where Mistress Lani is?"

"She was in the kitchen — but that was a while ago."

"Ah, thank you, Master Jacob. If you'll excuse me." August inclined his head then directed his next words to Luna. "If you have any questions later, come find me. I'd be happy to chat, from one submissive to another." Then he, too, walked away, leaving the two of them alone once more, despite the number of people milling around and trickling downstairs.

She half-turned toward him, though her gaze remained forward, and Luna mumbled something beneath her breath. He bent forward, his head placed closer toward her. "Hm-m? What's that?"

"Do I have 'sub' written on my forehead?" Luna sounded grumpy.

Jacob chuckled and straightened. "No, but I have to admit that everything about you does scream submissive."

She spun around, a slight frown on her lips. *No, more a pout.* Normally, pouts annoyed him, but on her, it was sinful.

"Well, for one, you chose to address any Dominant you meet as 'Master' or 'Mistress' or 'Sir' or 'Ma'am'. And most people here are experienced in the lifestyle, meaning they can read body language well enough to distinguish between the two."

"Oh."

It was adorable that she didn't realize she was being that obvious — which meant none of her actions were an act to try to entice or entrap. The innocence was refreshing.

"It looks like submissiveness comes to you naturally," he told her.

"That's what Mistress Lani said to Mistress Erica. I don't get it. I'm not like this normally. I mean, I don't just cave to people in my regular life. Hell, the other day at work, I volunteered to take the lead on an internal project."

He watched as she struggled to reconcile the conflict she perceived in her head. Placing a hand on her shoulder, he turned her around until she faced him in full. "Hey, take it easy. Those are deep questions and you have lots of time to sort through them. I'll help you. Okay?"

The offer slipped out before he had time to consider it. He was saying a lot of things before he gave them much thought. What was it about her that loosened his control? But, if he asked himself honestly, he realized that he didn't mind helping her work through her doubts. She was a delight to talk to.

"Okay."

"Good girl." Jacob winced. The first time he had used the term, he had been acting as her Dom to bring her back from subspace, but this time there was no excuse. "Sorry."

"For what?" Curiosity made her tilt her head.

"The phrasing. It's what I usually use with my sub or the partner I'm scening with."

"I don't mind." Her eyes didn't meet his but she gave him a small smile nonetheless, blushing. "I...like it."

God, does she have any idea of the effect she is having on me?

"Jacob..." Darryl poked his head up from the stairs. It looked like he had already been downstairs. "I think the first scene is starting."

He sighed, reaching to push his hair back, noting in the back of his mind that he was due for a haircut. For the first time, he was regretting not taking up Erica's offer to have someone relieve him for a shift or two. Not so that he could scene but just so they could talk more. She intrigued him, even more so than before, when she was just a gorgeous face.

"Duty calls. I'll see you later?" He hoped that was a yes.

"For sure" — the smallest of pauses — "Jacob."

He liked the sound of his name on her lips.

With greater reluctance than he'd expected, he made his way downstairs, already planning in his head all the ways that he could entice his little mouse to spend more time with him. Then he stopped himself short. He knew that once he was interested in a sub, he would become hyper-focused on her, like he was tonight, but the speed with which this was happening felt almost out of control. No, if he wanted to figure out the potential of whatever was growing between them, he needed to find some semblance of balance. Maybe he would have to speak with Lani after all.

Great, just great.

Chapter Six

At first, Luna hung back upstairs, sipping a glass of punch, but soon, curiosity got the better of her. As she took one step at a time, she could hear low murmurs mingled with occasional moans and squeals.

Midway down the flight of stairs, she paused and took a few steadying breaths, reminding herself of Jacob's instructions should the whole thing overwhelm her too much. One hand on the wall, she closed her eyes then opened them once more, and with determined steps, she made the rest of her way down before her imagination ran too far away and she lost her nerve.

In a lot of ways, Luna was glad she had prepared herself earlier by visiting The Playgrounds before the party. The scene that unfolded before she reached the last steps was not that different. Many of the stations were in use, but to Luna, it was more like a blur as she struggled to focus on any specific scene. Rather than smelling like sex, however, the room had the same vanilla scent as before, thanks to many of the flickering candles that dotted the place.

Most in the room were engaged in conversation or play. Luna kept her hand against the wall to steady herself and scanned across the room until she glimpsed Jacob. And just like that, the butterflies in her stomach settled and the world snapped back into focus.

Swallowing each breath of air then exhaling, she walked up to stand beside Jacob, shifting her weight from one foot to another. Now that she was there, she wasn't sure what to say or if she should say anything at all. The man next to her threw her off in so many ways.

Luckily, it took only a few seconds before he tilted his head toward her and flashed a quick smile, though he kept his gaze forward. That was understandable, since he had a job to do.

"How're you doing?" he asked her softly.

"I'm okay." The answer was automatic, but she soon realized it wasn't the most truthful, and she sensed Jacob as someone that valued honesty. "It's a little overwhelming, but I think I just need time to adjust."

A loud cry distracted both of them and Luna shivered when she realized it was from a woman in the throes of a climax. Then she did a double-take. It wasn't just any woman. Cassie was bent backward in half as her body twisted in a heightened mix of pain and pleasure, judging by the bright red marks blossoming all over her body. Heat rushed to Luna's cheeks.

A chuckle drew her attention and her blush only deepened as she wondered if Jacob was laughing at her. She wasn't a prude. Really.

"Glad to be of entertainment," she muttered beneath her breath as she fixed her gaze at the floor before she blinked as a hand touched her shoulder.

When she didn't look up, Jacob gave her shoulder a gentle squeeze. "I'm not laughing at you, sweetheart. I'm just remembering when I was in your shoes. You get used to it."

His words held enough compassion that she dared a peek up at him. The amusement was still there, but behind it was a warmth that made her let her guard down, *just a little.*

"If you want, I wouldn't mind if you stayed here for a bit and kept me company," he said.

Okay, a lot. "I'd like that."

She watched on, shifting closer. It wasn't until her arm brushed his that she realized what she was doing. If he'd noticed, he gave no sign of it.

But questions had formed in her head. As she stood next to Jacob, she judged herself grounded enough to study each act, noting her own physiological reactions in an almost-clinical manner. She flinched at the sound of a paddle nearby and tensed when she heard the yelp that followed. When an actual whip cracked in the air, she jumped and paled, grabbing Jacob's arm on instinct.

"Are you okay?" The earlier humor that had been there was gone, replaced with concern as he knitted his brows together.

She swallowed hard and nodded. Suddenly realizing her hand was on him, she started to move away. "Oh God, I'm so sorry. I didn't mean..."

He shook his head and took her hand in his, tucking it instead in the crook of his arm. "It's okay. I don't mind."

For the next half-hour, they kept their eyes on the room—Luna, to desensitize herself, forcing herself to study each scene. Steadied by Jacob's reassuring presence and support, it didn't feel so bad, more like to each their own. But it was the control play that evoked a different reaction. Watching a Mistress edge her submissive repeatedly until he was begging to come quickened her heart and made her stomach clench with arousal so much that she worried Jacob could smell her.

But there was also something strange happening in every scene, and over time, she worked up her courage to ask. "Jacob, how come no one is having sex?" *Damn it, I sound so naïve.*

"Ah, that's a good question. It's a pretty common rule, but it also depends on the venue. Sometimes no penetration of any sort is allowed, in order to meet certain legal or insurance requirements. Because this is a private party, Erica and Dominique can push a little further, so toys and other ways of stimulation are allowed. But they draw the line at genital-to-genital contact."

Is he always so clinical? Somehow Luna doubted it, but the way he explained things so matter-of-factly helped her process and understand without feeling embarrassed or pressured, even if he was…well…him. She appreciated that a lot.

After a little while longer, many of the scenes began to wind down and people trickled out of the dungeon in pairs or groups. However, Jacob would have to stay until the last scene, so the next thought came as naturally to her as breathing. "Are you thirsty or hungry? Want me to bring you something from upstairs?" It was the least she could do.

The look he gave her, a mixture of surprise and wonder, baffled her but made her duck her head a little until he cleared his throat.

"Ah, just a bottle of water. There should be some in the fridge. Thanks."

"Sure, no problem.".

It wasn't until Luna was upstairs, opening the fridge door, that Cassie came bounding to her. "Oh my God. What a rush!"

Cassie had on a pair of panties, a bra and little else. Red welts covered her body in a well-designed pattern. *Well*, like she'd thought earlier, *to each their own.*

"You...looked like you had fun." What else was she supposed to say? There was a moment of hesitation before she plunged ahead. "I thought, though, that you were a top."

The woman grinned and shook her head. "Now why would you think that, silly girl?"

"Well, just that" — Luna paused — "I heard you and August play and he mentioned he's a sub."

"Luna, Luna, Luna..." Cassie snatched a bottle of water from the fridge, reminding her to do the same. "Dominance and submission is not an either-or thing. It's more like a spectrum, and I'd like to think I'm a little more fluid. It keeps things fun."

Luna blinked.

"I'm a switch."

"Oh." That she understood.

A sly grin spread across Cassie's lips as she leaned in a little closer and lowered her voice. "So, you and Jacob?"

Luna's brows shot up. "What? No. I mean, he was just" — she flapped her hands in the air — "just helping a newbie like me out, you know? Being nice."

"Come on. I saw you two all cozied up. You know, Jacob's a trainer. He specializes in introducing potential and interested subs to the scene, helps them figure out what they want, that kind of thing."

"Oh."

"Besides, Jacob doesn't let just anyone cling to his arm all night, you know." Cassie waved the unopened bottle before unscrewing the top and taking a long swig.

"Oh." Luna flushed again, kicking herself at the one-word answers she was being reduced to.

"Now, come on." Cassie set down the now-empty bottle with a smirk. "I think the shibari demo is starting and we wouldn't want to miss that."

"Right."

By the time they made it downstairs once more, most had already gathered. Luna threaded her way through the guests until she reached Jacob. He gave her a nod of thanks as she handed him the water bottle, and they both remained silent as the demo started.

She lurched forward when someone from behind pushed past her. Almost losing her balance, she flailed, only to have strong arms encircle her.

"I've got you," Jacob whispered as he steadied her.

She leaned against him. As if taking it as a sign, Jacob kept one arm around her then tilted his head to one side. When she nodded her assent with a small smile, he grinned in return, keeping his arm around her.

On her other side, she sensed another familiar presence and turned to see Lani. When the Domme raised a brow with the cheekiest curve of her lips, Luna's face reddened once more and she wrinkled her nose at her mentor. Jacob didn't seem to notice once again. *Phew.*

On the platform, a tall Asian man, young with a slim, athletic build, stood in the center. Rather than fetish wear, the man wore a pair of black slacks and a crisp white shirt with the sleeves rolled up. Behind him, lengths of rope already trailed from the hooks above that Luna had seen above earlier. Next to him stood Erica, almost a full head shorter, despite the impossible stilettos she wore.

"Good evening, all. I hope you are enjoying the party so far. It's my pleasure tonight to introduce my dear friend Elijah Lee, who's an award-winning artist in the shibari arts. You may have seen his works featured in national exhibits and various publications. Tonight, he will show us live how he turns the human body into art, and he has also graciously offered to teach some basics. Without further ado, I'll pass the stage to you, Elijah."

A brief smattering of applause filled the air before dying away.

"Thank you, Erica, for that kind introduction." The man offered a slight bow, clapping both of his hands together. "It's always a pleasure to share my art with others and to introduce shibari. You know, the word 'shibari' means 'to tie' in Japanese and comes from a martial arts style used to restrain captives. The name of its erotic counterpart, as we know it in North America and much of the Western world today, is actually 'kinbaku.'"

Luna found herself once more itching for a notebook and she made a mental note to do more research when she got home.

He smiled, almost sheepish in his mannerisms. "But you aren't here for a history lesson. So instead, let me welcome my assistant to the stage. I have to thank Erica for so graciously letting me borrow Dominique."

Widening her eyes, Luna inhaled as the submissive strode across the stage in her full naked glory and with confidence that she envied. Dominique's legs seemed unending and her proud, larger breasts swayed, along with her hips. Luna could only hunch a little and lean closer against Jacob.

Another round of applause filled the air but Elijah was already a blur of motion. With deft movements, he looped different strands of rope around her body in dizzying ways and a hushed, almost revered silence fell on the crowd. When he next stepped back, he beamed as he showed the intricate harness he had threaded around Dominique's abdominal area in a crisscross pattern that framed her breasts. The sheer sensuality of it all made Luna's own breasts ache with need.

"Now, a party like this is also a rare opportunity for me to push my limits as an artist into more of the performance art variety. This is not something I usually get to do in my studio..." Elijah trailed off as he started working again, looping the rope around her limbs, creating a V that dipped between her legs. Once done, he began pulling the ropes dangling from the hooks in the ceiling to tie around Dominique before hoisting her. Her body hung horizontal, face-up, with her back arched, her hair cascading down toward the floor. The rope suspended one leg upward. The other was bent back while he tied her arms behind her back. He ran his hand along her body and, in response, Dominique moaned, closing her eyes in obvious pleasure.

"While the art form is a sensual display of the human body" — Elijah circled his thumb along each of Dominique's hardening nipples and Luna had to bite back a moan herself — "the act itself can be extremely arousing for the one being tied."

Luna's breathing grew shallow as he trailed his hand downward. Her gaze followed Elijah's, toward Erica, who gave a perceptible nod, likely for some permission. He trailed his hand farther down as he spun Dominique around until he was displaying her pussy to the crowd, a particular knot nestled against her glistening folds. He crept his hand with agonizing slowness and it was as if the crowd collectively held their breath for one of the goddesses of The Playgrounds.

Without thinking, Luna's own hand rose to cross her own chest, reaching to hold on to the one Jacob had laid on her shoulder.

"You see, the knot in the middle, along with the tension that the entire harness is under from the suspension, creates a particular friction. And with a simple move, I can provoke the most intense reactions."

Elijah gave a hard tap on the knot. Immediately, Dominique's body tensed and her face scrunched up. Encouraged by her reactions, he kept tapping, alternating in rhythm. As she began to writhe, he pressed the knot against her. Her lips parted in a wordless scream and her body spasmed in climax, causing all the ropes and Dominique herself to swing wildly.

Flushing now for a different reason, Luna tried to squeeze her legs together without drawing attention to herself. When Jacob turned his hand to engulf hers, giving it a reassuring squeeze, her stomach clenched and her core turned to a molten mess.

Moments passed in hushed silence before Dominique's body relaxed once more against the ropes, her body limp, and Elijah moved to stabilize her, stroking her hair and murmuring soft words into her ear.

A few people began to recover from the performance and started the applause. Others followed and soon, as Elijah helped Dominique out of the ropes and harness, Erica stepped on the stage, grinning like a Cheshire cat. With a tenderness that belied her usual mannerisms, she wrapped the taller woman in a blanket and escorted her off the stage.

"Thank you again to both Erica and Dominique." Elijah clapped his hands together and bowed again before turning back to the audience. "And now, can I ask for a volunteer from the audience to help me demonstrate some basics?"

If Luna were honest with herself, the entire rest of the evening had been a blur. She remembered excusing herself at some point and heading upstairs to sit on the couch. She remembered Lani coming to sit with her. And if she tried hard enough, she could recall the details, bit by bit, but none ever so vivid as her hand in Jacob's, struggling against her own arousal as they watched another woman orgasm. And through it all, one prevailing question kept circling her mind.

She'd never had a high libido. *So what is happening to me?*

Chapter Seven

They crashed into her apartment, their lips locked in a passionate kiss, fumbling beneath each other's clothes like horny teenagers. Heat emanated from Jacob's body as she smoothed her hand over his abs and shivered as he flexed his abdomen in response.

He traveled his hands upward, and with little ado, he unzipped her dress, helping her shimmy out of it. The dress hadn't allowed for a bra, and his eyes darkened at the sight of her nipples hardening in the cold air. But as if testing his control, he left them alone.

When he slipped his hands from caressing her shoulders to cupping her breasts, she moaned and pushed them more against him. When he kissed down her neck, licking the hollow where he could feel her pulse, Luna ground her hips against his, the hardened length of his member straining against his pants and pressing against her. And when she reached down to undo them, Jacob grabbed her wrists, holding them still before drawing them behind her back.

"No, Luna," he whispered, his licks turning into nibbles along her collarbone.

Pinned against him, she squirmed in his arms, whimpering with need as she soaked her panties from his ministrations. The rest of her body ached for his touch. Without the use of her hands, she did the only thing possible and tilted her head to nip at his exposed neck.

He hissed in return and bit down on her skin, drawing a loud yelp. The next thing she knew, soft cotton was wrapped around her wrists, as somehow he'd grabbed one of her scarves off the coat rack and had tied her wrists together behind her back. As he eased back, he smirked as he spun her around and eyed his handiwork. "Now, march. Show me your bedroom."

Luna giggled as she sauntered, hips sashaying, treating him to a full view of her rear. She squealed in surprise when he growled.

As soon as they entered her bedroom, he stalked toward her once more, pressing closer and closer until she fell back onto her bed. With her hands trapped behind her, she was only able to squirm her way up the bed. The sight of her body's movements must have evoked something in Jacob, because a low, guttural sound emerged from the back of his throat and he started climbing onto the bed, positioning himself to kneel over her.

He skimmed his fingers along her legs, leaving goosebumps in their wake. Still now, when her eyes met his, her body melted into the bed at the intensity she saw reflected in them. When he reached her panties and dragged them down, she lifted her hips for him and swallowed at the hunger she saw there.

"No coming until I tell you to." His voice rumbled in his chest as he dipped his fingers between her legs before raising them to his lips. "Delicious."

Oh God. Her body burned and she wasn't going to last. She needed him inside her.

Instead, he stroked her inner thighs, his weight keeping her legs from moving, from even parting for him. Unable to see what he was doing, she dropped her head back as he began to walk his fingers upward until they were parting her folds. He cupped her sex with his warm palm, the heel grinding against the general area around her clit as he slipped a finger inside her, rubbing against her inner walls.

"Oh God," she moaned as she thrust her hip against his hand, beginning to rock back and forth as she chased the impending climax that was threatening to close.

"Eyes on me, babe. I want to see you, and I want you to see how pleased I am when you come for me."

There was something about his words that struck a chord within her. "Please," she pleaded. When he paused and slowed his fingers instead, she whimpered and tried to grind her hip against his hand harder. *So close to the edge.*

"No-o-o," she protested, gasping as he sped up again. When her body began to tense and twitch, he slowed once more. The cycle repeated, over and over, until tears of frustration streamed down her face and he had reduced her to a bundle of nerves and desire.

Dear God, he was edging her — just like that Mistress at the party had.

"Sir, please, please," she pleaded, only semi-conscious of the words spilling out of her mouth, her hips thrusting. He smirked as he slowed for what felt like the gazillionth time, keeping her so close but not enough to give her the orgasm she so needed. He was going to drive her to the brink of insanity.

"Hm-m-m, since you asked so prettily..." He leaned in close, nipped her ear and whispered, "Come."

It was all she needed as she exploded into his hand. He covered her lips with his, swallowing her screams as she snapped her eyes open.

Open?

She stared at her ceiling as an orgasm rolled through her body, soaking her own fingers. Sometime through the night, she had kicked off her panties and her sheets had twisted around her legs. Sweat drenched her pillow.

As the climax faded, she slowed her hand and groaned. *A dream. A freaking sex dream featuring Mr. Just-a-guy.*

He was *so* not 'just a guy'.

She sat up and passed her cleaner hand over her face. *What the hell is wrong with me?* Sure, it had been a while since she had been with someone, but she had never really missed it. Sex had never been something to write home about. That was what food was for.

How was it that the dream with him was hotter than any actual real-life sex she'd ever had? Her damn imagination.

There is *something wrong with me.*

There was a giant wet spot on her sheets. Luna sighed and slid off her bed, making her way to the washroom to clean up.

Fifteen minutes later, she was sitting on the floor in the hall outside her bedroom, clothed in a fresh pair of panties and a cotton spaghetti-strap tank, watching her sheets swirling around in the washing machine. One arm braced against her knee, she continued to rub her forehead, too riled up to sleep.

What was it about that man that triggered such a change in her libido? It couldn't be just because he was a Dom. She'd met plenty of men in her life who at least acted that way. It couldn't even be the texts they had exchanged. She'd had questions after the first set of reading material he'd sent her, and those had led to another and another. Their discussion was academic with minimal flirting. So what could it be?

She grabbed the water bottle she'd brought from the kitchen and took small sips of the cool liquid. Maybe it was just the setting where she had met him. She admitted that many of the scenes she'd seen had turned her on. Maybe her brain had somehow created a weird association between those hot scenes and Jacob. *Yeah, that must be it.*

Whatever it was, the possibility of how much control she could lose around him was marvelously hot — and incredibly terrifying.

Her phone lit up with some stupid system notification. She exhaled, grabbing the phone then pausing as she saw a calendar reminder. *Right...* Climbing with Dylan was tomorrow... Today... Remembering his dimpled smile, Luna grinned a little. Going by the type she was usually attracted to, Dylan had an advantage. Then again, his type was not usually attracted to her.

Men were so confusing.

She gave up all hope of returning to bed and pushed herself up instead. It was time to fix herself a middle-of-the-night snack to accompany the reading she'd decided to catch up on. Some decent fantasy with wizards, faeries and demons would keep her mind off men — and help her stop questioning her damn wet dream.

* * * *

Only a few hours later, Luna yawned as she pulled open the door to the climbing gym. Although it was still early, she was surprised as she regarded the number of people already there, scaling the walls with ropes tied to safety harnesses around their waists. The image of the rope harness around Dominique flashed in her mind and she flushed, shoving the memory into a deep, dark box — and the box in a deep, dark hole. Why did it have to be top-rope climbing? Why not...not...tennis?

"Luna!" Dylan came bounding over, full of energy that made her grin. His obvious pleasure at the sight of her warmed her and cleared the confusion in her head.

"Come on. Let's get you set up." With a hand on the small of her back, Dylan guided her to the counter where, acting like a complete gentleman, he paid for her entry and equipment rental fee, despite her protests. She hadn't intended for the climbing adventure to be a date, just a casual hangout, but it was turning into one.

"Okay, so..." Dylan led her to the mats then steered her toward a particular wall. Unlike other areas in the gym with odd angles and portions jutting out, the one in front of them was almost straight up and down. "Before we start, I've got a few tips for you to make it easier." He moved closer to the wall and reached up with his left hand, stepping with the right foot. "First, push up with your leg. You will want to pull with your arm, but you'll tire yourself out too fast. Make sure that when you step, though, do it with your toes, not the side of your foot. Don't worry. The shoes will help and your toes have better grip than you think."

He pushed himself up before leaning back, hanging in a casual pose. Luna was trying to focus on his words but could not help but admire the way his arm muscles, exposed by the loose tank he wore, rippled with the easy effort of a skilled climber. "If you are resting or trying to figure out what to do next, keep your arms straight. Don't hug the wall. You'll also tire out faster that way."

He jumped back down and looked back to check.

"Got it. In theory," she told him and laughed.

Dylan chuckled. "Okay, so basic safety etiquette. I'll be belaying you, which means my weight will be what keeps you from taking a bad fall. That also means you and I need to communicate." Next, he explained the commands and terminology, making her repeat them to ensure that she understood. With his instructions completed, it was time to strap on the harness. He knelt before her and held it out. Luna stared at it for a moment, full of doubt, then, steeling her nerves, she attempted to step in.

She should have known better than to try without holding on to something for balance. As she stumbled, she grabbed Dylan's shoulder for support, even as he reached out to her hip to stabilize her. It was perfectly innocent and had nothing over the kinds of compromising positions she'd been in during grappling sessions in the dojo. But somehow, she blushed at the way his muscles moved beneath her palm, the warmth of his hand burning her hip through her yoga pants.

"Easy there," he murmured, then rose to his feet.

He stepped back to let her tug the harness into place, but Luna only struggled with all the straps and buckles, wondering what went where.

"Here… May I?" Dylan extended his hands in an offer.

Luna nodded with a sheepish smile. "Please."

Dylan wrapped his arms around her for a moment but made quick work of securing the harness. Then he looped one of the top ropes to it. Despite his hands remaining respectful as he focused on ensuring her safety, Luna held her breath, his nearness causing her heart to beat just a little harder. And she hadn't even started climbing.

Her breathing resumed as he stepped back to tie the other end to himself.

"Okay." He guided her back to the wall. "If you look up, you'll notice that the holds all have different colored tape. You want to pick one and go for only holds with that color. I was scoping the routes out earlier and I think that to start, you may want to consider going for the ones with the blue tape."

She tilted her head back and eyed the wall, trying to pick out the handholds with blue tape among all their peers. It was better than lingering on his comments about having been here early to prepare for teaching her. *Focus, Luna, focus.* There were a lot of choices.

The worry must have been obvious on her face.

"Hey, don't worry. If you get stuck, I'll shout out suggestions, and if you get tired, just let go." Dylan placed a hand on her shoulder. "I've got you, I promise. If you fall, I'll catch you."

There it was again, that slight mix of shyness and charm that made him so endearing. Luna's cheeks reddened and she nodded, helpless in not knowing how to flirt back. So she took a deep breath instead and placed her hand on the first hold.

"All right, I can do this."

Chapter Eight

Luna whimpered under her breath, wondering why she'd decided that going to The Playgrounds was a good idea when she was already so sore from climbing earlier in the day. Her limbs felt like limp, wet noodles and muscles she didn't know existed were already beginning to ache. To console herself, she had dressed in the most comfortable outfit she could imagine while still being acceptable for a club — a distressed black tank top, a short tulle skirt and heavy stomper goth boots. She was going for the industrial punk look. Yeah that was it. The mere thought of a corset made her cringe.

What she really wanted was a drink and a sit down. So when she spied August alone at the bar, Luna counted her good fortunes and walked over to join him.

"Good evening, Luna," August greeted as she eased onto the bar stool beside him.

"Hi, August. How are you?"

"Well…yourself?"

"Tired, but good." She sucked at small talk. Luckily, the bartender swung by and there was a pause in their conversation as they both ordered their drinks.

She remembered his offer at the party. "August, would you mind if I ask you some questions about... well...being a submissive?"

He chuckled, pushing his glasses up the ridge of his nose. Sometimes August struck her as an anime character who had been brought to life. "Of course. I offered before. Ask away."

Luna chewed her lower lip. As the drinks arrive, she grabbed her rum and Coke, taking a good swallow of liquid courage before speaking. "So, how did you figure you were a sub?"

August took a sip of his own drink, also a rum and Coke, and considered her question. "Well, not without a lot of time and exploration. I suppose in a way, though, it's no different from, say, sexual orientation. How does one figure out if they're attracted to women or men or both — or don't see gender at all?"

Her mouth dropped open, and she gaped at him. His words hit a core part of her and reverberated within her soul. Old memories stirred within, memories from before she'd tried anything in real life, before the relationship that had thrown everything into such confusion. Back then, she'd spent many nights reading stories of dominance and submission and she'd become so worked up that she would wear out the batteries in her vibrator. She remembered that when she first started delving into the world of kinks online, certain suggestions alone would send her imagination spinning.

The image of the shibari demonstration came to mind. She swallowed, her cheeks growing warmer, when she realized August was watching her. "Yeah, I see what you mean." That sounded lame, even to her ears.

A small smile tugged at his lips and Luna couldn't help but smile back. It was a smile laden with meaning, a shared understanding of two similar people.

"Is that the question you really want to ask?" August leaned in closer. "I remember that when I first started, I had a different question."

It was like he saw through all her hesitation and layers of doubts. "Was it 'how did you come to terms with being a sub?'"

"Precisely!" August took a much larger swallow of his drink and shook his head a little. "That's a much harder question. As you're aware, the traditional male role and image society has for us is one of authority and dominance. It took a long time for me to come to terms that being a submissive doesn't mean I'm any less masculine."

"How?" The word came out as a bare whisper but August only arched his brow at her. "I've worked very hard, all my life, to achieve what I have. I want to lead, to be that strong, independent woman who's successful with her own career, that doesn't have to depend on anyone—like a good little feminist." She made a rueful smile at that, aware of the modern societal pressures influencing her words. "But how do I reconcile that?" She groaned and rubbed her forehead. "All the Doms around here keep saying I'm a natural, so does that make me a failure?"

"Whoa, hey." August placed a hand on her shoulder. "Are you calling me a failure then?"

Luna's eyes snapped wide open and her hands flew to her mouth. "Oh my God, no! I'm so sorry. I meant…"

August chuckled and waved his hand. "Don't worry about it. I understood what you meant." Growing serious once more, he stared at his drink. "I think the only way to figure it all out is to understand what submission means to you."

Blinking once, then twice, Luna opened her mouth before shutting it again, her mind still processing his statement.

August continued. "It means that if you want to submit, to relinquish control, what are you getting out of it and what are you willing to put into the relationship in return? For some people, it's a thing in the bedroom. For others, it's beyond. How much power do you want to give to the other person and why? What meaning does it hold for you?"

She continued to gape at August, her mind spinning as she tried to summon some coherent, intelligent answer.

Before she could stammer a reply, August leaned in and patted her shoulder. "It's a lot to take in—and those are questions that take a long time and a lot of hard looks in the mirror to answer." He withdrew the touch and turned back to nursing his drink. Silence settled between them.

Luna stared into her glass. Unsure if it was the drink that had loosened her tongue, her next words surprised even her, but it was too late to take them back. "I'm not sure where I'm at yet, though I think I'm a submissive. Taking control doesn't appeal to me. I don't know if I want to give up control either, though. So I'm not even sure why the concept has been turning me on so much lately." She made a face at the memories that were resurfacing and knocked back the rest of her drink, letting the liquor smooth away the rough edges.

Something she said must have alarmed August enough that when he turned toward her, concern furrowed his forehead. Or maybe it was the way she was now attempting to drown herself in her own lightweight fashion. Whatever it was, it seemed to make him chew over his next words, each one enunciated with care.

"I don't know what happened in your past, and I won't pry. But I do know from experience that not every Dom is right for every sub. Everyone has a different style, and it may have been that the Dom you were with was not right for you. It's also rare to find someone who matches you completely, but when you do, serving that person becomes effortless."

There was a softness to his voice. Luna wasn't so far gone that she couldn't hear it. Curious now, she peered at August before her lips turned into a small teasing leer. It was a guess, but an educated one. "Lani?"

It was the reaction she'd hoped for. August's eyes widened and his back stiffened, his cheeks pinkening. He curled his hand into a fist and brought it up to cover his mouth as he made a sound to clear his throat. It was most adorable, seeing the well-put-together man flustered.

When Luna waited, he looked away and heaved a sigh. "Yes, I think she and I would do well together. But I don't believe Mistress Lani intends to settle on a particular submissive any time soon."

"Luna, August! Guess who I found!" Cassie approached, before Luna could question August more. The crowd parted to reveal Cassie, hanging on to Elijah's arm.

They both turned a little in surprise. "Master Elijah," August greeted with a dip of his head.

"Please, Eli is fine." The Asian man dipped his head in acknowledgment before smiling at them both. "It's good to see you, August. And I remembering seeing you at the party, but I don't believe we got introduced." He extended his free hand to Luna.

"Luna. I enjoyed your demonstration." She shook his hand.

Eli dipped his head again, beaming with pleasure. "I'm glad you did. I enjoy these demonstrations as much as sharing my art in exhibits."

Cassie's eyes flashed in a way that made Luna worry, enough that she started chewing on her lower lip again. "Guess what Eli's been looking for?" She nudged the man next to her with a mischievous smile.

August and Luna exchanged a look.

"Ah yes. I was telling Cassie here that I've been looking for some models for a new project I'm starting here. It's why I'm in town. But rather than flying in my usual partners, I'm looking for some locals to work with instead. It's an outdoor shoot, but I guarantee privacy for my models." He leaned forward. "Cassie has already said yes, but I was wondering if you two would be interested."

Luna's brows shot up. "Us?" Her voice squeaked.

"Why yes. August here is a perfect blend of masculinity and grace and would do well with various harnesses that will bring out his muscle contours. And you, little moon, would be a perfect foil with Cassie here — your pale coloring alongside Cassie's Asian dark eyes and hair."

"You flatter us, Eli," August murmured, though his voice carried all the same.

"Nah." Eli brushed their humble replies aside. "I'm an artist and I've got an eye for these things. In my public shibari art, I use the rope to bring out the beauty of the human body, to frame its strengths and vulnerability for capture with the camera."

When put that way, Luna could understand the man. It would be a lie to say she hadn't gone home after the play party and googled the man's work. What she'd found was beautiful—sensual rather than pornographic.

"If you're nervous at all, I'd also be happy to work with poses that keep the face hidden from view. For example, Luna, your hair can cover most of your face while you're hanging face down. I'd love to do a shot of you in a suspended crescent, like your namesake. See? You're already giving me ideas!" There was a feverish glint in his eyes. Luna recognized it. She had seen the same look on her own face when inspiration hit with her writing.

Damn it, that sounded hot and appealing on so many levels—some that she wasn't even sure she was ready to admit to herself.

"I pay my models too, and I pay well!" It was obvious that Eli really wanted them in his shoot.

"Come on. Say you'll do it with me!" Cassie released Eli's arm and grabbed Luna's hand with both of her own.

August cleared his throat once more, jolting Luna out of her lust-filled thoughts. "Thank you, Eli. This is really flattering. Can we have some time to think about it before getting back to you?"

"Of course!" Eli produced two business cards and handed them to Luna and August. "Here... Call me anytime, whatever you decide. The project starts in three days. If your decision is yes, we can discuss fees and schedules. I understand you all have day jobs, so we can work around that." He beamed again, as if pleased that their answers weren't an outright no.

Luna gave Cassie's hand a light squeeze before turning to take the offered card in hand. It was gorgeous in its simplicity, a single strand of rope tied in a loop against a black background, a sans-serif font used for Eli's name, phone number and email, as well as his gallery's location. Inwardly though, Luna sighed in relief, grateful for August's level-headedness. In her current lightly inebriated state, combined with Cassie's pleading expression, she wasn't sure what she would've agreed to. She had downed that one drink too fast — and on an empty stomach.

"Thanks, Eli." Luna bobbed her head, tucking the card away, aware that her cheeks were surely still bright red.

"You're very welcome, my dear. Now, if you'll excuse me, Cassie has promised to show me around." He offered an arm back to her and, with a wink and a wave, they were both off.

Shaking his head, August sighed again and held out his hand toward Luna. "Unlock and hand over your phone."

"Huh?"

August only made a come-here motion until Luna complied. Once the phone was in his hand, he typed on it and handed it back to Luna. The man had put in his contact details.

"Call me tomorrow when you're more sober and we can talk about Eli's offer."

Luna's eyes narrowed. "Are you sure you're not a Dom? Or at least a switch?"

That drew a genuine laugh from August. "Like I said, we all have different styles and different reasons to serve. I serve by protecting and putting order to chaos." He grinned and poked at Luna. "Besides, right now, you very much need protecting, given how tipsy you are."

Surprised at his sudden playfulness, Luna gaped at him before mustering up enough grace to close her mouth. He was right, but she would not give him the satisfaction of hearing her agree out loud. Instead, she stuck out her tongue. "Just for that, I'm calling you at seven a.m. tomorrow."

August only grinned wider. "I'll be waiting."

Chapter Nine

"So...how was your weekend?"

Oh, she knew that tone, that teasing sing-song voice that preceded the grilling session to come. Luna glared at Ted as she crammed in another mouthful of hot dog, if only to make him wait and squirm in suspense. He deserved it.

Lunch hour usually meant hanging out with Ted, and today, it meant hot dogs from the closest stand and a sit on a park bench to bask in the summer sun. If not for these brief periods outdoors, Luna would look even more like a ghost with her pale skin.

"Come on, Luna. Quit stalling. That hot dog won't last forever, you know."

Perhaps she should tell him about Eli's offer, just to spite him. But alas, being offered a chance to be a bondage model was not exactly shareable weekend gossip with someone outside the scene.

Do I already think of myself as 'in the scene'? How did that happen? When did that happen?

"Hello? Earth to Luna. Are you going to tell me? Or do I have to ask Brandon to judo-throw it out of you?"

She snapped back to attention and, swallowing the bite, she glowered at him. "Hey, that's an abuse of power and Brandon is too good of a sensei to do that." She sighed when Ted gave her a puppy-dog look.

"Fine. The climbing with Dylan went well, I think."

"You *think*? Details, girl. You're just as bad as a guy."

Which was ironic, considering who the comment came from. *Fine.* Turning, she batted her eyelashes at Ted. "Well, you know, 'cause like, he was super cute and just totally adorbs." Luna pitched her voice high and rolled her eyes, twirling a strand of hair around her forefinger.

"Luna Weir, I'm going to smack you." Ted lifted a hand in a mock threat, but she ducked her head all the same.

"Okay, okay!" She laughed a little. "Dylan was really cute, though. I learned a lot from him on how to climb and he pushed me just enough to challenge me without going overboard. And he was very supportive and patient."

Ted rolled his finger in the air, motioning for her to speed it up.

"Okay, he paid for my session and we flirted."

Ted sped up the movement with his finger.

"Um…he has a cute dimple when he smiles and he has some pretty strong arms?"

Her friend leaned in closer, his eyes starting to light up.

"Fine! He has a cute ass!" Luna blurted out.

"Hallelujah, thank you!" Ted clapped his hands together. "Finally, she proves she's warm-blooded after all!"

"Hey, I resent that!" It was turning into the lunch hour of death glares.

Ted waved off her protest with a laugh. "So, tell me... When are you guys meeting next?"

Luna hesitated before replying, if only because she didn't want more grilling. But she could already tell that Ted would not let it go, and he still might try to get Brandon to help pry the information out of her somehow. She sighed. "I'm not sure yet. We talked about climbing again and maybe dinner after. I need to text him back." She trailed off with a shrug.

Dylan was a complication she didn't need. August had been right in that she really needed to do some hard thinking about what her submissive nature meant and whether it was the right path for her. And Dylan represented an easy way out, to turn her back on it.

"Well, Luna, what the hell are you waiting for? Don't keep the poor boy waiting!"

Luna groaned and rose from her seat, wrapping the remains of her hot dog. With exaggerated motions, she checked her watch. "I need to get back. I've got a meeting!"

It was Ted's turn to glare at her, this time with suspicion. "Fine... But don't think you're off the hook that easily, missy."

"Of course not." Luna rolled her eyes. But despite being a complication, Luna didn't quite want to give up on Dylan yet. Something about that simple charm and his easygoing manner made Luna feel like she was basking in sunshine whenever she was around him — warm and safe. She would have to think on that more.

It was hard to sit through the afternoon, full of mindless edits and copy to write. Many times Luna rose from her chair on the pretense of getting water or snacks, just to stretch her legs and help keep her mind from analyzing further on whether she should say yes to Eli or not. The cautionary part of her was already protesting that she had gone too deep into the scene and that she should stick to a normal relationship with someone like Dylan.

But normal was the furthest thing from her mind as she walked into the coffee shop after a quick dinner at home. Luna scanned the room, spotting August amid the pods of other late-night coffee drinkers. It was surprising how many of those there were.

After their quick phone conversation earlier that day, Luna had come to realize that she needed more time to process and they needed more time to discuss her thoughts. Luna had suggested they meet up, going so far as to bribe August, who she found out loved his tea.

"Good evening, Luna," August greeted as she dumped her bag on the chair.

"Hey, hey come on. Let's go get our teas first." She had several thoughts and was eager to get started.

Once they'd sorted out their teas and desserts, Luna took out a notebook—her personal journal. She always processed her thoughts better with the pen. It forced order to the tangled web of her mind.

August inhaled the aroma of his tea with his eyes closed before taking a slow sip. "All right, tell me what's on your mind."

"Well, it just seems…a bit extreme as a first baby step to not only be naked but then be tied up and have pictures taken for public consumption. Isn't it insane to even consider this?"

She had said as much on their phone call, so August's immediate follow-up did not surprise her.

"First, let's consider how we view this. Do you think of this experience as sexual?"

Her first instinctive answer was 'yes', but she stared at her notebook. "The experience, yeah, in that it's arousing, but it's not 'play' to me, if that's what you mean." She chewed her lower lip. "I know, intellectually, that the naked body is not inherently sexual. But being naked and bound is a different matter."

"True. Let me ask you then, if someone asked you to pose nude for a life drawing class, what would you do?"

At that, Luna blushed with a sheepish smile and a small shrug. "Actually, I did a bit of that in college. It helped with the tuition."

"Ah-h."

No judgment showed on his face or in his words. August leaned back, instead, in his chair, cradling his mug still. "So, what's different about this?"

"Well, the rope..." It was a flimsy excuse. The rope framed the body. It was really only a prop. When she had called Eli with more questions, he had reassured her that the shoot would not involve sex or play of any kind, unlike the demonstration at the party. It was just a professional photography session. But that led to a different concern. Her gaze fell on the name she'd jotted down in her notebook with several circles drawn around it.

When she looked up, she found August's eyes on her and she swallowed once more.

"Jacob will be there," she whispered.

"Ah-h." August pushed his glasses up the ridge of his nose.

As an extra guarantee to his models, Eli had shared with her that he always insisted on having a neutral third party at the shoot to chaperone. It was a good policy, a way to make the models feel safe, and it also acted as a deterrent for any false accusations of inappropriate conduct on Eli's part. He was excited to tell Luna that he had secured Jacob's service, considering he seemed like a trusted man in the local community and he was one of Erica's dungeon monitors. The poor artist had no idea that Jacob's presence would, in reality, be making Luna more nervous.

"Luna, I understand you're attracted to Jacob and that may make things a little awkward, but he is a professional and very good at what he does."

When she still didn't reply, August sighed and took a sip of his tea. "Let's take a step back."

"Okay, sensei August." Humor was a good cover.

He stared at her and shook his head, even as he set his mug down, folding his arms on the table. "What's making you consider Eli's offer in the first place?"

Ah-ha! She had prepared for that in her list of pros and cons. Luna turned to her notebook and tried to flip the page, but August dropped his hand to close it. "From your gut, Luna, not your head."

She made a face at him before slumping her shoulders. "Because I've always been curious about bondage, and it's a way to try it with a master with no obligation beyond just the bondage part. When Eli did his demo, it was a huge turn-on. I want to see if there's something there, even if this time it's not sexual."

With that, August gave her a small smile of encouragement. "Focus on that instead. Don't let a bystander's presence deprive you of an experience you deem is right for you."

"You are going through with it too, right?"

"Luna..." He had already developed a way to say her name that sounded like scolding. Kind of like how he was with Cassie.

"Okay, okay, focus on myself. I know. But" — she paused and leaned forward — "you are going to say yes, right?"

August lifted the mug to his lips and chuckled, his eyes crinkling at the corners. "I already did."

"Wait, *what*?" The last word hit an octave higher.

It appeared that he was not going to dignify her exclamation with an answer. She dug her phone out and stared hard at it before unlocking the screen and typing before she lost her nerve. With a little more force than she'd intended, she set the device down.

"There. Done. I'm in."

* * * *

She might have sealed her fate that night, but reality didn't quite set in until Sunday afternoon, when she arrived on location. True to his word, one of Eli's assistants had met her, August and Cassie at a specific place on the side of the road then led them to a secluded spot in the middle of the forest. He had also taken extra caution in roping the area off with a white drop cloth along the side facing the road, despite how far away they were. His other assistant was setting up lighting while Eli himself was laying out his rope on a folding table, deep in discussion with someone whose back was toward them.

Still, Luna would recognize that silhouette anywhere. Her heart began beating faster, and she sucked in a deep breath. Then he turned around at their arrival and their eyes met, surprise and pleasure registering in those deep dark-chocolate orbs.

With that, the question switched from being about feeling shy and awkward to whether she could go through the session without embarrassing herself with her arousal. No matter how she denied it, Jacob was not just a bystander.

Eli looked up and delight blossomed over his features. "Ah, so glad you could all make it. I'm excited to be working with you three." Eli greeted each of them with a hug, and Jacob nodded a more subdued greeting from behind. They might be friends, but this was a job for all of them.

"Please." Eli gestured to the three portable changing rooms set up for them. "If you will undress in there… I've taken the liberty to prepare robes for you. You should keep your shoes on until your turn, given the rough terrain."

Luna heard the words, but it was Jacob's stare that held her rapt attention. Her breath caught as they held each other's gaze. Was that what Ted had meant when he'd once described eye-fucking? Despite the cool air under the forest canopy, her body temperature rose.

Beside her, August cleared his throat and Luna looked away, her cheeks warming. From the corner of her eye, she caught Jacob smirking. *The smug bastard.*

"Okay… Changing, right," she muttered under her breath and trudged her way toward her own pseudo-room.

Chapter Ten

The fluffy robe, combined with her going last, almost lulled Luna into a false sense of security. After they had changed, a makeup artist and a hair stylist descended on the three. Because most of the shots would consist of Luna's face being covered, they applied only minimal makeup on her but took the time to run her already-straight hair through a flat iron to take it to another level of smoothness. Eli had said something about making sure it simulated a waterfall.

Eli gathered them together once they'd all emerged dressed alike and made up in varying degrees. His team, knowing how their boss worked, had also joined them and Jacob had trailed behind a second later.

The artist clapped his hands together and bowed, a signature move of respect that Luna recognized. "I thank you all for being here today to help bring my vision to life. Without each one of you, my ideas would remain only as images in my mind. For that, I am grateful for your presence here."

He paused, fixing his gaze to meet each one.

"I want you to all remember that the body and all its reactions are perfectly natural, beautiful and should be honored. Because of the nature of what we are shooting here, there may be different comfort levels, so I ask everyone to be communicative and respectful. Let's make today's experience positive for everyone."

Everyone clapped. It was time to get to work.

It was fascinating watching Eli and his team work on Cassie and, not for the first time, Luna had to admire how limber the other woman was. By the time Eli had finished his first ties, he'd suspended Cassie face up in a similar position to the one he'd put Dominique in a few nights before, except both her legs and her arms were left to swing free, with her head falling back. Unlike Luna's hair, the stylist had done Cassie's up in a mass of curls that tumbled downward, trailing almost to the carpeted forest floor. There was a grace to her arched body that Luna envied.

As soon as Eli stepped back, the makeup artist stepped in again, murmuring as she dusted blush and toner on Cassie's body, bringing out the contours of her muscles.

On closer examination, Luna exhaled in relief. Cassie was flushed with arousal, but no one batted an eye or commented. Everyone had taken Eli's opening speech to heart, and the earlier tension drained from her body. There was such a body-positive, sex-positive attitude here that Luna could not help but relax a smidge.

When they brought August into the shot, Luna parted her lips in awe. Knotted with a harness that showed off his back, August was positioned to kneel beneath Cassie, her body framing him, almost like an arch. Cassie had curved her arms and legs with such grace that, not for the first time, Luna wondered if she'd had classical ballet training. Regardless, she had to admire the composition.

"Are you doing okay?" Jacob's whisper tickled her ear, and she almost jumped out of her skin. She knew it was important to remain quiet while Eli and his team worked, but did the man have to be such a ninja?

"Yeah." Just like dungeon monitoring, Luna knew that he had to keep his eyes on what was happening, but gratefulness welled in her for him checking up on her. "It's...beautiful, what Eli is doing."

A small smile tugged at Jacob's lips, wistful even, as he made a small noise of agreement. Another pause. "I'm surprised to find you here."

Ah-h. "I did some nude modeling before for life drawing classes. August convinced me that this wasn't any different. And he's right, with the way Eli is treating us."

With his nearness, she felt more than saw Jacob's nod. "I look forward to seeing what he will do with you."

There were so many ways to take that statement. On the spot, Luna came up with five on her own. But her body chose for her as her face warmed and moisture began gathering between her legs. *No, I can't be aroused just at the thought of Jacob watching me being tied up. Oh dear God, but I am.*

Jacob cleared his throat, a small sound almost escaping her notice. "If you've got some time after this, I'd like it if we could grab a cup of coffee."

She blinked. *Is he asking me out? Right now? When I'm dressed in a fluffy robe, about to show him my entire body in all its naked not-so-glory? When I can barely contain my lust for him as it is?*

"Sure." *Where did that easy, nonchalant voice come from?* She wasn't sure how she was managing it without being reduced to a quivering mess.

"Good." He grinned and, out of the corner of her eye, Luna noted how the smile was a little crooked. The man oozed a mischievous charm. It wasn't fair at all. *No, he's just a guy,* she reminded herself. She would do it. Besides, free coffee and maybe even free pastry for the win.

"Luna?" Eli motioned her over. August had finished his solo shoot and Cassie had been long released from her bondage. Now it was her turn.

She sucked in a breath. Two could play at that game. Slipping off her shoes, she walked toward Eli and undid her robe, letting it slide off her shoulders and down her back, revealing the curve of her hips until her full rear was in Jacob's view. She tossed one last glance over her shoulder toward him, smiled and sauntered to Eli, hips swaying, robe hanging on one arm, fully aware she was playing with fire. If only she could observe his reaction.

"Now, Luna..." Eli placed both hands on her shoulders and caught her eyes. "I know that of everyone here, you're the newest at this. I want you to know that I will treat you with the utmost respect and professionalism. This is not a scene. This is my work. I'm honored that you have trusted me. But also know that if at any time you are uncomfortable with anything or if you need things to stop, just say so. There will be no hard feelings and it will not offend me. Do you understand?"

The sincerity in Eli's voice and the earnest expression on his face made Luna smile. "I do. Thank you, Eli. That helps."

"Good. Now I will talk a little more than usual, both because you are new at this and because this suspension is also new for me. I've been trying to think of the best way to pose you like your namesake." He took a step back and retrieved a jute rope, holding it up to her. "Are you ready?"

Luna lost track of time as Eli built the harnesses and anchor points that he would use to suspend her, looping lengths of jute rope around her. It was, in a way, reminiscent of how Dylan had helped her into the climbing harness and attached the belay rope, but in a longer, extended fashion.

Each step of the way, Eli took care to explain what he was doing. By focusing on his explanations, she remained engaged on an academic level and that helped to keep her rooted so she didn't enter subspace. His touch was pleasant, light, but despite the nudity, it was not as arousing as she'd expected. It was more like a professional massage.

When he moved to work on the ties along her back, she glimpsed August and Cassie, clothed once more in their robes. Both smiled, August with a nod of encouragement and Cassie with a thumbs-up sign.

Then her gaze met Jacob's.

His body spoke of a tension she'd never seen before, his face schooled into a neutral expression. But there was something in his eyes. Her breath caught. The way they darkened, he seemed to be staring at her with an intensity that spoke of desire — for her.

But rather than making her want to cover up, it made her straighten, her own muscles tensing as her stomach clenched with a want of her own. Everything began to fade from existence and her focus narrowed to the sensation of the rope against her skin, heat radiating from her center—heat that he seemed to draw out of her with such ease. She scarcely registered Eli's hands on her.

"Luna? Are you okay?" The artist's voice cut through her thoughts and she blinked once, then twice before nodding.

"Yeah, I'm good." If her voice sounded a little hoarse, she hoped he only interpreted it as nerves.

"Excellent. Now, would you be okay with being suspended upside down?"

Surprised by the sudden question, Luna broke her eye contact with Jacob to focus on Eli. "I...haven't hung upside down since I was a kid on monkey bars."

Eli chuckled in response. "If it's okay with you, I'd like to try it. If it becomes uncomfortable, let me know and we can try a different pose. Okay?"

When she nodded her assent, he began attaching ropes from a nearby tree and tying them to the anchor points. His deft hands worked with swiftness and skill, but it wasn't until he hoisted her legs up that she flipped. Despite Eli's warning beforehand, she still gave a yelp of surprise. But before he had a chance to ask if she was fine again, she started giggling. Her hand flew to cover her mouth. "Sorry!"

Eli beamed instead, pleased by her reaction. "No apologies necessary, my dear. I'm relieved to see you are enjoying this." He spent the next few minutes adjusting her legs so that they bent back at the knee and over her head. The ropes forced her body to arc, though it was well within her own flexible abilities. Even in her mind, she pictured the crescent shape her body made.

"Now, your hands please."

Pulling her hands from her mouth, she let Eli position them to brace against her face, fingers apart so that they covered most of her features while her hair cascaded down. "No numbness in any of your limbs?"

"No, I'm good."

"Excellent." His vision complete, he took a step back and breathed in admiration. "Beautiful."

Luna's cheeks warmed, even as the makeup artist approached, applying similar treatment to her as she had with Cassie and August. Without realizing what she was doing, she peered through the gaps of her fingers to search for Jacob.

That was a mistake.

He had moved closer, as if to ensure he could see the details of what Eli was doing. Her gaze traveled to his crotch, where there was a visible bulge in his jeans. In an instant, the ropes went from pleasant and entertaining to kindling a fire inside her. Was it her imagination or did he tilt his chin up, as if aware and proud of the reaction he was provoking in her?

What would it be like if it was just the two of them? Would he touch her? In a dark part of her mind, she imagined his fingers slipping between her legs, parting her folds. What would it be like with his tongue licking her flesh? She grew wetter at the thought. At least upside down, it would not trickle down her thigh. But even she could smell herself. She attempted to shift her fingers with subtle movements, as if trying to cover her embarrassment.

The makeup artist gave a small smile, her next words jolting Luna from the sudden fantasy. "It's all right, hon. Your body's reaction is perfectly normal. I can't tell you how many models I've worked with who reacted the same way. It's nothing to be ashamed of. Okay?"

She gave the woman a nod and a grateful smile. At least she hadn't guessed the true source of her arousal.

When the woman stepped back, Eli lifted his camera and her photo session began. After several shots, they brought Cassie back in and they were posed together, Cassie sitting below, both of them positioned to cup each other's face like lovers.

The intimacy caught Luna off guard and she couldn't stop flushing.

"You're doing great, Luna. You're gorgeous," Cassie whispered and trailed a finger across her cheekbone while Eli was still preparing his camera. The tenderness Luna saw in her eyes stunned Luna. It was so contradictory to anything she'd ever expected from Cassie. But then the moment passed and she grinned with a wink. "Home stretch, right?"

"Yeah," Luna stammered, still not sure what had just happened.

Then it was over. Eli released her from the ropes and made sure she was stable. One of the other assistants handed her and Cassie their robes, even as Luna studied herself. There were rope marks on her body but nothing she hadn't expected.

When August approached, she grinned at him, exhilarated from the new experience. "I did it!"

"You did." August smiled in return.

"Everyone!" Once more, Eli motioned for them to gather around. "Thank you again for all your hard work today. I'll be developing these shots and send you all copies sometime in the next few weeks. It's been a pleasure working with all of you, and I cannot thank you enough for this experience we were able to share."

He clapped and bowed once more and Luna could not help but bow back, before they all dispersed to change or pack.

"Hey, August, can you come help me with my dress?" Cassie grabbed August's hand and tugged at it, batting her eyelashes.

August sighed and rolled his eyes. Laughter bubbling up, Luna gestured. "Go... I'll be fine."

As soon as they'd left, Jacob approached. "Ready for that coffee?"

Her cheeks heated, remembering the look in his eyes. With Herculean willpower, she managed to not look down beyond the man's face.

"Yeah, let me go change." When he nodded, she turned and started walking toward her own change pod.

"Hey, Luna."

She paused and spun around, tilting her head to one side.

"Good job today."

The smile that spread across her face was only matched by the warmth deep in her soul.

Chapter Eleven

He wasn't sure why he was so excited about getting coffee with Luna. No, that was a lie.

Jacob could admit his own desires as Eli's expert hands tied up Luna's naked form. What he didn't expect were the shots of jealousy that made him struggle through the session. Something in him wanted to claim her, to tell others to get their grubby hands off her. And while none of that was reasonable at any level, there was also no reason he shouldn't explore the mutual attraction between them.

He quirked his lips in amusement as Luna told August that she was leaving with him. August had only lifted a brow and nodded with a simple, "Text me later." It made Jacob wonder how Luna and he had gotten so close in such a short time.

Cassie, on the other hand, wouldn't stop smirking at them until, after a moment, to save Luna, he had murmured something about having to guide Luna out of the forest to his car. Still chuckling at the others' reactions, he'd allowed Luna to pick the coffee place and he drove there under her directions.

When they arrived, he opened the door to what seemed to be her favorite bakery and couldn't help but chuckle again at the excitement he saw. Luna had a bounce in her steps and she was quick to lead them to the counter. As the scent of butter and sugar greeted his nose, he understood why. His little mouse had a sweet tooth.

"The apple turnovers here are amazing. But if you want something a little less sweet, the croissants are also excellent."

Jacob smiled as he stepped up to the till. "An apple turnover, a croissant, a coffee and...?" He turned toward Luna.

"Two coffees." As she came to his side, she pulled out her wallet.

He disregarded her actions as he handed over his credit card.

"Hey! I wanted to pay and thank you for sending me those articles and answering all my questions!"

He waited until the woman at the till had left to complete their order before he replied, keeping his voice low. "And I just got paid to stand around and watch you get tied up."

Rewarded by the prettiest of blushes, he straightened and took his coffee and croissant, leading them to settle into one of the two armchairs by the window, also well aware of the self-satisfied smirk on his face.

"Well, thank you," Luna replied as she settled opposite him. Without waiting, she bit into her apple turnover and her eyes fluttered closed with a small *mm-m* sound, then another bite and sigh of satisfaction. A sip of coffee and she leaned back, a happy smile on her face.

He had never seen anyone relish a baked good the way she did. His jeans tightened, not for the first time today, and he shifted in his seat. In his mind, he wondered, if an apple turnover elicited that kind of reaction, what would she be like in the throes of pleasure?

He cleared his throat and she tilted her head to one side, a gesture he was coming to realize was uniquely hers. There was no guile on her face, no pretense — not even a smidgen of awareness of what she looked like when she ate. That was just how much the woman enjoyed food.

She was going to be the death of him.

It was best to create a diversion. "So what made you agree to be one of Eli's models?" He wasn't sure if she was going to answer but thought it was worth a shot.

"Well" — she set down her mug and curled up to tuck her legs beneath her in the chair — "I wanted to see what bondage felt like and thought it was a safe setting to try it, without obligation to…go beyond."

The urge to ask for more surged in him but he shied away from the more personal questions. "Now I understand why you were asking questions about rope earlier this week. I hope those articles helped."

"They did." She smiled again, tucking her hair behind her ear. "It helped a little to get a picture of what to expect" — she held up her wrist — "down to knowing that these marks would happen and that they would fade pretty soon. So…thank you."

"No problem." Jacob took a bite of his croissant and a sip of his coffee. Outside the window, a sudden parade of people in costumes walked by.

"Is the convention this weekend?" Luna's eyes widened as she stared out of the window.

"Looks like it. Hey, that's a pretty good Wolverine."

"And the yellow spandex version too! That guy's got guts."

Their gazes met and they shared the same grin, as one comic book nerd recognizing another. Excitement flashing in her eyes, Luna leaned forward. "Okay, favorite *X-Men* character."

From there on, conversation flowed. The constant attraction was there, but the lust faded into the background as he focused on enjoying her company and getting to know her. There was no mention of kink or lifestyle, and they ranged from topic to topic, finding more in common than not.

A woman, different from the one who had taken their orders earlier, approached their table. "Excuse me. My apologies, but we'll be closing in fifteen minutes."

They had been there for hours. Jacob blinked in surprise but smiled as Luna did the same. "Ah, thanks. We'll get out of your hair so you can close up."

They rose at the same time and Luna smiled, ducking her head. "Sorry for nattering away all this time."

"Not at all... I enjoyed it." Jacob rose and offered a hand to her. A glance of the clock showed that it was almost a quarter to five.

"I was wondering..." Now Luna blushed, as if her shyness was returning, and she looked down, avoiding meeting his eyes. "Would you be interested in dinner? I'd still like to thank you for teaching me so much." Her voice was growing softer and softer, even as her words came out faster and faster. "I cook a mean piece of fish and I bought too large of a filet of salmon for one person yesterday. Oh, unless you have a seafood allergy, in which case I can make something else, or — "

"Luna" — he placed a hand on her shoulder and ducked his head a little to catch her gaze — "salmon sounds great, and it would be a pleasure to try your cooking."

They swung by a nearby grocery store to pick up a few more things for dinner — potatoes, ingredients for a salad... He'd been on his own for so long that the sheer domesticity of their errand together caught him off guard. It was nowhere near how he imagined a first date would go, but it felt natural, normal, as if they'd done it before, as if they'd always done that.

When they'd arrived at her apartment, with him insisting on helping with the bags, Jacob was curious and pleased at the same time to see her place neat and tidy. The dinner was an impromptu invite, which meant what he saw was how it was usually.

And one could tell a lot from a person's home.

His gaze swept across the apartment. The living room held a small couch and a larger armchair, which was angled toward the wall-mounted TV. Along one wall stood a line of bookshelves, stocked with several novels and knick-knacks, including an impressive collection of Funko Pop vinyl figures. Next to where he stood by the entrance was an open-concept kitchen with a large island where two bar stools stood along one side. A large poster depicting a silhouette of a spaceship dominated one wall as decoration. Jacob recognized it as the Firefly anniversary poster. On another wall, a map of Middle-earth hung in a distressed frame.

"Can I get you something to drink? I have water, Sprite and beer."

A woman after his own heart. "I can use a Sprite." Damn his addiction. He could never turn down an offer of pop. He followed her movements as she took a two-liter bottle from the fridge and poured a glass before offering it to him. Only when he took it did she do the same for herself.

"Please, make yourself at home." Luna gestured toward the couch.

He shook his head and moved to the kitchen sink instead to wash his hands. "Why don't you let me help instead." A Dominant, he was. A male chauvinist, he wasn't. When she looked as though she was about to protest, he offered his puppy dog eyes and a slight pout. It was enough to make her laugh, which turned his pout into a grin.

"Okay, okay. Can you deal with the potatoes while I prep the salmon?"

It turned out to be the most fun he'd had for a while. They worked well together, despite his unfamiliarity with her kitchen. Perhaps it was the way she adjusted to work around him or her careful directions of where things were, as if it were second nature to her. And, in the meantime, she kept him chuckling with anecdotes of her more adventurous cooking and baking experiments. Before he realized it, they had dinner ready.

Luna kept her eyes on him as he took the first bite, sitting side by side on the high bar stools next to the kitchen island. Well aware of her scrutiny, he made a show of sampling his first bite of the potato first while keeping a poker face. He chewed with exaggerated slowness before taking another bite. Then, at last, he tried the salmon.

She had cooked it to perfection, with a simple balance of lemon and dill. He had spied pots of herbs to one side of the kitchen and realized that the freshness of the dill was a strong differentiating factor. He savored the bite then took another with more gusto.

Out of the corner of his eye, he caught a glimpse of her taking her own first bite, although she kept stealing peeks at him. Keeping her in suspense, he decided to ignore the unvoiced question that hung on her lips.

"Well? How is it?" Luna burst out, anxiety making her voice squeak after a minute longer.

Oh, she was fun. He couldn't help teasing her. It was only after he took another bite that he took pity on her and relented. "Fantastic." He paused then grinned, well aware of the mischief tugging at the corners of his lips. "If this is what I get for answering some questions, is there anything else you'd like me to teach you?"

The ill-timed comment provoked a more intense reaction than he'd anticipated. Luna, mid-bite, began coughing. Her face turned red while she flapped her hands in the air.

"Crap!" Jacob turned and started patting her back until she appeared to recover. As her coughing subsided and her face began to return to more normal coloring, his patting slowed to rubbing in small circles. Grabbing her glass of Sprite, he held it out to her. "Here, slow sips."

She drew in deep breaths and leaned a little back against his hand even as she took the glass and brought it to her lips. When she began drinking, taking slow sips, he let out a sigh of relief. "You okay?"

She turned toward him to nod and gave him a wan smile then blushed as their eyes met. Caught in the startling crystal blue, Jacob found himself unable to look away. Instead, he slowed his hand until it stilled behind her back, watching as her lips parted. *Those very, very kissable lips.* He leaned forward and had to suppress the urge to pull him to her when she did the same.

With the most willpower he'd ever had to exert on himself, he brushed his lips against her temple instead. Somehow, however, the gesture came out much more intimate. "Good."

She had closed her eyes at the gesture and it took seconds longer before she fluttered them open once more. Jacob held his breath, wondering at how she would react next.

"Thank you," Luna whispered and ducked her head again.

A part of him mused over just what she had in her mind when he made his teaching comment that made her choke on her food, but rather than tease her further, unwilling to ruin the moment, he let it drop for now. "Eat your food before it gets cold."

Once more, she nodded, turned and started eating again. *So responsive to commands.* Even as he returned to his own meal, he chewed over his thoughts. She was a natural and he could see how easy it would be for someone to take advantage of her submissiveness. Besides education, there must be something else he could do to protect her.

For a time, he fell silent as he ate and pondered the woman next to him.

Chapter Twelve

Her heart was pounding so hard that Luna wasn't sure how she'd managed to eat the rest of her food at all. She had thought he was going to kiss her. She wanted him to kiss her. A tinge of disappointment tainted the otherwise perfect day, just a wee bit.

When he'd finished his meal, she gave him a quick smile as she reached to collect his plate and fork, bringing it over to the sink.

"That was great. Thank you."

Luna beamed at Jacob's compliment and gave a slight nod, beginning to rinse the dishes. Then she tilted her head, watching him as he left his seat to walk toward the fridge. *Maybe for more pop?*

"Wait... I have a bit of a surprise for you." With his back turned toward Luna, she couldn't quite tell what he was up to until he stepped back from her fridge with a small white box in his hands. When he placed it on the kitchen counter and motioned her over, the intensity of his gaze as he watched her every move threatened to overwhelm her. "Open it."

Luna pried the sticker loose with slow care and lifted the lid of the box, her eyes widening at the six-inch tiramisu cake that sat inside, topped with delicate scrolls of cream and an abundance of chocolate shavings. A small whimper escaped her lips. It must be a bribe of some form. For what, though, she had no idea.

"Good."

Something must have shown in her face. Luna looked up, gaping at Jacob a little, even as his lips curved upward in a self-satisfied smile.

"How?" She had so many questions but she only managed that one word. Was the man some sort of ninja? How did he know it was her absolute favorite?

"Your eyes kept going to the little tiramisu cups in the bakery, and when you were busy picking out potatoes, I picked it up from the bakery side."

She blinked at him.

"No, I'm not a mind reader."

Luna managed a small squeak of happiness.

Jacob chuckled while rubbing the back of his neck. "Normally I'd bake something for a dinner like this, but since this was more of a last-minute thing…"

Oh dear God, the man bakes. He had already proven more than capable in the kitchen. The way he'd held his knife alone had told her that he cooked often enough, and now he was claiming he could also make sweets. In her mind, his title changed from Mr. Just-a-guy to Mr. Chef. It had taken all her willpower to not call him Mr. Dream Guy. She was not in the business of putting anyone on a pedestal like that, but he was making it mighty hard.

Her gaze returned to stare at the cake. Gorgeous. She resisted the urge to take out her phone to snap pictures to add to her food porn collection. Ted had made fun of that enough. She didn't want to give Jacob more of a dorky impression of her than she already had.

"Luna, go fetch us some plates and forks." Jacob's voice remained gentle as he chided her, but the command behind it was enough to wake her from her thoughts of the cake.

Her body responded before her mind registered how fast she'd obeyed. As she moved to the cupboards, she extracted two plates and grabbed forks and a cake knife from the drawer. She kept darting her eyes back to the cake, to Jacob, then to the cake again. Relinquishing the knife to Jacob, she moved to sit once more and stared as he cut a large slice before handing it to her. "Eat."

Heaven on a fork. She swayed a little in her seat from the first bite.

"How is it?"

She should tease him back. She should not answer. But somehow that felt wrong. "Amazing." Her voice was hushed with reverence.

He chuckled, and she basked in the sound. "Good. I've done my job for the day."

"Job?" Another tilt of her head in question.

"Well, let's see. I made sure you were safe and happy."

Her cheeks heated and her lips made an O shape, but no sound came out as she stared at him. His job as monitor for Eli had meant that he'd ensured everyone's safety — but the second...

He's flirting with me. Oh my God, he's flirting back with me. What do I say? What do I say?

"Thank…y-you…" she stammered, still flushed. In her head, she facepalmed at her own awkwardness.

They finished the cake, Luna savoring every bite, then retired to the couch to pick a movie, finally settling on an old *Hellboy* rerun. They started on opposite ends of her small couch. As the evening chill of the early summer settled in, Luna began hunting for her knitted throw, finding it on the other side of Jacob. At first, she curled into it without another thought but soon, Jacob reached over to tug at the opposite end.

"Cold?"

"That looks way too comfortable. Share," he ordered.

With a small laugh, Luna scooted closer so they could both huddle into the blanket. Once they had both resettled underneath it, Jacob took the liberty to adjust it over both of them, to ensure maximum coverage.

Somewhere toward the end of the movie, lulled by the combined warmth of Jacob and the throw, Luna came to cuddle against him, laying her head on his shoulder, her eyes half-closed in sleepiness. At some point, he had wrapped an arm around her shoulder, much like the way he had kept an arm around her during Eli's public demonstration with Dominique. A part of her mind registered that she should blush like mad, but half asleep, she found it hard to care. It felt natural, like they had cuddled a million times before.

"Luna, sweetheart, it's time to wake up."

His lips brushed by her hair. *When did I fall asleep?* She opened her eyes to the Netflix home screen then turned to gaze up at Jacob, even as he leaned back a little, his smile tender. Her breath caught as they stared at each other, both seeming unwilling to pull away.

With slow tenderness, he leaned forward and pressed a small kiss on her forehead. "I have to get home and you have to get to bed." She wasn't sure if she'd imagined the regret she thought she heard.

With a small exhale, she leaned back too and, with limbs lethargic with reluctance, Luna pushed aside the throw so that they could both rise from the couch. She rubbed the sleep from her eyes and followed as Jacob made his way to the door.

"Thank you for spending the day with me." Shy once more, she managed a small smile for him but kept her gaze down a little. Luna feared that if she looked into his eyes once more, she would do something rash, like ask him to stay.

"Thank you for making me the delicious dinner." Jacob reached out and tucked a strand of her hair behind her ear. He trailed his fingers down, brushing his knuckles along her cheek until they met her chin and he could tilt her face toward him.

Despite all her misgivings, she looked into his eyes. The affection in those warm chocolate orbs threatened to break down every defense she had.

He leaned in to brush his lips against hers. They were warm, gentle—almost teasing in how light his kiss was. He tasted as delicious as the tiramisu they had shared earlier.

Her entire being melted at his touch and she closed her eyes, opening only when he withdrew, which was much too soon for her liking.

"Good night, Luna. I'll see you soon."

She smiled at him, her cheeks rosy once more. "Good night, Jacob."

Her heart was still pounding when she closed the door behind him with a soft but audible click. She felt almost floaty, like the whole day had been surreal. When she began to recognize what was unfolding between them, she drew in deep breaths, working through the exercise that Jacob had taught her to ground herself. The man was making her enter subspace with just a kiss alone—and a closed-mouthed one at that. What would it be like if...?

With vicious urgency, she slammed the door shut on those speculations. She needed another sex dream like she needed a hole in her head. With a grumble to herself, she stalked to bed.

Luna was still a little floaty the next morning, all the way through work until lunch.

"Over here!"

Luna turned to glimpse a bounce of curls and an enthusiastic wave of arms, and she grinned as she spied Lani at a corner table. They had agreed to meet up for brunch, and Luna salivated at the thought of eggs and bacon. Even as she sat, her stomach rumbled with anticipation.

"Hi, hi! How are you?"

"I'm good!" And she was. In truth, she hadn't been able to wipe the stupid grin off her face. How often had she touched her lips all day, savoring the memory of Jacob's?

Lani arched a brow and Luna blushed at the scrutiny, but as luck would have it, a waiter coming by to take their orders saved her from having to say more. The servers obviously understood that the lunch crowd needed to get back to work quick enough.

"So, August told me that you guys were planning to model for a photoshoot for Elijah? It was yesterday, right? How did it go?"

Traitor. "It was fun—all very professional." She knew, however, the warmth that spread across her cheeks belied her words. A distraction... She needed to distract Lani. "So, you and August talked?"

Lani sniffed and took a sip of her tea. "We talk often. I rather enjoy the lovely company. We'll see where we go from here, but I'm unsure if I can give him what he desires."

"What do you mean?"

A delicate shrug. "Exclusivity." A mischievous grin spread across her lips. "I'm not ready to settle yet. There are too many pretty dollies to play with." Lani leaned forward and peered at Luna. "That was a nice attempt at a diversion, my dear. Now tell me... If things were so professional at the shoot, why are your cheeks so red, hmm-m?"

Luna could see that Lani was trying to stifle her giggles. *Busted. Distraction failed.* With a sigh, she stared down at the table and mumbled. "Well, it was fine until..."

"Until?"

"Until I realized Jacob was watching." Now she was muttering under her breath.

"Well, Luna, my dear, of course he was looking. He was doing his job."

Luna sneaked a peek at Lani, and while her friend was keeping her expression neutral, her eyes gleamed with humor.

"Lani...."

"Okay." The other woman laughed and shook her head. "Let me guess. Was he looking at you like he wanted to eat you up?"

"Lani!" Luna squirmed in her seat. Her fantasy from the session, his face between her legs, replayed in full color in her mind. It was just a brief flash of an image but enough to make her stomach clench. *Where the hell is the lust coming from?* She swallowed, shoving her libido away to focus on the conversation. "How?"

"I've known Jacob for a very long time now." Lani chuckled. "I saw how he looked at you at the party."

Her lips formed a small O. She would protest, but the memory of their cuddling then his kiss resurfaced. There was no denying that Mr. Chef was interested.

"Did something else happen?"

Luna winced when she realized she was touching her lips again. There was no hiding anything from Lani. It figured, considering the woman was a counselor by trade. "We hung out after. He kissed me." Her whisper was full of wonder and awe.

A high-pitched squeak broke through her shyness. "Oh, you've got his attention and the dear boy finally made a move!" Lani was almost bouncing in her seat and she squealed in delight. Luna's eyes widened, overwhelmed by her friend's enthusiasm. A couple from the next table shot them an annoyed look, but Lani paid them no heed.

"One coffee-crusted pork belly hash and one breakfast quesadilla. Is there anything else I can get you two?" The server came, arms laden with food, saving Luna from having to reply. She breathed a discreet sigh of relief and shook her head, even as Lani did the same.

"Excellent. Enjoy."

The waiter stepped away.

"Luna?" A second later, Dylan appeared beside their table, a dimpled smile on his lips.

Surprise almost made Luna spit out her drink. Instead, she recovered with a small wave. "Dylan! Hi!" The greeting came out more like a squeak as her heart hammered. The last thing she'd expected was for her two very distinct and different worlds to collide.

"Hi."

The two of them stared at each other until Lani cleared her throat with a dainty sound.

"Oh, Dylan, meet my friend Lani." Luna turned toward the Domme, resisting from chewing her lower lip out of nervousness.

Lani extended a hand and Dylan reached across to shake it. "Nice to meet you, Dylan." Giving him a beaming smile, she nodded. "Have you known Luna long?"

"Ah-h. Actually, Ted and Brandon just introduced me to her a few weeks back. Have you met them?"

"No, I don't believe I have."

"Dylan taught me how to climb a few weeks ago," Luna interjected before the conversation delved more into her various social lives. How the hell does every superhero do it? Oh wait, Tony Stark didn't even bother. And Batman didn't have a social life, not as Batman.

"Oh, that sounds like fun!"

What is with that speculative gleam in Lani's eyes?

"Well, I won't keep you girls from your food." Dylan gestured to the table. "Luna, are we still on for dinner and drinks tomorrow night?"

She kicked herself. *Right...* At Ted's urging, she had reached out, and they had agreed on the date before things had gotten intense with Jacob. *Was it even intense?*

"Sure." Maybe the word came out with more forced enthusiasm than she'd intended.

"Awesome. See you then! Nice to meet you, Lani." He nodded once more then turned and walked away.

Luna was still watching him when Lani spoke. "So, he seems cute. And it sounds like you've got a big date tomorrow."

With a hard swallow, Luna turned. "I swear that I booked the date before the kiss. I mean, I didn't even know Jacob was going to ask me out to coffee. And —"

"Whoa! Easy, girl." Lani shook her head and placed a hand on Luna's arm. "You don't have to explain anything. You're exploring right now and haven't committed to anything, much less any*one*. What you're doing is healthy."

Luna released the tension building up in her shoulders and ducked her head a little. "Thanks. I've never been in this situation before."

"How so?"

"Well" — Luna paused and swallowed, gazing toward where Dylan had walked off — "just having two guys interested in me at the same time. Dylan and Jacob are very different."

"Ah-h…" Lani's features softened with understanding, her tone sympathetic. "As long as you're honest with everyone, including yourself, simply take your time to explore, to see what seems more right to you."

Luna nodded. "Thanks." The unexpected kindness made her want to give Lani a big hug, but she refrained, lest she make a scene.

"Now eat. Your food's getting cold."

Luna straightened and gave a small laugh. "Yes, Ma'am."

Chapter Thirteen

It was just drinks and dinner. Luna smoothed a hand over her black drapey tank top with a deep V neck, having conceded to dress a little nicer than her usual T-shirt and jeans. With a firm nod to herself, she grasped the handle of the door, pulled it opened and let herself into the restaurant and lounge she had picked for their date. It screamed casual but chic and she had been dying to try their steak. Now she wondered if they would have both been better served going to the neighborhood diner instead.

The place was packed with multiple gorgeous hostesses in tight black dresses and glossy lipstick talking to several waiting guests. More self-conscious than ever, Luna stood in one corner until she caught sight of Dylan, waving at her from one of the two-seater tables in the lounge. Well, she'd dug her own grave — now she must lie in it.

"Hi, Luna." Dylan rose from his seat and swung around to envelop her in a hug.

Caught by surprise, she hugged back then gave a small smile, noting with approval the simple gray short-sleeved shirt and black slacks that he wore. He cleaned up well. And he smelled good, with a hint of aftershave.

When they stepped back and took a seat, Dylan grinned. "You look amazing."

Right on cue, Luna's cheeks warmed. Compliments were never her strong suit. "Thank you," she stammered, even as she picked up the drink menu. Unlike the impromptu coffee date with Jacob, she felt a lot more nervous as she racked her brain, trying to think of a topic for small talk. Instead, her inner dialogue ran a litany of curses aimed at Ted.

"How did you find climbing the other day?"

Luna schooled her face, hoping she wasn't looking too relieved that he'd brought up a safe topic. "It was fun. I was pretty sore after, but it was worth it."

"The soreness will happen. Climbing uses some pretty specific muscle groups that don't get used a lot in other sports."

"You're telling me! I was hurting in places I didn't know existed."

Conversation flowed with more ease after that but stayed focused on climbing. They finished the first round of drinks and moved to the main dining area for dinner. Luna's eyes lit up as she found the fabled steak on the menu.

"Found something you like?" Dylan had on a different smile, one that was teasing.

Luna smiled as she looked over the menu, also realizing that he was looking at her. "Guilty as charged. I heard their steaks are ridiculously good."

Dylan chuckled and closed the menu. "Well, I'll follow your lead. Steak sounds good to me."

It was an odd turn of phrase. In the back of her mind, Luna wondered if Dylan was in the scene somehow as another submissive — or maybe he was a closet one. Or perhaps she'd been reading too much about the lifestyle in the last while and was seeing everything through that lens. She made a mental note to ask both August and Jacob about their opinions when she next saw them.

"Are you okay, Luna?" There was a slight knowing tug of the corners of Dylan's lips as he leaned forward a little.

Realizing that she had been staring, Luna nodded and flushed again but was a little surprised as she checked herself. There was attraction — Dylan checked almost all her boxes — but her libido wasn't kicking into high gear like it was in Jacob's presence. It was something worth puzzling over later.

"Hey, don't be embarrassed. There's no need." Dylan's voice had gentled.

"Ah, sorry." Luna chewed her lower lip.

"Hey, am I making you nervous? There's no pressure. We can take it as fast or as slow as you'd like." Dylan straightened. Luna wasn't sure in the dim lighting but she thought she saw his own cheeks pinken. "I like you, Luna. I mean… What's there to not like? You're gorgeous, smart and fun. I'd like to continue hanging out to see where it takes us, but I don't want you to feel pressured into anything."

Where has he been all my life? Not only was he adorable, but he was sweet and every bit a gentleman. And he was giving her the reins, to stay in control. It was safe and normal. He was someone who had the potential to be a long-term partner if he proved to be consistent in how considerate he was. Luna owed it to herself to see it through. "I'd like that. Thank you." She smiled even as she looked up at him — though her chin remained pointing downward.

"Awesome."

A waitress looking almost identical to the hostesses outside dropped by to take their orders, interrupting their conversation. As soon as she'd left, Luna lifted the Bellini to her lips and took another sip, savoring the cool sweetness on her tongue.

"Now that's just wrong," Dylan muttered under his breath.

Luna had just managed to catch his words and turned toward the direction he was looking. Two tables over, there was a couple dressed as though they were on a date, but they had a toddler in tow. She watched in fascination as the mom had all but abandoned her food, trying to cajole the toddler to be quiet while the dad ate, oblivious to the distress the rest of his family was in.

"How so?" Luna had several opinions herself but she remained curious as to where Dylan stood. Lots of people thought parents shouldn't bring their kids to places like the one they were in. She was pretty against that point of view and was already preparing to argue her side

He shook his head and sighed. "I've seen too many dads expecting the mom to do everything with their kids. It's frustrating to see. I mean, I don't have kids, but even I can tell that's wrong. Look… He's eating away while her food's getting cold."

Surprised, Luna turned her attention back to Dylan, beaming. There were no arguments from her there, but now she was even more curious. "Do you identify as a feminist?"

"I suppose you can say that. When I was in Sweden a couple of months ago, there were as many men pushing strollers together on play dates as there were women. I guess that when push comes to shove, I believe in gender equality and think traditional gender roles are dumb. We're all humans. A woman should get as much of a say in things as a man, especially in a partnership." Determination steeled his voice. "It shouldn't be just the man calling the shots."

Luna nodded and found herself agreeing with his opinion. It sounded wonderful. How many times in her short career so far had she had to fight for equal treatment? There had been nothing major, just microaggressions like not being heard or being talked over. But in a relationship, to make all the decisions? It sounded...exhausting. A twinge of guilt plucked at her soul.

"What— What if the woman doesn't want to call the shots?" she asked in a small voice.

"I find that hard to believe." Dylan scoffed and waved a hand in the air. "Besides," he offered an accompanying impish smile, "I find a woman who takes charge incredibly sexy."

Was that how she came off? Or perhaps that's how Ted and Brandon had been selling her? Part of her wondered if she should hook Dylan up with Lani instead, but no, she wouldn't do that to August.

The food arriving saved her from coming up with a response. Her eyes widened as she devoured the artful display of the steak before she even had her first bite. Soon, eating made them both too busy to talk.

Only when the wait staff had cleared their plates and they'd ordered desserts did her phone light up with a incoming messages. As soon as Dylan excused himself to use the washroom, Luna grabbed the device and unlocked it.

Ted had sent the first one, asking how the date was progressing. That one she ignored. He could grill her tomorrow. The second, however, came from Jacob — a casual check-up, asking her how she was.

Good. On a date actually.

She hit Send before her brain caught up with her fingers. *Shit. Shit. Shit. Why did I type that?* The Bellini… She blamed the Bellini. Perhaps it wasn't the first one, but the second must have been the culprit. The sugar must have hidden how much alcohol the drinks each contained. She scrambled to search for a 'delete message' function, only to remember that the text message system had no such feature.

I see. Thank you for being honest with me.

Honesty. Lani said being honest was important, right? Which also meant she needed to keep being honest with him. Well, if the drink had gotten her this far… She grabbed the glass and gulped down the rest of it in one large dose of liquid courage.

I'm exploring. I'm not sure yet if the lifestyle is right for me, but it doesn't mean I'm not insanely attracted to you.

Why the hell had she used the word 'insanely'? She could picture the smirk on his face already.

Easy, Luna. I understand. It just means I have a little competition. I'm not afraid of that.

How the hell could a man sound so confident and sexy over text? Before she had another chance to reply, another text came in.

Besides, if you're texting and thinking of me as insanely attractive during your date, I don't have that much to worry about.

That ass! Just for that, she put her phone down without replying. And if she tried hard enough, she could even convince herself that the heat in her cheeks resulted from the damn alcohol she'd drunk—and nothing else.

Dylan returned as dessert arrived. The rest of the date turned into a fuzzy pleasant blur. At some point, Luna checked herself. She was still functional and still had her full faculties and memory. But her nerves had dulled. So if she was freer with her tongue and louder with her laughter, it was for the best.

Dylan walked her home and the next thing she knew, they were sitting on her couch sharing a bottle of prosecco. Dylan's boyish charms had her laughing with more of his comical climbing stories, while he also laughed at all the right places during her retelling of all the ins and outs of judo trainings. As the night wore on, he became more touchy-feely and, rather than worrying, Luna allowed herself to enjoy the pleasantness of it.

He was running his fingers through her hair when he leaned in, catching her gaze. "You're so beautiful," he whispered but he paused in his movements. It was

Luna who had to push forward so that their lips touched.

That was also pleasant and gentle. There was a slight hesitation in his actions until she snaked a hand to the back of his head. Their kiss lasted until she guided his head down toward her neck, where he could kiss and lick as he pleased. She closed her eyes and tilted her head to one side, exposing more of her skin with a small moan when he got the hint. Her body warmed a small tinge as he took more initiative.

"Give me a chance and I'll worship you like a goddess." His words caressed her skin, his breath tickling her.

But it was as if he had poured a cold bucket of water over her. She didn't want to be worshiped. Valued and treasured, but not put on a pedestal. Luna could understand how much of a turn-on that line would be for other women, but like other times, that, combined with his earlier timidity, caused her libido to take a dive downward instead. She tried to recover her arousal, so much that she pulled Dylan's head closer to her neck, urging him to devour her, to show some aggression rather than the careful gentleness. Unbidden, her mind brought up the image of Jacob to help.

No, it's all wrong. Even in her inebriated state, she knew that.

She dropped her hand from his head and pushed his shoulder away with gentle pressure. Dylan took the cue and eased back, his eyes glazed over with desire.

"I'm sorry. I'm *so* sorry. I can't do this right now. It's. It's too fast." *Lamest excuse ever.*

"Hey, hey, it's okay." Dylan took her hands in his and gave them a gentle squeeze. "No pressure, remember?"

She didn't meet his eyes, guilt gnawing at her.

"Look... It's getting late. Why don't I head home and we can talk tomorrow or whenever you're ready?"

Grateful for his understanding, she gave him a weak smile and rose, a little unsteady on her feet. "Thanks. Yeah, that sounds good."

"Awesome." As they made their way to the door, Luna could only focus on putting one foot in front of the other. While she'd felt buzzed after dinner, wooziness informed her that with the prosecco added to that, she had entered the nearly drunk category now.

"Good night, Luna." Dylan leaned in and kissed her cheek. With a last, brief smile, he let himself out.

With enough clarity still to lock the door behind him, she turned and leaned her back against it before sliding down until she sat on the floor, her head in her hands. Dylan was a nice guy and damn good-looking. Luna could find no reason to not be head over heels for him except he was like every other guy she had dated, wanting her to take charge. Then, there was Mr. Chef.

Luna groaned. Jacob had ruined her for all other men. One little kiss... That was all they had shared so far.

She was doomed.

Chapter Fourteen

Why the hell had she thought that drinking that much on a weeknight was a good idea? The alarm jolted Luna out of sleep and into consciousness, but as soon as she'd cracked her eyes open, sunlight had stabbed like daggers into her pounding head. Her phone rang and all she could do was hiss at it. With her eyes still closed, she groped along her bedside table until she grabbed the infernal device and picked it up. A vague part of her was even impressed with the feat, even if the rest of her was full of regret.

"Good morning, Luna."

Jacob's voice startled her so much that her eyes snapped open and she shot right up, sitting upright in bed before whimpering in pain.

"Maybe just morning."

He chuckled and she thought him laughing at her would annoy her. Instead, she warmed at the sound and found it eased the pounding in her head a little.

"Jacob?" Her own voice sounded hoarse. It wasn't her sexiest moment by far.

"You asked me to give you a wake-up call this morning to make sure you didn't miss work."

"I did?" She rubbed her temple in slow circles, trying to recall when she would have made such a request.

"Let's see...and I quote." There was a pause, a bit of a shuffling as he must have put her on the speaker to pull up her message. "*'I'd love it if a Dom kicks my ass in the morning and makes sure I get to work on time'*. So here I am, reporting for duty."

"I said *what*?" Luna spluttered and pulled her own phone back to scroll through her text messages. The exact quote stared back at her. She scanned the subsequent texts, which were even worse — even if, out of mercy, Jacob hadn't read those out loud.

I mean, besides all the other smexy things that the Dom would do to me in the morning if he was here. Interested?

She had drunk-texted him the previous night.
Oh. Dear. God.

"Luna? Are you still there?"

"Yes." She scrambled to put the phone back to her ear. "Jacob, I'm so, so sorry." Not only her cheeks but her entire body was also heated in embarrassment, and she wasn't sure if she could ever look Jacob in the eye again. "I had way too much to drink. It's not something I normally do. I don't even think I've ever drunk-texted anyone, ever."

"Well, I'm honored to be your first, I think?" She could hear the smug smirk in his voice and wanted to hide in her bed forever. When she didn't reply, he spoke again. "Hey, Luna, listen… Don't worry about it. Now go have a hot shower, make sure you drink lots of water today and try to eat something light, like a piece of toast when you think you can stomach it. Okay?"

"Okay," she replied in a small voice, although her stomach churned at the thought of food.

"Good girl. Now do all that and I'll come give you a ride to work and save you from the bus."

Right… They had talked about work before. Despite the less-than-appealing prospect of seeing Jacob at the moment, the bribe of a ride, coupled with the pounding headache that protested against the thought of public transit, was too good to resist. "Okay."

"I'll be over in about forty-five minutes. Is that enough time for you?"

"Yeah."

"Good. See you soon."

Long after they'd hung up, Luna stared at her phone, torn. On one hand, she feared to discover what else she had texted Jacob. On the other hand, her morbid curiosity urged her to peek at what his replies were.

No, she didn't have time to dither. Despite her entire body's protests, she climbed out of bed. She swore to never drink again.

By the time Jacob rang the buzzer, she had showered, dressed and was taking slow sips of water out of her water bottle. Unable to stomach food yet, she had packed a bagel in her bag for later. When she'd found out that, sometime the previous night, she had finished that bottle of wine by herself, she groaned with self-hatred.

Shuffling to open the door, Luna tugged at her hoodie. Despite wanting to dress to impress, she had settled on a pair of tight jeans and an oversized *Doctor Who* T-shirt. At least it wasn't her cargo shorts, and the jeans made her butt look perky — or so she thought.

What greeted her was a paper bag from her favorite bakery and a cup of coffee, along with the sexiest crooked grin. Self-conscious and wishing she'd dressed up more, Luna ducked her head and flushed.

"Drink before your hangover turns into a caffeine-withdrawal headache." Jacob passed the coffee to her, and she tried to still her quick-beating heart when his fingers brushed hers. "This can be for later, when you're up for a little sugar."

The smell wafted to her nose. *Apples.* He'd bought her an apple turnover. Luna wanted to kiss him. Instead, she took a sip of the coffee, licking the side of the rim to catch a drip that was threatening to spill on her hand before she set it and the turnover down.

When she looked up once more, the smile she had mustered for him faded. There was an intensity in the way he looked at her. *Like he wants to eat me up.* Lani's words came echoing back in her mind and she bit her lower lip hard.

"Stop chewing on it." His thumb came to rub her lower lip, tugging it with gentleness back from her teeth. Despite the hangover, Luna had to resist the urge to lick his thumb, to see what he tasted like.

Jacob was the first to clear his throat. "Are you ready to go?"

The fog threatening to cloud her mind receded a little, enough for her to nod. While he waited, she turned to throw her water bottle into her messenger bag then grabbed the coffee and apple turnover. "Yeah."

As Jacob opened the door, she followed him out, remembering at the last second to lock up behind her.

The car ride was quiet at first, except for her giving him directions to her office. Luna kept opening and closing her eyes behind the sunglasses she wore. Now and then, a bump in the road would jostle them and she would wince.

"Did you take a painkiller?"

Luna wasn't sure how he could tell the headache was still there, as he had kept his eyes on the road. "I forgot," she answered, ducking her head. Hangovers were such a rare occurrence for her, because she usually kept tight control over how much she drank.

"Glove box. There's a bottle of Advil."

She flashed him a grateful smile, helped herself and popped an extra strength tablet into her mouth, washing it down with her cooling coffee. "Thank you."

Without warning, her phone buzzed, almost startling her into spilling the remaining liquid on herself. Luckily, her drink saved, she juggled the cup and phone until she could pull up the text and she gave a soft sigh. *Dylan.*

"Everything okay?"

"Yeah." Hesitation made her pause but she remembered to not chew her lower lip this time. With another exhale of breath, she shook her head. "It's Dylan, my date from last night."

"Ah-h."

"We shared a bottle of wine but not much happened." Luna wasn't sure why she felt the need to explain.

"Luna, you don't owe me any details about your date." Jacob's forehead had furrowed, though he kept his eyes looking forward.

"I know... I just..." She groped for the right words. "I just wanted to be honest." A glance outside. "Pull in here. This is the building." It also meant that she needed to be honest with Dylan soon.

Jacob nodded as he turned into the parking lot. There was a tension between them that Luna disliked.

"Jacob, what's wrong?"

Sighing as he parked and turned off the car, he shifted toward her and offered a tight smile. "Don't worry about it. Okay?"

"Jacob, please." Luna hated the pleading tone in her voice, but she missed the comfort and ease they'd had with each other the last time they'd been together. She needed to clear the air.

He gave another sigh and ran a hand over his hair. "Luna, I know you're still exploring and I'm trying to give you the space to do that..." Now he moved his hand to the back of his neck. "But, I have to admit that you haven't made it easy."

"I'm sorry," she replied in a small voice, wilting.

"Luna" —he reached across and laid a hand on top of her head—"none of this is your fault. You have nothing to be sorry for."

Confused, she blinked at him once, then twice.

"You're just being you. But you being you is something I find very attractive, especially as a Dom."

"Oh." Luna's cheeks grew hot. "I—" Her heartbeat sped faster until she was sure they could both hear it. Before she lost her nerves, she blurted out, "I want to try scening with you."

Her eyes widened and she raised her free hand to cover her mouth.

Jacob's eyes grew rounder in surprise. Luna was sure his expression mirrored her own bewilderment. Her words hung in the air between them.

"I mean..." Stammering now, she began to try to dig herself out. "That was presumptuous. I'm sorry. I meant...only if you would be interested. It would help with exploring, right? Help me figure out if... I mean, if you don't mind. It can be casual, no commitment. But I mean, just, if you're comfortable and okay with it." Oh God, she was babbling. With a Herculean effort, she clamped her mouth shut.

"Luna" — he breathed out her name out as he reached to cup her cheek — "it would be my pleasure to provide you with that experience, but I want you to be clear that it is what you want. I want you to take a few days to think it over and let me know Saturday morning if you still want to go through with it. Okay?"

Unsure whether to be excited or disappointed by his answer, Luna could only incline her head in acknowledgment. His palm felt warm against her cheek, soothing her nerves. In an even smaller voice, just above a whisper, she asked, "May I have a kiss?"

His answer was not what she expected. With a new ferocity, he surged forward and crushed her lips with his. It was nothing like that brief, chaste kiss he'd given her the last time. The one he gave her now spoke of a barely leashed passion as he moved his hand to the back of her head, pulling her closer. When her lips parted for him, he slipped in his tongue to entangle with hers. And when he tilted his head to nibble on her lip, she moaned. Her panties dampened at the searing kiss alone.

As they pulled apart to catch their breaths, Luna stared at Jacob, while he only smiled at her with smug satisfaction. He leaned forward once more, pressing a gentler kiss on her forehead. "Have a good day at work, sweetheart. Don't forget to drink more water."

"Okay. You too." Still dizzy from the kiss, her body went on autopilot as she opened the door and let herself out. With a last wave to him, she slung her bag over her shoulder and walked to her office then turned to watch him pull out of the parking spot only after she was inside.

Luna was still in a daze when she spun around once more and smacked headlong into Ted.

"Whoa!" Her friend held her shoulders, steadying her as she blinked at him. "Luna?"

"Oh, Ted, hi." For some inexplicable reason, she started flushing again.

"Was that someone dropping you off?"

"Um…yes?"

Ted's grin widened like the Cheshire Cat's. "Was that Dylan?"

"Um…no."

"Another guy?"

"Um…yes?"

"Dayam. Weren't you on a date with Dylan last night, though?"

Ted's line of questioning kicked in after a few more seconds. Her mind snapped back into reality as she lifted her hands and tried to wave it off. "No, no, no, it's not like that. I was just hungover from last night and Jacob offered to drive me to work."

"And nothing happened with Dylan last night?"

"Well…" The memory resurfaced. "We made out a little, but nothing beyond that."

"So, let me get this straight. You went on a date with one guy, got sloshed, made out then sent the guy home and called another guy up to give you a ride to work in the morning."

Luna opened her mouth to protest then closed it. Ted wasn't inaccurate in describing the last twelve hours. She shrugged instead in a weak response.

"Wait! Did you make out with this guy too? What's his name again?"

"Jacob, and no!" Luna protested but her cheeks grew even hotter.

"You did!"

"No, we just kissed!" She hissed at Ted then groaned.

"Wow, Luna..."

It was like her conscience was talking. In defense, her back stiffened, and she drew herself up. "I'm a free agent!"

Now it was Ted's turn to hold up his hands. "Hey, I'm not judging here. I'm just admiring your game."

Luna only groaned once more in response and stalked across the lobby with Ted following at her heels.

"So are you interested in something longer term with either Dylan or Jacob?"

"Maybe," she muttered—but in her heart, she already knew.

Chapter Fifteen

Luna exhaled with a deep sigh and slumped into her seat at the food court of the mall. She had begun to compose a response to Dylan, deleted it before sending, then started again. It had taken about five tries before she had given up crafting something meaningful and sent a simple *I'm okay* instead. It had started as a conversation over text that had lasted most of the day, but they were both dancing around the elephant in the proverbial room.

She was staring at the blank text box, unsure of what to type. That was ironic, considering she had chosen word-smithing as a career. Out of nowhere, a voice made her jump out of her seat.

"Why the long face?" Cassie leaned over her shoulder, trying to glimpse her phone.

Luna hit the Power button, blacking the screen.

"Aw, come on!" Cassie straightened and moved to take one of the other seats at the table.

"Cassie..." It seemed like August, who had come up from behind and taken another empty seat, was forever warning Cassie off her case, but Luna only gave a small shake of her head. They had agreed to meet at the mall to shop for birthday presents for Lani, for her beach party the coming weekend.

"Let's get some food first," she suggested and stood.

By the time they'd regrouped, Luna was staring at her phone again. Something in her was reluctant to bring up the discussion of where they were at, but Dylan deserved an explanation. She still wasn't sure her heart was set yet—or at least that was what her brain was saying. But she couldn't stop wanting to explain.

"Okay, Luna, what's up?" Cassie asked, the first to come back with food.

For a moment, Luna debated saying anything at all and chewed her lip until Cassie sighed and reached out a hand to place over Luna's. For once, she looked serious.

"If you want to talk about it, I'm here. Everyone may tease me all the time, but it also means I'm experienced and I know the community well. I promise you that whatever you say, I won't laugh and I won't blab."

She already trusted August and kept him up-to-date with phone calls and texts as to her thoughts and feelings. Even earlier that morning she had texted August in a panic for advice after Jacob had dropped her off, but her fellow sub was busy and said it would be easier for them to talk tonight. She wanted to trust Cassie, considering the experiences they'd shared so far. Perhaps another woman's point of view would be beneficial.

In the end, it was Cassie's speech that made her decide. She nodded.

"I've gone on a few dates with this guy, Dylan. We made out last time but..." Luna wasn't sure how she was going to put it politely. Her words trailed off as she looked down at her cooling burger and fries.

"Let me guess. Too vanilla and turned you right off."

Right on target. Luna winced. "Yeah. I stopped things and said it was too soon." She left out the fact that her brain had kept thinking he was Jacob instead. The memory of the intense kiss resurfaced.

"Talking about Dylan?" August set his tray of food down and slid into the third seat.

Luna glimpsed a pout on Cassie's lips and wondered in the back of her mind what that was about, but she only nodded in misery.

"Well, what have you said to him so far since this morning?"

"Not much. It's been small talk. Work was busy today."

"Well, if I were you, with Jacob being interested, I wouldn't even bother with another guy, especially a vanilla one." The smirk from Cassie underscored her words.

Luna's jaw dropped a little. There was a lot to unpack in that statement alone, but her immediate question was how did Cassie know? *How does everyone know?*

"You went home with Jacob after the modeling session with Eli." August cleared his throat and dabbed the corners of his lips with a napkin after his first bite of food.

Oh. That's true.

Still, August shot a rather disapproving look at Cassie, who held up her hand. "Okay, okay, I was just kidding...sort of. Look... If you want a partner who's a little more aggressive, ask yourself if this Dylan guy has it in him, and if so, ask yourself if it's something you can bring out in him — and if he's worth the effort." She gave a slight shrug and popped a piece of sushi into her mouth.

Luna took a bite of her burger while considering Cassie's words.

"Whatever you decide, I think that no matter how hard it will be, it would be best to tell Dylan face-to-face."

August's words resonated deep within her. She'd known all day that it was the right course of action, even if every part of her wanted to take the coward's way out. She nodded as she swallowed her food. "I know."

"Come on. We have little time before the mall closes." August glanced at his watch. "Let's finish up."

August's anxiety at picking the right gift for Lani had come right through his texts the last few days, although the man had tried hard to hide it. So, with a nod, Luna refocused on her burger and fries.

Silence filled between them as they busied themselves eating.

"Why aren't you considering Jacob, anyway?" Cassie, ever the bold one, asked.

"I'm not *not* considering Jacob!" Luna protested. "It's just" — she struggled for the right words — "that I like him...a lot. But how I am around him scares the crap out of me." Her voice grew soft with the admission.

"Oh, Luna." Cassie breathed out her name, a blend of pity and concern. Luna had mixed feelings about her reaction.

"That is a normal response for a sub just discovering herself." August pushed his glasses up the bridge of his nose. "Remember what I told you in the beginning. Figure out how far you would go and your reasons. The rest will come."

It wasn't like she hadn't thought about it. It was just that every time she tried, her mind drew blanks. She took a deep breath, pulled out her phone and shot a quick text to Dylan before she lost her nerve.

"There."

"What did you do?" Cassie and August both leaned forward at once, peering at her.

"I texted Dylan back, asking to meet up for coffee after work sometime next week. I'll talk to him, face-to-face."

"And what are you planning to say?" That question came from August.

"I'm not sure yet, but I have time to work on that." Despite the doubts in her head, she had to smile at the slight pout and looks of disappointment from both her friends. She couldn't tell them things she didn't know yet. But at least now she'd given herself a deadline to figure some parts out. *No more procrastinating.*

Speaking of... "Come on. Let's go shopping," she said.

Only an hour later, they had all somehow managed to pick out their own gifts for Lani. Luna, having shopped with the birthday girl before, was the only one who had ventured a clothing item — a pair of ankle boots that had stiletto heels and studded straps. Cassie had opted for a piece of stone art that resembled a woman being embraced by two men—or so she claimed. August remained aloof, refusing to share what was in his bag.

They completed their shopping much earlier then they'd thought they would. Cassie grinned wide and tugged Luna in a very specific direction. August trailed behind the two, hesitation in his steps as he held both his and Cassie's bags. Luna had refused to let him hold hers.

"Come on. There's this new lingerie store I want to check out!"

Luna glanced back over her shoulders with a helpless look, only to see August shrug a little. "I'll be at the bookstore. Come find me when you're done."

Traitor!

As if sensing her reluctance, Cassie stopped and lowered her voice. "You'll want to pick up some stuff. Trust me. I've heard that Jacob's a bit of a lacy lingerie guy."

It had an immediate effect. Luna's pulse raced as blood rushed to her cheeks. She swallowed, her body temperature rising. There was no reason that the comment made her want to buy a few sets of lingerie herself all of a sudden, except she had asked to scene with him. And she wanted to please him, so very much.

She wanted to please *him*.

The realization hit her like a ton of bricks. There had been only one other person that she had ever felt that way toward. Except Jacob was here, available and interested. *Dear God.*

"Come on!" Cassie giggled and, taking advantage of her dazed state, ushered her into the store until Luna found herself arms full of bras, panties and a baby doll or two.

"Go forth and try!" Cassie had her own pile and was already entering her own changing room. "And don't forget to show me!"

Luna stared at the pile, sorting through the items to put order to how she would try each one on. Some she took off as fast as she could and others made her giggle at their ridiculousness.

"What's so funny? Come on! I'm waiting," Cassie called out. It was obvious from the direction of her voice that she was standing, tapping her foot with impatience, in front of Luna's changing room.

"Okay...one sec!" Luna changed into another set then gasped, brushing her fingers against the black lace. She poked her head out to make sure no one else was outside besides Cassie.

"Come *on!*" Her friend made an impatient huffing sound and, with a sigh, Luna pulled the curtain aside.

"Oh my, I think we have a winner."

"You think so?" Luna asked.

"Definitely. Jacob's going to be in trouble."

Luna could protest. Part of her wanted to. But another part of her wanted what Cassie said to be true.

"Get that set in red too. Here... I'll go find it."

She really needed only one set. It was only one scene, she told herself. Nonetheless, she ended up buying three—and two baby dolls. The silky material had felt too nice and cool against her skin to resist.

"Lingerie," Cassie started, launching into a lecture as they walked out of the store, "is not just for your partner. That's really just a bonus. A nice set gives you more confidence and helps you be more aware of your body's sexuality. I find I always stand a little taller when I'm wearing a good one."

Luna had never thought of it that way before.

"Watch out!" A loud cry from behind made both of them stop and turn in surprise.

Luna's eyes widened as she saw a man clutching a plastic bag barreling down the corridor toward them. Behind, two mall security guards were giving chase. Everything slowed and, without thinking, she dropped her bags, pushed Cassie behind her then, with her instincts still guiding her, pivoted with a swing of her hips. *Tai sabaki*. She lowered her center of gravity and timed her movements toward the man, a wide step just off to the side. She placed her left hand across her body, palm outward, to protect herself while she extended her right hand, curling her fingers in as she thrust the heel of her palm upward at the man's chin. She slid her foot behind the man's, preventing him from taking a step back to regain his balance.

The move worked, better than it could have in the dojo. It was as if her hand was the fulcrum. The guy's legs went flying first and he landed flat on his back. By then, the security guards had caught up and Luna took a step back as they pinned the man down.

One of them got on her walkie-talkie as soon as they'd managed to restrain the man to radio their colleagues. Luna stood there, watching the entire scene unfold. At first adrenaline kept her upright, but as it started to leave her, she began to shake.

"Luna?" Cassie wrapped an arm around her but Luna only shivered more.

"Miss?" One guard approached the pair. When Luna didn't respond, the woman spoke into her radio again, asking for backup before turning toward Cassie. "Can you help your friend to the bench over there? I think she's going into shock. I'll make sure she gets some space until it wears off."

She heard the words but, lightheaded, she had trouble registering them. Instead, Luna let Cassie guide her to sit. As her friend rubbed her back in slow circles, Luna began to draw deep breaths until her heart rate returned to something closer to normal.

After a little longer, the woman in uniform returned. "Thank you for all your help, miss. When you're ready, we'd like for you to come to the security office with us. The police will want both of you to give your statements." The voice sounded kind and Luna nodded in response.

"What happened?" The other guards kept the small crowd that was forming away, but they must have let August through when he'd indicated he was their friend.

"Luna's a freaking superhero, that's what. She just stopped a shoplifter." Cassie was grinning now.

The words sounded weird to Luna's ears and she could only shake her head a little, not ready yet to speak.

August crouched down, catching Luna's eyes as he reached to clasp her hands. "You okay? You need anything?"

She cleared her throat and nodded once more. "Yeah." Another breath. "I'll be fine." She mustered a wan smile. "I can't believe that worked. I guess Sensei'll be proud."

Or something like that.

Chapter Sixteen

An hour later, Luna was sitting in one of the office chairs—the best that security had to offer—with a cup of tea in her hand. It wasn't the best tea, but it served its purpose, calming her nerves. August sat next to her in another chair, while other security guards milled around them, coming and going with their usual routines while one remained to monitor the screens streaming footage from cameras around the mall. From time to time, one guard would flash Luna a smile and a thumbs-up or some other sign of approval. The incident had already started to become a bit of a legend among them—how a five-foot-three girl took down a six-foot man with one move. *Great.*

From the room next door, she heard the low muffled sound of Cassie speaking with the two cops who had come to take their statements. Luna found comfort in the fact that no one had asked them to go down to the station like she had imagined at first, although they said they might still require her help there at a later time. For now, it was enough to sit in the chair and huddle over the comfort of the hot beverage, contemplating how she'd even gotten there in the first place.

The door opened once more. It was happening with such frequency now that she paid it no heed as she stared into her mug, until August rose next to her. Curious, she looked up.

"Jacob?" August was the first to offer a greeting, surprised to see Jacob as he entered the already-cramped office, escorted by another guard who must have guided him there. One cop opened the other door to allow Cassie to step out. Luna looked from Jacob to Cassie. By the look of Cassie's beaming smile, Luna surmised that she must have had a hand in him coming. When her friend mouthed a silent 'you're welcome', it confirmed her suspicions.

"Are you guys okay?" Jacob may have been polite in including everyone, but his eyes remained on Luna alone, as if he could discern her condition with visuals alone. She swallowed a little under the scrutiny and nodded once, lest he inspect her further. *Would the inspection be so bad, though?*

"We're fine, Jacob, but I think Luna is a bit shaken up." Cassie was only all too gleeful to inform Jacob of her state.

Luna shook her head, taking another sip of the tea to wet her dry lips. "I'm fine…really."

One of the police officers cleared his throat. "I'm sorry to interrupt. Thank you for your assistance. I think we've got all we need for today. If anything comes up, please feel free to call us." With a polite nod, the two left.

"Come on. Let's get you guys out of here." Jacob motioned toward the door and, setting her tea down, Luna trailed after him and the others with a last goodbye and thank you to the security guards.

"So, what happened?" Jacob asked.

"Well" — Cassie took a breath, her eyes flashing with excitement — "this guy, the shoplifter, was running toward us with the security guys chasing behind. There was this loud yell and the next thing I knew, Luna had pushed me aside and did some move. She had the guy flat on his back in less than a second." She turned and fluttered her lashes at Luna. "My hero."

Luna's ears heated, and she ducked her head. As she looked to one side, she jammed her hands in her pockets, unable to meet any of their eyes. "I'm not a hero. It was a fluke. I wasn't even thinking. It just happened. I didn't even think it would work." She was mumbling under her breath now.

"Luna." August spoke, as if ready to admonish her, but it was Jacob who walked back until he stopped before her, halting her in her path.

"Luna... Look at me, sweetheart."

Unable to resist, she tilted her head up. Her hair had fallen to veil her face and now he brushed the strands back until he could catch her eyes. "You did something amazing. Don't minimize it. Be proud of it. Can you do that for me?"

Put that way, how could anyone say no? She nodded, her cheeks now warming for an entirely different reason, Cassie and August forgotten. "Yeah, I can do that," she replied and stood a little taller.

"Good girl." He didn't move his hand for a moment but stroked her hair instead. The warmth of him was soothing, draining some of her remaining tension.

"Well, August's going to take me home. Later!"

They both looked up at the same time to see Cassie already tugging at August, who was still looking back at them with a tinge of doubt. Jacob chuckled, the sound drawing a confused look from Luna.

"What?"

"Cassie's trying pretty hard, isn't she?"

"Oh...I'm sorry."

"Don't be." Jacob grinned at her. "I don't mind." Before Luna came up with any awkward reply, he placed a hand on the small of her back. "Come on. Let's get you home."

The ride almost felt too short. When Luna unlocked the door to let both of them in, she lapsed back into hostess mode, moving toward the kitchen to pour drinks. Since she had learned of his fondness for pop from last time, Luna had started the habit of making sure she always had some stocked in the fridge.

"You, sit. Are you up for more tea?"

"Okay. Yeah, you sure?" Luna asked. Already the man was bustling around in her kitchen, seeming to remember where everything was.

"Yes, I am," Jacob replied as he put the kettle on the stove. He paused to make sure Luna was sitting on the couch before resuming his preparations.

"Thank you."

Comfortable silence settled until the kettle whistled its readiness. He filled her teapot with hot water then, after a minute of steeping the tea, poured the contents into two mugs, along with a generous spoonful of honey each. *How does he know?*

He joined her on the couch and they sat side by side. Luna took a sip and exhaled a sigh of contentment. By now, the immediacy of the events had faded, enough for her to think straight again. That was, until a sudden siren startled her enough that she jumped, spilling a good portion of tea on herself. With a yelp, she set the mug down with haste and stood, lest any of it get on the couch, wincing at the scalding liquid seeping through her T-shirt to her skin.

Jacob rose and retrieved a tea towel from the kitchen before handing it to Luna, who tried to soak up the tea that had spilled on her. "Are you okay?" Concern filled his eyes.

"Yeah." She winced as the siren went screeching down the street until it faded away before offering him a wan smile. "I guess I'm still more skittish than I thought." She glanced at the front door then her bedroom. "I should go change."

"Go. I'll wait for you."

With a nod, she made her way to the bedroom and closed the door behind her. On a logical level, she understood that she was safe at home. But she couldn't shake how pear-shaped the whole situation could have gotten instead. Her breath shortened, and she closed her eyes, trying to draw deeper breaths. There was no reason she should have been that shaken — but she was.

"Get a grip," she muttered beneath her breath then changed her shirt.

When she emerged once more, the relief she felt seeing Jacob still on her couch was palpable. Everything calmed once more, just knowing he was there.

"Are you going to be okay?" Jacob stood as she walked back toward him.

"I..." Luna opened her mouth to say she was fine but the words would not come. Instead, she imagined being alone in the apartment, glancing at the door every five minutes. Unreasonable scenarios played out in her head. The shoplifter was going to escape and come to exact revenge. He was going to call a friend to kidnap her. Damn she was getting paranoid. She might as well sit up all night with a baseball bat. Part of her wasn't sure she wouldn't.

"Luna?"

"I guess I'm still a little scared." Her voice was just above a whisper. It was not something she would admit to just anyone, but Jacob wouldn't laugh. Admitting it to him would not be a weakness.

"Oh, sweetheart" — he opened his arms — "come here."

That was all it took. As she stepped into his embrace, he folded his arms around her and held her tight. She inhaled his scent, closing her eyes, and wondered at how safe and natural she felt nestled against him. Somehow, they fit together.

He stroked her hair then nuzzled the top of her head. "It's all right, Luna. It was a scary thing. You're safe now."

They remained that way, for how long Luna wasn't sure, but in the end, she stepped back, albeit with reluctance. "Thanks."

"You're welcome." His soft smile coupled with his tenderness melted her heart. How could she even think about being with anyone else? He glided his hand down to cup her cheek, his palm warm against it. "I need to get going. I have an early morning at work tomorrow." There was reluctance in his voice.

"Okay." She stepped back to clear the path to the door but inside, she quaked at the thought of being alone. It was odd. She'd never had that problem before. When he walked, she trailed behind, dragging her feet.

They both paused at the entryway, Jacob turning to check on her for the last time. He leaned forward and pressed a light kiss to her forehead. "If you need anything, just call me. Okay? It doesn't matter what time."

Luna nodded once more, struggling with a knot that was tightening in her stomach. When he turned to open the door, she reached out and tugged at his shirt. "Stay. Please."

A pause. Luna tensed before it hit her how he could interpret those two little words. "I... I mean...in a pure platonic way, not like a scene. I just— I just need someone else here tonight. I can take the couch. Or if you're busy, it's okay. I can call a friend, maybe Ted or August."

"Luna." Now Jacob turned around, her name on his lips putting a stop to her rambling. "Didn't I just finish saying *'whatever you need'*?" Head still tilted down, Luna snuck a peek up. Humor crinkled the corners of his eyes. "It's not a problem. I can stay, but only if you let me take the couch."

Ever the gallant one. She sensed that it was a condition he would not budge on. Her shoulders slumped with a whoosh of a breath leaving her lips before she smiled at him.

"That's better." Then he paused. "If you don't mind, though, can I borrow your shower? I was in the warehouse today. My clothes are clean but I'm pretty sure I don't smell great, with all that dust."

This is him not smelling great? Dear God. She swallowed, hoping he wouldn't notice the subtle movement—or at least as subtle as she could make it. "Ah yeah, sure. Bathroom's to the left. I'll go get you some towels."

"Thanks."

It wasn't until she heard the shower turn on that Luna froze, standing in her living room with arms full of a pillow and a large throw, in the middle of preparing the couch for him. *He's in my shower. Naked.* Her mind dove into the gutter as she imagined water sliding down his body, over the muscles she'd sensed underneath, down the V of his hips, lower...

All of a sudden, it became boiling in the apartment. Willing herself to move, she laid out the pillow and throw then straightened to fan herself. The temptation to peek was strong. *Just one little peek.*

Instead, she forced herself to march to her bedroom with every intention of changing into her sleepwear. Despite her best efforts, however, with her bedroom and the bathroom separated only by a thin wall, the nearness did nothing to calm her libido. The washroom was an interesting design with two doors, one facing the hall, the other leading to her bedroom. She stared at that latter door and almost had to slap her own face.

"PJ's," Luna muttered under her breath. She had brought her bag of just-purchased lingerie in and she resisted the urge to put on one of the baby dolls. *No.* She'd asked him to stay for platonic reasons. Putting that on was wrong — not to mention that it would send mixed signals. But oh, she wanted to give that signal.

With a sigh, she pulled on an oversized T-shirt instead, her usual summer uniform for home lounging and sleep. By then, the water had shut off but that had escaped her notice.

They both stepped out into the hall at the same time.

Jacob was shirtless, with the bath towel over his damp dark locks. Luna wasn't sure if the way he'd framed himself was on purpose but her lust couldn't care less. A need to taste him, to trail her lips along that bare chest filled her. His gaze swept downward in admiration of her bare legs, his muscles tensing, as if he was a predator that would spring any second.

Her breathing grew heavier, and his seemed to do the same. It appeared that she might be having the same effect on him.

It was Jacob who broke the silence, his voice tight. "Saturday."

Luna nodded, not trusting her voice.

"Good night, sweetheart."

"Good night, Jacob."

He didn't touch her. Clearly they both knew that if he did, it wouldn't end with just kisses.

Luna retreated to her bedroom and closed the door behind her. Lani had once mentioned that Jacob was a legend with his control.

At the moment, she could almost curse it.

Chapter Seventeen

It had been one of the hardest things to walk away from in his life. Jacob had understood what Luna had offered, what she would have given him. His little mouse had started to blossom, and although he was an experienced trainer, something in him was afraid of messing it up.

Which was how he found himself spending his lunch hour in Lani's office. Over the years, he had seen her as his counselor, trusting her professional advice and her instincts as a fellow Dominant with a similar style.

The office was not a large one but it was well furnished, with a bookshelf to one side and a modest desk next to it. A set of matching couch, armchair and coffee table took up the remaining space, and it was here where Lani sat with most clients as they tried to work out their problems.

When they had finished their sandwiches and were sipping on their coffee and tea respectively, Jacob ventured to the reason he was here. "So, what do you think of Luna?"

Lani raised her brows. "I'm not sure if my opinion matters much here, Jacob. What do *you* think of Luna?"

Pest.

"She…" He was not one to struggle with words in normal circumstances. Sometimes he was too blunt. But for the first time, he was trying to give voice to the tangled feelings he had toward his little mouse. "There's something between us, a strong pull that goes beyond just attraction. I think we can be good together."

"But?"

He had learned long ago to stop asking how Lani knew that there was a 'but'. She was perceptive. It was what made her damn good at her job. "But she seems fragile and unsure still, like she's not sure if the lifestyle is what she wants. I don't want our attraction to start her on a path that she regrets."

Lani tapped her lips then she set her tea down on the coffee table between them. She leaned back in her chair, folding her arms in her lap over the open pages of her notebook. "This is not a recent development, so why come see me about it just now?"

There was no dodging her perceptiveness. Jacob felt a momentary pity for her subs — or her 'dolls', as she liked to call them.

"Luna asked to scene with me."

"Ah-h." That single word was laden with subtle meaning. Jacob waited until Lani elaborated, both of them baiting each other with the silence that followed.

"Jacob…" There was warning in Lani's voice. It wasn't the first time she had used that tone with him. He was in her domain, asking for her help. With a sigh of exasperation, Lani tucked her curls back behind her ears. "It's a single scene. Why so much hesitation?"

Now it was Jacob's turn to sigh, and he rubbed his face with one hand. "Because my gut is telling me that it won't be just a single scene. She might not realize it herself, but I'm pretty sure Luna would get emotionally attached."

"And you're afraid of that attachment?"

"No. I'd take her on as my sub in a heartbeat if she wanted." He hadn't meant to confess that, but Lani had a way of drawing confidence from people that made them let their guard down, himself included. Still, in for a penny, in for a pound. "We're compatible. I'm sure of it. But I also need to know that she wants to submit because that's what *she* wants, not because she wants to be with me."

As soon as he gave voice to the doubt, everything snapped into focus. That was it, wasn't it? He couldn't stand the thought of making her into something she didn't or wasn't ready to be. The very potential of that happening sickened him.

"Remember, Luna's not new to the scene. She has had previous experience."

"I know." She had mentioned as much, but something nagged at him. "She still feels to me like she's unsure, though."

"Okay." Lani closed the notebook and leaned forward resting her elbow on her knee and her chin in her hand. "You've trained others who were new before. How did you assess that they were sure?"

Jacob's mind flipped through those he had worked with in the past. "I test them, before the contract. Push their limits just enough and watch how they react. See if they chafe or thrive under the control. See how far they want to go."

"So…scening."

"That's part of it."

It took only a split second for him to realize where Lani had led their conversation. Damn it. Of course he wanted to go through with it and Lani was right. So how come his brain was throwing up excuses and roadblocks for him to not do it?

"I told her to think about it and get back to me Saturday." *Tomorrow.*

He felt Lani's eyes on him, studying his reactions and his expression before she spoke again. "I think your protective instincts are getting the better of you."

Surprised by the sudden comment, Jacob leaned forward himself, stiffening. "What do you mean?"

"You and I both know that Luna's a natural, which means we both want to protect her. Heck, you told me even Erica asked you to look out for her before. Your dominant nature urges you to do whatever it takes to make her safe, to clear away all persuasive distractions, including yourself, so she has a safe space to make an important decision about her life."

Lani paused then continued when Jacob nodded his agreement. So far, what Lani had said was nothing he hadn't already shared.

"But what you're forgetting is that Luna's smart, and she has her own agency. If she was letting only her heart lead, she would have asked to scene with you a long time ago. That it took this long should be a sign that she's already being careful."

"What're you trying to say, Lani?" She didn't give strong opinions in her sessions often, preferring to lead her clients to their own conclusions. That she was taking on a more aggressive approach meant that her own dominant instincts were rising.

Lani set the notebook and pen aside. "As a friend, Jacob, I'm saying that perhaps you should start respecting and trusting her as a strong, independent woman who is capable of making her own rational decisions. If she decides that she wants to scene, support that and help her build confidence as a sub." A small smile graced her lips, taking the sting out of her next words. "Stop second-guessing her choices and take her at face value. And go have some damn fun."

* * * *

Hours later, Jacob was still chewing over Lani's words as he sat at the bar in The Playgrounds, nursing a glass of cognac in one hand, his poison of choice.

"You're not the brooding type." Darryl appeared before him, a towel slung over one shoulder.

He glared at the larger man but there was no ill will behind it. "Ha ha," he replied instead and took a long draw of his drink.

"What's going on?"

The crowd had yet to gather, and Jacob was rather enjoying the quiet. A glance backward showed only a few people milling around and a sub or two sitting in the lounge. The tourists had yet to make appearances.

"I'm just trying to figure some things out with a sub." He hadn't discussed his dilemma with anyone else other than Lani, but Darryl was as close a friend as Lani was.

"That white-haired girl you've been hanging with? Luna, right?"

Jacob arched a brow.

"Cassie's been hanging out with her too. She's been pretty tight-lipped about it, which is surprising, but she mentioned something about her being a natural sub and that she thought this girl would be a good match for you. I warned her not to stick her nose in and try to play matchmaker." Darryl rubbed the back of his neck. "It seems she's taken a shine to the girl."

"So have August—and Lani." Something about Luna drew people to her.

"She seems like an interesting girl. I wouldn't mind meeting her some time."

Someone at the end of the bar must have waved for Darryl's attention as he nodded and moved toward them. Over the years, Jacob had gotten used to the rhythm of conversation and interruption with Darryl as he manned the bar of The Playgrounds. His friend took the order and fixed the drink with well-honed skills.

"So, what's the problem?" Darryl asked when he returned once more.

"Lani said I'm being overprotective to the point of second-guessing and not trusting Luna's decisions." There was a peevishness to his tone, like a child sulking from a scolding. Jacob wasn't sure if it was her words or his own reaction that annoyed him more.

Darryl laughed, a single bark that had Jacob snap his gaze up, even more irritated. When the bartender smirked, Jacob glared harder. *If only looks could kill — or at least do some bodily harm.*

"Okay, sorry, man." Darryl held up both hands in surrender. "It's just that that is *so* you. Lani has you nailed, one hundred percent."

Jacob growled at him.

"Hey, man, go growl at your girl instead. I'm sure she'd find it hot." Mirth danced in Darryl's eyes.

153

My girl. Jacob found he liked the sound of that in reference to Luna. A part of him hoped Luna would still want to go through with the decision to scene with him tomorrow. A large part of him.

The thought distracted him enough from coming up with a suitable retort. Darryl leaned over the bar, bracing his hands against it for balance. "Look, man… Maybe I'm over-simplifying things here, but if she likes you as much as you like her, I don't see a problem. It's time you take on a sub, and who knows what you might learn from this one? From how Cassie describes her, she seems like a girl who can take care of herself. And I know you'll treat her right."

"Thanks," Jacob muttered then, with one long last draw, finished his drink. The vote of confidence was almost flattering. Now he just had to make sure he lived up to it.

Chapter Eighteen

Saturday. Luna was a bundle of nerves, even as she arrived early by transit to help set up at August's request. It was late in the afternoon, and the 'toasters' had already started petering out, leaving the beach emptier than usual. She tugged at her oversized T-shirt before setting the bags she'd brought with her aside to slip her sandals off before picking them back up. She scanned the beach and, sighting where Lani had already staked out their territory, began trudging her way toward it.

However, she itched to pull out her phone instead to read the earlier text message exchange with Jacob for the umpteenth time, despite having it already memorized.

Good morning, Jacob.

Morning.

She remembered the pause and the butterflies in her stomach before she typed those fateful words, the ones that took all the effort she had to steel her nerves for.

I want to go through with it.

There wasn't much of a wait for a response after that.

I'm pleased to hear that. Tonight?

Yeah, I'd like that.

Tonight then. I need to get going. Got to get some stuff from the store to make the damn pasta salad for the party.

See you there?

Yeah, see you there, little one.

It had been the first time *he'd* called her that. She remembered glowing a little when she'd read it. Okay, she still was. *That means something...*

"Luna!"

In the distance she spied Lani, who was waving her down. With no hands to spare, she gave a wide smile instead, hoping to convey a returned greeting. As she got closer, she saw August in the background, setting up a charcoal grill. Her stomach rumbled in anticipation.

They had already stacked beach towels to one side, with frisbees and beach balls piled against a large log. Another cooler sat at the foot of the grill and it was in it that she dropped off the heavier bag of meat before turning to hand the gift bag to Lani. "Happy birthday!"

"Aw-w!" Lani accepted the present but set it aside quick enough in favor of throwing her arms around her in a tight hug, almost setting both of them off balance.

Luna laughed and hugged back. "I hope you like it." She spared a glance over the Domme's shoulder toward August, who was arranging the charcoal, and she lowered her voice. If Luna was right, they would have spent a bit of time together already by now. "How's it going?" She jerked her chin toward him.

Lani giggled. "He's quite lovely. I'll have to show you the card he got me later. He rented a cottage nearby for the weekend too and gave himself to me as a birthday present on op of the gift he got me." She grinned like the Cheshire Cat. "And he did all that without even being sure if I would accept the invite."

Luna considered for a moment August's way of serving and found she could picture herself doing the same for Jacob. *When is his birthday? No, focus!* "Oh my God, Lani, so you're going to take him up on it?"

Her eyes softened as she glanced over her shoulder. "Yeah. We'll see how this weekend goes, but I think maybe it's time to take a partner, to see where it takes us."

Luna almost squealed. It was a pairing she supported and she could not wait to see August's wish come true. She covered her mouth, lest her excitement gave it away too early.

"What are you two gossiping about—and should I be concerned?"

All thoughts fled from her mind as she recognized the voice behind her. Her eyes widened, almost like a deer in headlights, even as Lani's lips curved into a knowing smile. *Wait! Just what does she know?*

"Nothing that concerns you." Lani sniffed, though she was hard-pressed to suppress the mischief that shone in her eyes.

Luna turned around, her prepared hello turning more into a squeak at the sight that greeted her.

Jacob was clothed in swim trunks and flip-flops, a light white linen shirt covering his upper body, with the top few buttons undone. A gentle breeze tugged at the material, enough to give hints to the chest and abs underneath. The memory of him emerging from the shower the other night surfaced in her mind and she almost whimpered.

"Pest," Jacob muttered under his breath then held up a gift bag of his own. "Happy birthday."

Jacob and Lani exchanged hugs and kisses on the cheek before Jacob turned to Luna. Lani eyed the two and murmured something about needing to put the gifts someplace safe. Luna hardly heard with the roaring in her ears.

"Hello, little one." Jacob's voice, however, came through loud and clear. *A second time that he has called me that.* Just hearing it verbalized, coupled with that crooked grin of his, did crazy things to her pulse. She wasn't sure how she was going to survive the party.

"Hello." Her second attempt at a greeting came out better. At least she had enunciated.

He leaned forward with care, brushing his lips against her forehead. "You look delicious. I'm going to enjoy eating you up later."

She needed to jump in the ocean, like right then. To cool off, for sure, but then she would also have an excuse why her bottom half of her bikini was already wet.

With a smirk, as if knowing the exact effect he was having on her, Jacob guided her toward digging tools lying next to all the supplies. "Come on. Let's go dig out some seats."

Doing something to busy herself and expend her nervous energy was a great idea. She shrugged off her backpack and grabbed one of the hand shovels before picking a spot to shape the sand.

Soon, Jacob knelt down to work beside her and took up casual conversation, easing the knots that had wound tight in her stomach. For a little while, she even forgot what lay ahead and instead enjoyed his company, much like when they had been at the café.

People began trickling into the party. Someone turned on a radio. Chatter ebbed and flowed around them. Jacob settled them into one set of the seats they had built before continuing to chat. Knowing many more of the guests than her, Jacob often had to break their conversation to wave or greet someone, but he remained by her side.

That, however, was not to last. Known for his culinary skills, Jacob was called on by the others at the party to man the grill and get the dinner started. Luna followed on instinct, hovering to help as a sous chef. The position felt natural to her and, like the first time when they'd made dinner in her kitchen, she marveled at how easy it was to work with him.

"Hello, Luna." August approached to put together a plate, likely for Lani. They had waved at each other earlier, but on purpose, Luna had stayed away, noting how August had hovered around Lani, waiting on her hand and foot, from holding her drinks to ensuring she had sunscreen on. It was adorable, and she wanted to give him space, knowing what was to come for him and the birthday girl—or so she told herself. It had *nothing* to do with her own interests at the moment. *Nope, none at all.*

"Does Lani want a burger or hot dog?"

"A burger, please."

"Cheese?"

"Yes, please."

Luna turned to prepare the bun, handing it to Jacob to toast on the grill. When she turned, August glanced over her shoulder then lowered his voice.

"How are you?" His eyes flickered once more toward the man behind her.

"Nervous," she admitted in a whisper, cheeks already warming. Her own gaze traveled to catch sight of Lani, laughing at something Erica just said. "You? Lani told me about your offer."

"Same as you. I'll text you on Monday?"

"Tea after work?"

"Yes, let's." August straightened as Jacob called to him from behind. The bun and patty were ready and Luna held up a plate for it before passing the food back to August, who nodded in acknowledgment, his face once more smoothed to a more neutral expression.

Soon enough, everyone at the party had their orders. Last to eat, Luna followed as Jacob took their own hot dogs and burgers back to their original spot. As if by mutual unspoken agreement, they remained more friendly than affectionate, though Luna contented herself with the feel of his arm brushing against hers. It made sense. Until they were certain they were compatible in a scene, there was no point in advertising their closeness as anything beyond friendship. But inside, she hoped that the sexual tension that had been obvious between them all along was a sign that things would be good.

"Hey…" A little while after they had finished their meal, a larger, muscular man with intricate tattoos covering one shoulder down his upper arm to his elbow joined them, settling down on the other side of Jacob. Luna recognized him as one of the regular bartenders at The Playgrounds.

"Hey, Darryl." Jacob leaned back against the log behind them and draped an arm around her shoulders.

Surprised by the move, Luna leaned into him a little.

"This is Luna. Luna, meet Darryl."

"Hi." He held out his hand and Luna had to reach across Jacob to shake it, brushing against his chest. Warmth radiated from his body.

"It's nice to meet you," Luna said.

"Likewise. It's good to put a face to the name. I've been hearing a lot about you."

Wait! Who had been talking about her? She raked her fingers through her hair and gave an awkward chuckle. "Ah, well."

"Darryl, stop making Luna nervous," Jacob admonished. He shifted his hand and gave her shoulder a reassuring squeeze.

"Sorry 'bout that." A sheepish smile on his lips, Darryl rubbed the back of his neck. It made Luna smile. He was more of a gentle giant.

"Darryl's one of the bartenders at The Playgrounds. If ever you need someone to go to, just head to the bar." Jacob's tone had turned more serious than she'd expected and she turned to look at him.

"What he means is if any Dom bothers you, I can scare them off for you." Darryl dropped his voice in a loud stage whisper. "What he really means, though, is he'd prefer you where I can keep an eye on any competition for him."

In response, Jacob growled, a low rumble of his chest that she felt as much as she heard. Luna wasn't sure if her sudden warmth was from Darryl's teasing or from the sexiest sound she'd heard from Jacob yet.

"All right, that's enough from you. I'm going for a dip before it gets too cold." He rose in one swift motion, turned and offered a hand to Luna. "Join me." It wasn't a request.

Her heart beating in her throat, Luna placed her smaller hand in his and gasped as he hauled her up with easy strength, catching her as she fell, a little off balance, against him.

Next to them, Darryl chuckled and held his hands up in surrender. "All right, all right, go have fun, kids."

Without another word, Jacob grabbed two of the beach towels and led her away

"That...wasn't very nice," she ventured as soon as they were far enough from earshot.

"I'm not trying to be nice," he retorted. Closer to the beach now, he dropped her hand to ever-so-slowly unbutton the rest of his shirt. Whatever witty reply Luna may have had never quite left her lips as he stripped off his shirt. The man knew how to frame himself in the best light.

"Take off your jeans and T-shirt, little one. You don't want to go swimming in those."

Her hands moved to obey before her consciousness caught up. With a lot less grace, she tugged her own clothing off until she stood in her simple black bikini with a halter-style top and strings that held up the bottom on the sides. She folded her clothing and bent over to place everything on top of a log where Jacob had placed the towels. A sharp inhale drew Luna's attention as she looked up, catching sight of Jacob's eyes devouring her.

After a moment, he cleared his throat, enough for Luna to straighten. "Come on." She felt the warmth of his palm as he placed a hand on the small of her back, leading her toward the ocean. As they ventured into the water, the burning heat of his skin against hers in stark contrast to the cooling waters lapping at her feet only reminded her of his nearness. Under his guidance, she propelled herself forward until she could submerge most of her body, her feet just touching the ocean floor. Seconds later, Jacob joined her.

Luna closed her eyes in contentment for a moment, savoring the weightlessness of her limbs, which was how Jacob caught her by surprise as he came up from behind to wrap his arms around her.

"So beautiful," he murmured, nuzzling along the side of her neck. "All mine tonight."

Luna was pretty sure the wetness that gathered between her legs had nothing to do with the ocean they were swimming in.

He kept one arm around her midsection and moved his other hand to caress her neck, trailing his fingertips down to trace the outline of her bare shoulder, then lower along her arm, leaving goosebumps in their wake. "Jacob." His name came out as a sigh, a plea, though she wasn't sure for what.

"Yes, sweetheart?" He traveled his hand back up and traced from her neck down along the edge of her top, dipping low to her chest.

She had no answer for him. Her body was on fire and all she wanted was him. Without thinking, she pressed back against him and, feeling his hardness against her ass, she ground against him without reservation. Something about him drove her crazy, made her lose all her inhibitions. She had been right before. She would lose all control around him, but for the first time, it seemed to matter little.

"Minx." Once more he growled in her ear and cupped one breast possessively. "Teases get punished." He scraped his teeth against her skin. Then, without warning, he clamped down where her neck joined her shoulder, biting just hard enough to leave a mark. The briefest of pain melted as his tongue swept along the bite, sucking hard on the same spot while he pinched her nipple through the cup of her bra then tugged.

Oh God. She was going to come from his touch alone.

"Mine." There was satisfaction in his voice as he repeated the statement then eased off, gentling and shifting his fingers to once more caress her breast, leaving her nipple hard and yearning for more. She whimpered in protest—and he chuckled in return.

"Later. That was just to whet your appetite." He leaned back and circled her until he was in front once more, a proud grin on his face.

In response, her body shivered. He was the most infuriating man on earth. But there was no question... All she wanted was him.

Chapter Nineteen

They swam for a little while longer but he did not tease her anymore. He didn't need to. Every time he caught her rubbing the spot where he'd bitten her, he felt a satisfied smirk tugging at the corner of his lips. Jacob wondered if Luna realized that he had left a mark and that as soon as they rejoined the party, many would recognize it for what it was — a temporary claim. He knew on a logical level that Darryl wouldn't try to move in on his interest, but some deeper, primal part of him had urged him to let the other Dominants know.

As the air around them began cooling, they made their way back to shore. He was just grabbing the towels when he noticed Luna wrapping her arms around herself, shivering.

"Here." Jacob tucked the thicker one around her and drew her into his arms. She relaxed into the embrace, almost melting against him. How long had it been since he'd felt a woman's body surrender to him so sweetly? He found himself reluctant to let go.

"Jacob! Luna! Come on. We're doing s'mores!" Lani called out, waving.

When Luna eased back, Jacob loosened his arms and smiled at her, admiring the pretty blush that seemed to perpetually tinge her cheeks pink.

"Come on. Let's not keep your sweet tooth waiting any longer."

The laugh that got him warmed his heart. He was getting a good grasp of her nature and he was rather proud of that.

Someone had started a bonfire by the time they had dried off and gotten dressed. People in ones, twos and threes huddled by the firepit, toasting marshmallows. The party had already thinned out, some opting to leave a little earlier, probably for longer drives home.

"Please, let me." When they settled down and retrieved their own supply of sticks and marshmallows, Luna took them out of his hands. Amused, he nodded his permission and smiled to himself as she speared the marshmallows then began toasting them.

Warmed and satisfied, Jacob leaned back and once more wrapped an arm around Luna, enjoying the ebb and flow of conversation around them. His smile turned into a smirk as August raised a brow at them. Beside him, Luna tilted her head to one side then blushed as August tapped his own neck, mirroring the spot where Jacob had left his mark.

Luna's hand flew to her neck. Jacob frowned and lowered his head to whisper in her ear. "Don't cover it up. Wear it with pride, Luna." With more reluctance than he would have liked, she dropped her hand. It would be something he'd have to work on with her if they entered into a contract.

"We should play a game!" Cassie was lounging on the other side of the firepit, resting her head in Darryl's lap.

"What do you have in mind?" August asked, wariness in his eyes. By now, many of the remaining guests had gone off for walks or were sitting a bit away. The only ones left were him and Luna, Lani and August and Darryl and Cassie.

The grin on Cassie's face did not bode well for any of them. "Why, truth or dare, of course!"

"Cassie." Darryl growled a warning, leaning over her.

Rather than being intimidated, she pouted up at him then grinned when Lani laughed.

"Sure, why not?"

"All right, is everyone in?"

"I'm in," Luna offered.

Surprised, Jacob turned to admire Luna and re-evaluated his internal nickname for her. His little mouse was not a mouse anymore. Or perhaps she just had no idea what she was getting herself into. With a chuckle, he turned toward Cassie. "Sure."

They were all in.

"Okay, birthday girl first!" Cassie clapped her hands together in glee. Jacob chuckled, wondering how that girl always got what she wanted.

"All right. Hmm-m, let's see." Lani's eyes danced with mischief as they swept around the loose circle they made. "Darryl."

He grumbled under his breath and nodded once in acknowledgment. "Truth. I don't trust you."

A peal of laughter, from more than just Lani herself. "Oh, Darryl, I can't help it if you make it so easy. Fine.

An easy one to start. What's one kink you've been wanting to try that you haven't yet?"

With a sigh, Darryl rubbed his face and Cassie shifted to give him a kiss on his knee in sympathy.

"Taser," he admitted. "I've been thinking about talking to Colin, to get some tips from him."

Cassie's hand shot up. "I volunteer as tribute!" she quipped. Jacob chuckled and heard a soft laugh from Luna. It had very different connotations than the original quote used in *The Hunger Games* books and movies, but it was good to know that they were all pop culture nerds here.

Darryl caught Cassie's hand and nipped at her finger, which produced a squeal from her. "I'll keep that in mind." Then Darryl appeared to give a moment's thought before he said, "Jacob."

Things were about to get interesting. With a lift of a brow, he turned to Darryl and straightened. "Truth."

He could almost see the disappointment on his friend's face. Darryl hardened his features with determination, and in response, Jacob only eased back with a nonchalant shrug. *Challenge accepted.*

"Okay, you two, this isn't a staring contest. Get on with it!" Lani's voice, accompanied by stifled giggles, cut through the silence.

"Fine. So what drew you to Luna?"

It was not the question Jacob had expected, but judging from his friend's now self-satisfied smug expression, Darryl must have thought he had caught him off guard. Far from it. Instead, Jacob looked down on the woman nestled against him, noting the way she was now trying to bury her face against his side to hide. It was endearing, and it tugged at him that she was trying to find safety in his arms. *How much more I can make her squirm?*

"Well, that's easier than I expected." Watching Darryl's face fall was almost as good as watching Luna torn between hiding and peeking at him, curious about his answer. "Let's see. First it was her curiosity about everything, but also how she's shy about it. But then there's that big independent brain, as well, behind all the adorableness."

By then, Luna was shifting this way and that on the sand, red as a tomato, Lani was giggling, Cassie was making googly eyes and Darryl was scowling. Even August was looking on with a raised brow.

"Moving on," Luna muttered under her breath.

With a chuckle, Jacob pressed a light kiss on top of her head. "Yes, dear. Okay... August, truth or dare?"

August pushed his glasses up along the ridge of his nose. Until now, he had remained quiet but there was a slight upturn at the corner of his lips. "Dare."

"Really?" Luna pushed off from him, leaning forward instead.

It seemed to be enough to distract her from her embarrassment, but the way she had fidgeted had been delightful. He couldn't wait to see how else he could make her do so tonight.

"Hmm-m." Pretending to think, he traced light circles on one of Luna's bare shoulders, loving the way she shivered at his touch. Her sensitivity was going to make things even more fun. "Okay. I dare you to add 'in bed' to the end of everything you say until the end of the game."

Next to him, Luna burst out into giggles while August only humphed and adjusted his glasses again.

"Oh, good one." Cassie grinned and offered him a thumbs-up sign, which he acknowledged with a slight dip of his head. Coming from the always-serious August, the dare should keep things comical.

"Fine, in bed."

It drew laughter from everyone and August's ears pinkened.

"Lani, truth or dare…in bed," August said.

"Yes, dolly?" The queen of the party tilted her head back to look at them all with languid grace. "Hmm-m… Truth, I suppose."

"What are your most sensitive parts…in bed?"

The girls giggled again and Jacob couldn't help but snicker. He had picked a good dare.

Lani pouted and shook her head. "Now that's cheating."

"Merely using the game to my advantage, Ma'am, in bed."

"Fair enough. I can respect that. I would say, besides the usual places, ears and neck." The answer came without hesitation. Out of all of them, Lani was the most comfortable speaking about her sexual preferences, practicing what she preached. "Luna, truth or dare?"

Jacob felt Luna stiffen, her breath quickening as she bit her lower lip for a moment. "I'll regret this but" — her chest rose as she drew in a deeper breath — "dare me."

Not sure if her answer disappointed him as, like August, he had hoped to use the opportunity to learn more about Luna, Jacob grew all-the-more conflicted at Lani's next words.

"I dare you to give Jacob a lap dance."

"What?" Luna spluttered, while Lani just looked on her, composed and calm.

"I... But..." Still trying to form a sentence, Luna flapped her hands in the air.

"Come on, Luna. I think Jacob is waiting...in bed." *Damn...* August was using his dare to his advantage again.

Luna snapped her mouth shut, and she glared at both of them before rising to her feet and turning to face him. "Fine. Only because I never back down from a challenge."

Jacob was resisting grinning like a kid in a candy store but remained at ease as he leaned back to admire the view. The fact that Luna did not attempt to get out of the dare impressed him, and he more than looked forward to the performance until he noticed the way she was chewing her lower lip raw. He sat back up, reached out to take both her hands in his and began rubbing slow circles on the backs of them with his thumbs. "Eyes on me, sweetheart. Ignore all of them. I've got you."

With a slight nod, Luna closed her eyes. After a moment, Jacob discovered why as she began to hum. She must have paused to find the right song in her head to dance to. Her hips began to sway and when her eyes opened again, he saw only himself reflected in the startling blue. It was as if the dare had removed her inhibitions.

As she drew nearer toward him, her movements grew bolder. Every few beats, she would bend her knees, circling her lower body wide before she would straighten her legs again. She let go of one of his hands to spin around, repeating the hypnotic movement, which only resulted in an ample front-row-seat view of the way her ass would shake. Luna, tossing a look over her shoulder, spun around once more and took another step closer until she could straddle his lap.

She laid one hand on his shoulder and snaked the other around to run through his hair. As she trailed her fingers down to stroke his neck, she began rolling her hips, ending with rising off him, only to grind down again. He wasn't sure where this side of her came from, but it was a side he was very interested in exploring. Before him was a woman who understood and celebrated her own sensuality.

A soft moan escaped his lips and his cock hardened in his swim trunks. By then, Luna had switched tactics, shifting closer to grind hard against him, her rolling movements growing smaller and smaller until she was resting, pushing up against him. Her heat and dampness were obvious and it took all his control to not just sweep her off her feet and insist on them leaving right then and there.

"Oh my… It got rather warm here." Lani breathed out the words and, glancing over Luna's shoulder, he saw her fanning herself.

"He's one lucky guy," Cassie murmured — and he couldn't agree more.

Luna was still sitting on his lap but now she had buried her face in his shoulder. He raised a hand to pet her hair. "You okay, sweetheart?"

He felt more than saw her nod but could just make out her muffled words. "I don't think I can look at any of them yet."

With a small laugh, he wrapped his arms around her and kept stroking her hair. "All right, sweetheart, but it's your turn to ask."

She only shook her head.

"Want me to take your turn?"

A nod.

"Okay."

The game continued on, with Jacob holding Luna for a good while longer before she could detach herself enough to settle back next to him. No one commented on her embarrassment and she relaxed once more. The game kept things just on the side of naughty, but it also gave Jacob time to recover from what was one of the sexiest dares he'd ever had the pleasure to experience. He made a mental note to thank Lani one day. *Maybe.*

As evening turned to night, the fire faded to embers, and a chill settled in. They remained to help pack up, then there were no more reasons to wait any longer.

It was time.

Chapter Twenty

It was one thing to have it happen spontaneously, or even on a dare, but quite another when it was prearranged. Luna had agreed to Jacob's suggestion that they return to her place right away rather than his. It made sense. If things didn't work out, he could just take his car and leave.

Somehow, Luna doubted that it wouldn't work out, judging by how wet she was—at least as long as she didn't go into panic mode or her libido didn't take a dive again for no reason. Doubts and nerves stiffened her posture and she picked at a loose thread from her T-shirt.

Jacob's hand enveloped hers.

"Luna, relax."

Easy for him to say. He must have done this a thousand times.

He gave her hand a squeeze then shifted to rub the pad of his thumb in slow soothing circles over the back of her hand, much like he had when Lani had dared her to give the lap dance.

"Talk to me." Although he kept his eyes on the road, Luna was well aware that he could sense every line of tension in her body. She had long stopped trying to hide it.

"I..." Luna swallowed, struggling to find the right words. "I'm worried. Things are... I want it to work out but I haven't had a great history with sex."

"How so?" His thumb never ceased its movements but she thought maybe she heard a note of disbelief in his voice.

"I just... It..." She'd never had to admit it, not out loud, but Jacob deserved to know. "I don't have a great sex drive. It takes a lot to make me...come." There, she'd said it! *Oh God, I said it.* He was going to leave as soon as he dropped her off. They were nearing her place too. Maybe she should just walk the rest of the way home.

"Luna." With little warning, Jacob pulled over to the side of the road then put the car in Park. Luna's heart pounded, wondering if he was going to kick her out of the car now. Was he angry? Nothing about what she knew of him so far would have hinted he would be — or that he would be so cruel.

He cupped her cheek, forcing her to face him.

"Luna, sweetheart, do you trust me?"

Surprised by his question, she nodded.

"Good." The smile that spread across his face was tender and sweet. "Then trust me. Trust me enough to make you feel good, to allow you to let go of your worries. Whatever happens happens, and however your body reacts, it's a part of a woman I'm very attracted to, so just let me take care of you tonight."

There was no other way to describe the effect his words had on her. Everything in her melted and her entire body relaxed as knots unwound themselves. Her lips parted as she exhaled.

"That's better," he whispered. He began to stroke her cheek. "Remember... No matter what happens, you will always be in control. At your word, we can stop everything — no harm, no foul. It doesn't mean we don't try again later if you want. It doesn't mean I'll be angry or upset with you. Do you understand?"

Jacob had given her enough reading on that topic to last a lifetime. It was one of the first things they had covered. She nodded again.

"Good, so tell me your safeword."

"Um...the traffic light system?" It was a common one. "Red for stop, yellow for unsure and green for go?"

Jacob nodded. Even in the dark, their faces illuminated only by streetlights, Luna recognized the crooked grin that followed. "Except if things are going really well, I'd prefer my name instead."

The comment was enough to break the tension and build up a whole new kind. Luna flushed and felt a shot of pure lust straight to her core. As if sensing the change in her, Jacob leaned forward. He didn't wait for permission but pressed a soft, almost teasing kiss on her lips, flicking his tongue to lick her lower lip.

Luna moaned, and it was as if the sound was all he needed to proceed. He ran his hand down to her neck as he deepened his kiss, lightly scraping a nail at the likely fading bite mark. The sounds that spilled from her lips grew louder and she arched her back.

Her body's encouragement must have worked. He took the invitation and moved farther down, cupping her breast. He shifted to pin her wrist down as he pulled away from the kiss, watching her as he, with infinite slowness, began rubbing her nipple through her clothes in those same maddening slow circles.

The effect was instantaneous. She bucked from the seat with a loud groan then whimpered as he withdrew.

More. She wanted...no, needed more.

"We need to get back to your place now or I'm going to take you right here." There was a slight growl to his voice and Luna sucked in a breath.

Jacob didn't exactly drive the rest of the way like a demon but it was pretty close. By the time they were at the apartment, the butterflies in her stomach had returned, but more with anticipation as she unlocked the door. And when they entered, Jacob reached to take her hand before she could flick the light switch on. "Take me to your bedroom," he whispered in the dark, sending shivers down Luna's spine.

Not trusting her voice, she gave a slight nod and began to make her way there, tugging Jacob to follow. On purpose, she kept her pace even and measured, challenging herself to not look so damn eager.

The hall to her room had never seemed longer, despite the smallness of her apartment.

As she opened the door, a soft, warm light from a bedside lamp she always kept on flooded into the hall and she paused, drawing a deep breath to ready herself. Jacob let go of her hand and stepped through first, surveying the room before giving a slight nod.

"Come here, sweetheart." He extended a hand toward her.

Him standing there in the middle of her bedroom was almost surreal. She stepped to him. That morning she had made sure fresh sheets were on the bed, already half-turned down. The scent of lavender, just a hint, permeated the air. Her closet door was closed to hide the mess in it, though that meant the mirrored doors would show everything happening on the bed. Her cheeks heated at the thought.

"Luna." There was a slight note of impatience in Jacob's voice that drew her attention back to him.

"Sorry," she muttered, only to see his eyes flicker toward those mirrors.

"Sh-h-h." Jacob drew her to him, wrapping his arms around her in a comforting hug even as a hand rubbed her back. As her body melted into his under his ministrations, he began pressing small kisses, first on her forehead, then on her cheek before placing another one, more heated, on her mouth. She parted her lips and tangled her tongue with his as she slid her hands underneath his shirt to trace the muscles at last.

Instead of letting her continue, he withdrew from the kiss, reaching to grasp both of her wrists to pull them away from him. "No, sweetheart...not yet." He undid the rest of the buttons of his shirt but left it on, giving tantalizing glimpses as he backed up to sit on the edge of her bed. "Take your clothes off for me," he crooned.

What she really wanted was to run to him and pull the damn shirt off, to explore the contours of his body. But fully in the throes of the scene now, she remained rooted to her spot, beginning to tug her T-shirt over her head. Before they had left the beach, she had exchanged her swimsuit for one of the black lacy sets she had bought at the mall and only the unpadded bra remained on her upper body. When she saw his eyes darken and heard his sharp intake of breath, she sent a silent thank you to Cassie.

He rose once more, as if unwilling to only sit back and watch any longer. He caressed her shoulders, stroking while leaving fire in their wake before he trailed his fingers down to trace the edge of the lace. "Did you dress for me, little one?" His tone delved deeper, taking on a more commanding quality than his normal easygoingness.

"Yes. I... Do you like it?" Her voice felt small, hesitant.

"It pleases me."

She caught his eyes flickering toward the mirror and her gaze followed. The image was seared into her brain, his body towering over hers, his warmer skin tones contrasting against her pale one. Her body was flushed, the red traveling all the way down as she swallowed hard. At this rate, those lace panties would be straight up destroyed.

With a dark chuckle, Jacob shifted to stand behind her, positioning them both so that the mirror captured the reflection in full. He brushed her hair back, exposing a bare shoulder for his lips to explore, and with his other hand, he cupped her breast, the pad of his thumb now inching closer, rubbing in wide circles like he had to calm her down. But there was nothing calming about the movement now. Instead, when he grazed her nipple with his thumb, her body stiffened and a small whine emerged from her throat.

"Mm-m, I love those sounds you make." His words tickled her skin but it was the sight of them together that she couldn't tear her eyes away from. The way he stared at her like he wanted to devour her, the possessive way he held her body, knowing where to touch to draw out her desire, coupled with the words that set her aflame, created the image of an aroused woman whom she barely recognized.

His gaze turned toward their reflection and, with a wicked smile, he began ever-so-slowly to unbutton her shorts. Her breath hitched as he tugged them down, brushing his hand along the edges of her lace thong. At his touch, her stomach clenched with a new shot of heat straight to her core, soaking the fabric. *Yep, ruined for sure.*

He didn't remain idle. He slipped down the shoulder straps of her bra and loosened the clasp. Soon, the bra drifted down to join her pants and T-shirt on the floor. He returned to grasp one bare breast.

Then he dipped his fingers between her legs, pushing the small piece of cloth aside just to run along the length of her slit once. "So wet," he groaned in her ear. "Oh, the things I want to do to you, sweetheart."

Her body shivered with delight, her eyes half closing as she reveled in his touch. She felt on edge already, her body so keyed up that it would not take much to push her over. But he was being oh so slow. Never had she just wanted someone inside her so much. "Jacob." She breathed out his name like a plea.

"Soon, little one. Good things come to those who wait." With bated breath, she watched as he tugged her thong down, giving her a slight nudge to step out of it and the shorts.

Once done, he took her hand and led her to her bed. "Lie down for me."

As she crawled up, she heard a soft growl from behind and only then did she realize how her rear was on full display for him, swaying as she crawled. At the center of the bed, she turned to lay on her back, bracing herself with her elbows, her legs bent and pressed together.

Half expecting Jacob to be naked by then with his weight upon her, she was surprised to find him still clothed as he was before, standing at the foot of her bed. Rather than jumping on her, he bent forward, watching with an intensity that made her rub her legs together.

"Lie back and open your legs. Let me see you."

She gave a shy smile and relinquished sight of him, albeit with reluctance. With more slowness than she'd intended, she shifted, revealing her glistening sex, and she shivered at the cold air.

He reached across to take her hand, leading it to between her legs. He positioned it, cupping her mound with their combined warmth. With a soft moan, she arched her back and was unable to resist brushing one finger along her slit.

"That's it, sweetheart. Show me."

His words urged her on, and abandoning the last of her inhibition and caught in the web of his commands, she dipped her fingers low to spread the wetness upward. As his hand left hers, she began to rub along her slit, the length of her stroking lessening more and more until she was circling the flesh around her sensitive clit. With her other hand, she grabbed her breast and, without conscious thought, began rolling her hardened nipple back and forth between her fingers.

This was nothing like when she played with herself in the middle of the night, holding faceless lovers and ill-defined fantasies in her head — not even when those lovers and fantasies merged to become an imaginary him. The awareness of him watching spurred her on until liquid heat pooled to her center and her body began to tense. *So close.*

"Not yet, little one."

His stilled her hand and she let out a whimper of frustration. She snapped her eyes open to search the familiar face and seeing his dark chocolate eyes regarding her with a softness she didn't expect. *When did he move to the side of the bed?*

"Just a little longer, I promise." As he spoke, he smoothed a hand back over her hair and pressed another light kiss on her forehead. "You did good sweetheart, so good. Still green?"

She struggled to find her voice but gave up and nodded instead. *More than green.* Was this how sex was supposed to be? How many times tonight had she almost come already, each time taking less and less effort?

"Good, because now you get your reward."

He helped her sit up. His directions kept her off balance but it was clear that he'd had a plan from the beginning as he slipped into bed behind her. His weight shifted as he adjusted until he was sitting against the headboard, then tugged at her to scoot up against him until she sat between his legs, his hardness pressing against her back. One arm encircled her, pinning her to him and his nearness made her squeeze her legs together with want.

"Keep your legs open." There was a warning in his voice and she parted them once more. There was just something about him in this mode, something that tugged at her very being, demanding obedience. In this space, in this moment, there was only him and his next set of instructions.

He hooked his legs around hers, keeping them apart. In the new position, his body entrapped hers, leaving her exposed. In terms of all the kinky sex she had ever read about, this was on the more vanilla side, but for now, she and her body couldn't care less. Held vulnerable by nothing but his strength, she could only submit.

"Perfect. So pretty and open to me."

She tested his hold, just a slight tug against his legs. When she found herself trapped with very little give, a delicious shiver passed through her body. This was nothing like the rope experience from before and nothing like any sex she had ever had.

With her still held against him, he began sliding a hand down her side, tracing idle patterns along her stomach before dipping lower until he was smoothing it along the crease of her upper thigh. As she twisted her hips with whatever limited movement she had to entice him, he groaned in her ear.

"Behave." He scraped his teeth at her shoulder in warning and she held still once more. In return, he parted her labia with two fingers, his middle finger dipping just below, teasing her opening. Her body tensed and she whimpered once more in anticipation.

He spread her nectar across her slit and began to trace along her folds upward until he was teasing the flesh around her hardening nub. In response, she squirmed, the whimpering giving way to moans and gasps as he explored her, testing where she was most sensitive. As he scraped his fingernail against her clit, her hips almost bounced off the bed if not for him holding her down, his strong muscles keeping her to him.

"I... Oh God," she gasped, reaching her hands up to cling on to his arm in almost a death grip.

"Yes, sweetheart?" His breath tickled her shoulder, and he stilled his hand to a slow stop until he was applying just enough pressure to keep her poised on the edge but not enough to give her the orgasm she so needed.

She groaned, trying to thrust against his hand, anything to relieve that sweet ache building deep in her core. But he only tightened his hold, making a *tsking* sound in his ear. "You'll have to tell me what you want."

She caved then, anything to get his hand moving once more. "More, please..."

He nipped her ear, restarting his hand with the lightest of pressure. A remote part of her brain cursed the truth or dare game earlier. Later in the game, after she'd learned her lesson and had opted for truths, she had been subjected to many more intimate questions, from turn-ons to secret fantasies. Now he was using every single one of those answers against her.

"More...?"

"I need..." She struggled to form a single coherent sentence, her mind beginning to float on the edge of desperation.

"You can do it. Tell me."

"Come... I need to *come*," she blurted out in a rushed whisper, making another frantic attempt to drive him to further action.

"Ask."

Her cheeks flushed. No one had ever demanded her to seek permission to come. Never had her orgasms been withheld from her. And she had never felt more turned on. The complete submission he demanded was what her mind and body needed all along.

"Please." Her hoarse whisper came, accompanied by a small whine in the back of her throat. When still it changed nothing he did, she swallowed and tried again. The words did not seem like her own. It was too surreal. "Please, please let me come."

"Come."

The single word was accompanied by sudden hard flicks across her clit back and forth. It was all she needed as she lolled her head backward onto his shoulder, her eyes squeezed shut as a hard climax rolled through her body, causing it to jerk and spasm. In that moment, she fell apart in an utter loss of control as he drove her higher and higher until she couldn't recognize the screams of ecstasy that emerged from her throat.

He slowed his fingers after what felt like an eternity, allowing her to begin coming down, enough to regain some semblance of mind. Just in time to hear his next word.

"Again."

He shifted his hand, delving a finger into her and crooking it to press against her G spot. He resumed rubbing his thumb over her clit again and again. Still sensitive from her first orgasm, Luna found the new onslaught to be almost too much, and she bucked against his hand, coming even harder than the first time until all she could see were stars and dark spots.

She had no idea how long he held her suspended in that moment of raw mindless pleasure. Eventually, he relented, slowing his fingers until he was cupping her mound, massaging more than arousing as she slumped against him, panting for breath. She floated, riding on an endorphin-produced high that left her wanting to just curl up and purr.

"Good girl," he whispered in her ear, stroking her hair. He continued to whisper soothing words of encouragement as he cradled her in his arms, making no attempt to move either of them. When she stirred, he looked on her with a tender smile then slipped out from behind and pulled the covers over her.

"Don't move. I'll be right back. I promise."

She nodded, registering his words. When she returned, he held a glass of water to her lips. "Slow sips."

She did as he'd instructed, savoring the coolness of water against her raw throat. When she leaned back, he set the glass aside and crawled back into bed, drawing her close to him. "Rest."

"But…" Regaining thought once more, Luna looked at him in puzzlement. He hadn't entered her, hadn't even come yet.

"Later… Rest up now." He grinned and kissed her temple. "We have all night."

All night. Dear God.

Chapter Twenty-One

Luna yawned and rubbed her eyes, still heavy with sleep. The darkness had lightened but still permeated the room enough to let her know it was not yet a decent hour.

"Mm-m, good morning," the sexiest sleepy voice murmured, and an arm reached out to pull her close. A pleasant warmth surrounded her and, unused to another's presence, she took a moment to remember. As soon as the memory of how hard he'd made her come the previous night surfaced, her body warmed further and her cheeks flushed. None of her fears had surfaced. Rather, her body buzzed with an almost-unfamiliar sensitivity.

"Morning," she whispered and curled her body against him, shifting to nuzzle along his neck, drawing a surprising moan. *That's right.* She remembered him being sensitive there.

"Now that's a nice way to wake up." He glided his hand along her side to her hip, giving it a playful tug.

It made her shiver with need, her libido still on overdrive.

"Even better." His voice had turned hoarse with desire, as if sensing hers. In the darkness, he closed the distance to nibble along the ridge of her ear. "How are you doing, sweetheart? Still green?"

"Mmhm-m." Green was one way of putting it. As she tilted her head back to expose more of her neck for him, she slid one bare leg along his, pouting in dismay to find that, though his shirt was off, his cargo shorts were still on. With a slight grumble, she shifted, putting her weight on him until, with a chuckle, he rolled on to his back.

After a moment of hesitation, she indulged herself, trailing kisses along his chest, memorizing his contours with her lips. When she drifted toward the button and zipper that held his pants up, she looked at him, a plea ready on her lips.

"You may." His permission sent a thrill through her and a fresh gush of wetness between her legs. Her inner thighs became slick with her arousal as she undid all those pesky fasteners then tugged his pants down, freeing his already hard member as he lifted his hips.

It was her turn, payback for the previous night. She scraped a nail upward, trailing it along his inner thigh with teasing slowness, and was rewarded as she heard his breath hitch. On purpose, she avoided touching what she desired deep down and, instead, made her way down the other side. His body tensed but he only chuckled in her ear. *Damn that man and his control.*

Unable to resist any longer, she moved her fingers to trace the outline of his cock, moaning as it twitched in reaction. With much anticipation, she wrapped her fingers around him, giving his length a long stroke as she flicked her tongue over one of his nipples.

Without a warning, he surged forward, bolting up and clutching her shoulders to move her off him. She gasped, scrambling away, but before she'd even had time to formulate doubts or fears that she'd done something wrong, she found herself flipped over onto her back, her hands pinned on either side of her head, his weight on her preventing her from escaping — not that she really wanted to.

"Minx," he muttered then began to kiss and nibble his way down, starting along her sensitive neck. He took his time, feasting on the little sounds his touch drew from her and flashing her a wicked grin, circled her areola with his tongue, never quite touching her nipple. She thrust her hips upward to grind against him, leaving a trail of her juices along his thigh and cock.

He growled, pushing her hips back down with his, his length pressing hard against her slit, the hot length making her crave him inside all the more. "Mine." The grip on her wrists tightened as he rubbed against her entrance.

But instead of entering her, he continued to tease, torturing her upper body with his lips until he drove her mad with lust — until all she could do was whimper and squirm beneath him. She wasn't sure how long it was before he closed around one nipple and he sucked hard, sweeping his tongue across it at last. She almost cried in relief but let out a long moan instead, tossing her head back as her body tightened.

"So sensitive." He grazed his teeth against the hardened nub before switching his attention to the other.

Close, so close. "Don't stop… Please don't stop," she begged as he continued to grind against her, his length rubbing hard against her clit, providing much needed relief.

Her breathing grew ragged as she teetered on the edge — then nothing. He rose from her body and, exposed to the sudden cold air, she let out a long groan of frustration, a single tear rolling down her cheek.

"Ah, sweetheart, soon," he murmured, smoothing a hand over her hair and leaning to kiss the tear away before leaving the bed. From her left, she heard a rustling of movement.

And he was back, tracing one finger up her slit. She braced herself on her elbows to see that he had paused to put on a condom. That could only mean one thing. Her body trembled with anticipation and, unbidden, her legs parted farther.

"Still green?" He positioned himself between her legs and she nodded so fast that she almost gave herself whiplash.

"Mm-m good. So eager." Before she could reply, he kissed her — a hot open-mouthed one that burned her with a release of all the pent-up tension they'd both felt since they'd met the very first time. He began to enter her, stretching her to fit around him. He moved with almost-agonizing slowness, making sure she felt every inch as he pushed into her. A remote part of her brain wondered at how he could still exert such control.

At last, buried in her to the hilt, they both let out long groans, and she savored the sensation of them being joined at last. It felt right to Luna, like they always belonged together. She began to berate herself for such thoughts, but as he started to move, there was no more room to think at all.

He brought his hands to hers, raising them once more, this time higher above her head. With one hand, he held both of her wrists together, freeing one to glide downward once more. She wrapped one leg around his hips as he gripped her ass, using it as leverage to thrust harder. She moved with him, and their rhythm pushed her higher and higher as she approached the precipice.

It didn't take long before her entire body tightened, her inner muscles clenching around his cock. Her fingers curled into fists as she let out a strangled moan, recalling almost too late his previous order to ask first. "Please, I'm so close." She bit her lower lip hard, hoping to hold her climax at bay just a little longer.

"Come for me."

His words undid the last of her control. As she surrendered to the sensations that overwhelmed her, every nerve came alive as the orgasm surged. Pinned as she was to the bed, she could only jerk against him, crying out his name, though her body felt as if it were coming apart. Almost as if from a distance, she registered a faint long, delicious groan as he thrust hard into her one last time and held himself there, shuddering from his own climax.

With one last gasp, Luna slumped backward, and he almost fell on top of her, though he braced himself on his elbows at the last second. Head down, he buried his face in the crook of her neck and nuzzled, drawing more shivers from her. Everything felt so sensitive.

They spoke no words as they both struggled to catch their breath. Her body tingled, still high from the most intense climax she'd ever had, her mind floating on nothingness.

"Luna?" Jacob released her hand and brushed her hair back. When she refocused on his face, he smiled, tenderness softening his features. "There you are."

"Hello," she murmured, still not quite present.

His soft laughter melted her insides in a different way. "Stay here. Let me go clean up. I'll be back in a sec."

When he withdrew from her, they each let out a long moan. Luna's gaze followed him to the washroom before she closed her eyes. This was nothing like the sex she'd ever had before. Was the power exchange the reason? Whatever it was, equal parts of fear and desire mingled in confusion. She wanted him more than anyone she'd ever wanted and the intensity of that emotion scared the shit out of her. But in her sleepiness, she pushed the doubts away, unwilling to ruin the afterglow.

"Luna?"

She snapped her eyes open as he returned.

"Open your legs, little one."

She did so, not sure when or how she'd even had the strength to close them. A sigh escaped her lips as he pressed a warm, damp washcloth against her mound and she relaxed at his gentle cleaning.

"You okay?"

A small smile spread across her face and she nodded. "Mm-hm-m."

"Good." He crawled back to bed and scooped her up once more into his arms. When she shifted to lay her head on his shoulder, it felt natural. And when he started tracing random patterns across her shoulder and along her arm, she relaxed enough to succumb to slumber once more.

"Luna, come on, little one. We can't stay in bed all day."

She groaned and buried herself closer against the body of warmth that surrounded her. "Can too," she mumbled.

"What if I said I can make you French toast?"

Bribery. Not fair. She cracked her eyes open to see Jacob grinning down at her. It was the sexiest morning grin ever, and her heart skipped a beat.

"Good morning – or afternoon."

She smiled and ducked her head a little. Despite their mutual nakedness, a sudden shyness overtook her.

"Hey, where's my sexy minx from last night?"

She only flushed deeper at that.

"Hmm-m, do I have to coax it out of her again?" He dipped a finger below her waist

"Again?" she squeaked. Why did she keep squeaking around him?

He hovered his finger over her pelvis, teasing her, and she groaned. "You're insatiable."

He laughed then and kissed her. "Maybe. Definitely, when it comes to you."

His comment made her forget all her doubts earlier. Instead, she returned the kiss, nipping at his lower lip. "Are you sure you still want me? I don't go where I'm not wanted, you know."

Luna had meant it to tease, so the last thing she expected was the growl that rumbled in his chest, right before she found herself flipped over onto her stomach.

"Doubts about my intentions when I've made myself clear also get you punished," he whispered in her ear as his weight pressed down on her once more, though there was a lightness in his voice, showing more playfulness than actual anger. As if to emphasize his actual mood, he gave her ear a light nip.

He massaged one ass cheek then placed the flat of his palm against it and she stiffened with a different kind of tension. As if sensing her sudden nervousness, Jacob returned to kneading. "Luna, talk to me."

She had been spanked by things — but never bare-handed. It had never been pleasant, if she had to admit it to herself, but she also trusted Jacob to make her feel good. He made her feel better than any man ever had.

"Yellow," she breathed out.

"Are you sure you want to continue?" He stilled his movements.

Luna checked herself. She was curious. Jacob's hand was warm and felt pleasant against her skin. It was no cold, cruel tool. And she trusted him to stop if she needed him to. His earlier reassurances rang in her head. What would it be like to be at his mercy? "Yeah."

"I'll go slow," he confirmed and kissed her shoulder.

She nodded and willed her body to relax underneath him. It was easier than she expected as he continued to rub and knead. "All right, sweetheart. Just five. Ready?"

She exhaled and nodded once more.

The first one stung, but no more than if she'd landed wrong in the dojo. It was pain that she was familiar with, even felt good about sometimes, like an exercise burn. A yelp and an accompanying shiver turned into a moan as he rubbed the spot where he'd slapped, smoothing away the sensation.

Another one. She gasped and, only half aware, she spread her legs a little more. Her ass burned pleasantly, and she wiggled it at him. Again, he took his time, rubbing away at the spot for a good while before proceeding.

The third one was more of a thud, a different sensation on another spot that had her growing wet. Very little of what was happening made sense to her but, then again, she didn't bother trying to understand for now. Instead, she reveled at the way he would always soothe the pain after, while the hurt itself never rose beyond what she couldn't handle. By the time the fifth spank came, she was making soft mewling sounds that she didn't quite recognize, full of want for him.

"Now, in case there were any more doubts in your mind…" He trailed off as he shifted to rub his length between her legs once more.

In the end, they didn't get to the French toast until dinner time.

Chapter Twenty-Two

Luna cupped a glass of cold tea in her hand and sat slumped in the chair, staring at nothing in particular, wearing what she knew had to be a rather silly grin. It had been that way since Jacob had left her place Sunday night and she had been having a hard time concentrating at work, every little thing reminding her of something Jacob had said or done. She almost hadn't even noticed Ted's teasing over lunch — and that was saying something.

Her eyes snapped back to focus when August pulled out the chair opposite her and eased himself into it. When she saw the same silly grin on his face, her own spread even wider.

"So...Lani," she started.

"So...Jacob."

They stared at each other then burst out laughing. August seemed more relaxed than ever, losing some of that seriousness that made him look older than he was. Her heart soared for her friend.

"You first," Luna urged, reaching for her mango iced tea, more as an excuse to not talk, and she hoped he would take the bait.

"Well, without going into all the details…"

He heaved a sigh when she pouted at him. The whole point was details! Or perhaps she'd just been around Ted too much.

"Fine. We played. And that's all the detail you get." Adjusting his glasses, he held his own tea up, inhaling the scent before taking a long sip. "A gentleman does not kiss and tell."

The pout remained on Luna's face and she bit back her words, hoping silence would encourage him to say more. She doubted she would have any more success with Lani.

August sighed and set his drink down. "Fine." His voice lowered. "Lani's drawing up a longer-term contract."

Now it took Luna all her effort to not squeal out loud and draw unwanted attention to them. She bit her lower lip instead and grinned until August looked away, blushing, "I'm unsure why you're making such a big deal out of this," he mumbled into his tea.

"Are you kidding me?" Luna wasn't sure if he was trying to downplay it or if he was being serious. "This is huge. You've wanted this for a while, right? You and Lani are going to be a thing!" Babbling on, it took Luna a moment before she realized she was making August uncomfortable, so she cut herself off, taking a small breath to curb her enthusiasm. "I'm just really happy for you two."

"Thank you," August replied, and she glimpsed his eyes softening. It was the sweetest thing she'd ever witnessed from a guy.

Her phone buzzed, interrupting their moment. Her breath hitched. Was it him? She hadn't heard from Jacob all day but he had warned that work was going to be ridiculously busy.

Hey, sweetheart, just finally got off work. How was your day?

There was that silly grin again as she typed a response.

Good, out having tea with August. Are you heading home to rest?

Actually, can I swing by later? I left my watch at your place.

Smooth. Real smooth. The pitter patter of her heart sped up.

Sure.

Was he really coming over to pick up the watch? Or was he staying the night? How should she ask?

Great. Do you need a pick-up from the cafe?

I'm okay. Home's not far.

K. Text me when you're home. Say hi to August for me.

She hadn't asked, but that didn't stop her from hoping in secret. Her body thrummed with excitement and she had to swallow a few times to calm her racing heart. When she looked up, she saw August with a brow raised and sank a little in her chair. "Um…Jacob says hi."

Luna thought August was above smirking but she was finding out that he was indeed not. Muttering something about 'a smug bastard' under her breath, she sank even lower in her seat.

"It's your turn," August stated.

Turnabout's fair play but Luna still couldn't help the deepening heat across her cheeks. "We played," she mumbled beneath her breath, so much that August had to lean forward to catch her words. "It was…different."

"Different?"

She spoke with a thoughtful slowness. Forced to put words to her feelings for the first time, she chewed over each with care as her brain struggled to process the churn of emotions inside. "It was good. Sex has never been that good before. In some ways, I guess that's why I've always fixated on food. It's always been a substitute."

August nodded, folding his arms over the table. "You seem hesitant, though."

"I'm worried." The two words took a lot to admit. "I don't understand why this is such a turn-on."

"You're just starting to explore as a submissive. It's okay to not know all your own kinks yet."

"Losing control like that scares me." That was the easiest part to admit. Who wouldn't fear giving someone else that much power over them, in particular when that person could make them feel things they'd never felt before?

"It's balanced by trust." The answer came swift enough. "It's important to not give just any Dom that much power over you. You have to trust her or him first. That's why it's so important to pick the right partner. For example, having a good partner to help you explore your limits and kinks is a part of it. They have to be someone you trust enough with your own safety."

Trust made sense. She could understand that. There were people she trusted already in her life, so it wasn't that far to make that leap to the bedroom. Yet... "What would they get out of it?" That was bugging her too. Jacob had been so giving that previous weekend, so generous as a lover that she felt as though she had given him nothing in return.

"I don't pretend to understand a Dominant's mindset," August ventured with less certainty in his tone. "But perhaps it's less about what he's getting out of it and more about what you want to put in. Have you figured out why you want to submit and how far you want to go?"

Luna pushed herself up, sitting straight in her chair once more as she grew aware that their conversation had shifted from teasing to serious.

"I want to be like you."

August stared at her, mouth agape, and Luna couldn't help but return his reaction with a sheepish smile. "I saw what you were like all day with Lani at the party. I... If I was to submit, I want to serve someone that same way, to take care of them." Luna took a deeper breath, the words now coming in a rush. "The thought of putting their needs above mine, knowing they would do the same for me? It just seems right to me. I want to trust someone enough to give them power over me, but I never want to be the type that just passively receives it. I have agency and I want to use it to make them happy." She ducked her head and looked to one side. "Sorry... I must sound like an incurable romantic — or a huge idiot."

Silence. When Luna found the courage to venture a peek at August, she was startled to find him smiling at her. "If it makes you feel any better" — he gave a slight nod — "if I believed having a philosophy like that makes someone an idiot, then there are two idiots at this table."

"Oh." Her beliefs were her own, but somehow acknowledging them out loud and having someone she respected so much agree with them relaxed her. It was as if the final piece of a puzzle had snapped into place and though she was aware that she was only beginning her journey, at least now there was a foundation to build on. "Thank you."

"You're welcome."

They sat in companionable silence for a little while longer until Luna felt ready to tackle her next question.

"I'm still worried about whether I'm good enough to serve, though."

"Why?" August watched her, and maybe it was something in his eyes — or perhaps it was the gentleness in his voice, but every defense Luna had ever built broke down at his single-worded question.

"I thought I knew everything when I first started out. I had a Master online once. He was so sweet, so charming. I was head over heels. But when we met in real life, I tried so hard to please him." Her hands began to shake, and she had to clasp them together. "It didn't work out, and he left, just ghosted. How…" A tear rolled down her cheek, and she rubbed it away. "I can't even hold down a vanilla relationship, so how can I be sure I'm good enough to serve? The wobble in her voice was getting worse.

"Luna." Warm hands grasped hers. "Luna, look at me."

Fear coursed through her but she forced her gaze up, anyway.

"Luna, we all start somewhere, and any Dominant would be damn lucky to have you." It was rare for August to swear and she heard anger in his voice but didn't understand why. "Whoever was your Master must have been a piss-poor one if he didn't even stay to explain why he left, leaving you guessing like that. Please don't use him as a standard to measure yourself." August's hands were trembling as he inhaled to calm himself. "Okay? Promise me. Promise me you will not let your past hold you back."

Although she was still shaky as she nodded, August relaxed a little, enough that he let go of her hands and leaned back in his chair.

"You're angry." She feared she might cry again, but his anger jolted her from her own downward spiral.

"I am. I despise Doms who do that to ruin subs before they even have a chance to understand themselves. It's why those of us who have been around for a while become so protective over any new subs. We've all seen what a bad Dom can do. We're lucky you didn't just turn your back on the whole lifestyle."

Oh. Luna wasn't sure if she agreed with his sentiment about her past Dom, but August seemed adamant—and she lacked the energy to argue. She nodded with some reluctance, at least to show she was following his words.

"Besides, if Jacob's the one you choose, he's not like that. He's one of the good ones, and the subs he trains in the three years he has them all matched with good Dominants afterward. I can vouch for that."

It wasn't the first time someone had told her about Jacob as a trainer. Perhaps three years wasn't a bad thing. A time limit could let her see where things could go with no need to worry about further commitment. And who knew what would happen in that time? Luna blinked then shook her head. It was rather presumptuous to anticipate that he would offer her a contract at all. It was also early. Way too early.

"If you're thinking about it, talk to Jacob."

"I'll think about it." It was all she could commit to at the moment, overwhelmed still both by her confession and by August's near-visceral reaction. Her mouth dry as a desert, she took the glass and downed the last of her tea, letting the sweetness soothe her agitation.

"Luna, thank you for telling me."

"You're welcome." She paused then sighed, recovering enough now with her head clearing. "Promise me you won't tell anyone. I don't want anyone to know. I don't want them to see me differently."

She could see the protest in his eyes but he nodded. "I promise. I won't break your trust." He paused, hesitating for a moment. "But if I may suggest, go see Lani about it. As a counselor, she can help you sort through some of that."

She wasn't ready for that yet, for sure. All Luna wanted was to move forward, not dwell on her past. "Maybe...when I'm ready."

"Okay."

"I should get going. Jacob needs to come over and pick up something."

"Of course."

They both rose from the table at the same time. It wasn't until they were stepping outside that Luna realized what it looked like. That would not do. "Hey, August."

"Yes, Luna?"

She didn't wait for permission but stepped up to wrap her arms around him in a tight hug. "Thank you for everything—or being a friend and a mentor to me, for believing in me."

As she felt the tension melt from his body, Luna surmised that it had been the right move, the right words to say. And she'd meant every one of them.

"Always, Luna. I will always be in your corner."

"Ditto."

They grinned at each other for a moment before, with much lighter hearts, they parted ways.

Chapter Twenty-Three

"Jacob, hi. Come on in." Luna was breathless when she opened the door wide to welcome him, and it made him wonder what she was up to until he noticed her damp hair and a hint of lace peeking above the deep V of her tank top. Coupled with her jean shorts that showed off her long legs, it took a minute for him to gather his thoughts. *Did she rush home to shower and dress up for me?*

"Thanks. How's August?" He stepped into her home. A good part of him wanted to press her against the door and have his way with her. But that wasn't what he was there for. His watch, yes. There was that. There was also a burning need in him to make sure she was okay on an emotional level, that perhaps she'd enjoyed him enough to invite him back into her bed. Because, despite him being the Dominant, the submissive held all the power in this matter.

"Good. Really good." She was shy. He noticed it in the way she rubbed her hands up and down her jeans, but it only drew his attention to her legs. Damn, she was distracting, even when she didn't mean to be, but, nonetheless, he knew how to deal with shyness.

"Hmm-m… They must have had a good weekend. Maybe even as good as ours." He gave her a cheeky grin and a wink that left her gaping at him.

"How?"

"I was talking to Lani today. She was trying to hide it, but I've known her too long to not spot that spaced-out dreamy look of hers." He chuckled as he guided them both toward the couch, taking advantage of her being stunned.

"Well, I don't think I've ever seen August grin quite that hard." Luna was giggling herself.

"And you?" He kept an easy smile on his lips, his tone almost teasing, and was rewarded by the blush he found so adorable.

"Okay, so I was grinning like an idiot the whole day too."

His smile shifted to more of a smirk and he leaned in closer now, draping an arm on the back of the couch behind her. "Oh? And just what precisely had you grinning so hard?"

She was squirming and sinking into the couch. It delighted him to draw out such reactions with words alone.

Leaning in farther, he nuzzled, running the ridge of his nose along the outline of her ear. "Tell me, little one."

"You." With a soft sigh, she closed her eyes. "The things you say. The things you do to me." She trailed off, her voice growing quieter.

He warmed and perhaps he may have even puffed up with pride. To know he brought such pleasure to her was heady stuff. "Good girl," he whispered in her ear and pressed a kiss on her temple as a reward. "Do you want me to stay tonight?"

Jacob felt more than heard her intake of breath, thrilled by the shiver that coursed through her body, and he tried not to grin again as he noticed her press her legs a little closer together and wondered if she was even conscious of the movement herself.

"I'd like that."

It was the sign he was looking for. Tilting her head toward him, he leaned in to nip her lower lip. When her lips parted for him, he deepened the kiss, slipping his tongue in to taste her. She was every bit as sweet as he remembered.

"Come on. Let's head to bed." His lips brushed by hers as he spoke then tugged her off the couch at her eager nod.

By the time they'd made it to the bedroom, they had already left behind a trail of clothing — both of their tops and her shorts. As he pressed her against one wall, he busied himself, splaying his hands across the lace, exploring the interplay of the red against her pale skin while he kissed and nibbled along her bared flesh. Her moans were music to his ears.

He ran his lips downward, even as he tugged the straps of her bra off her shoulders then undid the clasp. Rather than making them both wait, he moved to one nipple, sucking it hard before drawing back, leaving it shiny as it hardened in the cool air. He trailed a hand downward, cupping between her legs, and he grinned in satisfaction at feeling how wet she was. Her sensitivity was becoming one of his favorite things about her.

She whimpered and shivered as he played, tugging at her panties before pushing the material aside to rub along the length of her slit. As he sank lower to the floor to kiss along her stomach, she moved her hand in an attempt to take his and press it tighter against her.

"No, sweetheart." He stopped. The key to training was to start early before bad habits could develop. Every moment was a tug of reward and punishment in the bedroom. He leaned back to catch her eyes. "Just because I'm on my knees in front of you doesn't mean you're in control."

He studied her as the words sank in and a great tremor passed through her body. With visible effort, she dropped her hands to her sides, even as her breathing grew heavier.

"Good girl." She learned fast. "Now, your job tonight is to hold still and count."

With hooded eyes, he watched as her breath quickened, but it took a few seconds for her to find her voice. "Count?"

"Yes." He took his time to peel those panties away, enjoying the slow reveal. The last time, he didn't quite have a chance to study her, but he fully intended to rectify that missed opportunity. She was already glistening with wetness. "Out loud." He parted her with a finger, and she widened her stance to spread her legs farther. "Every." He inhaled, his face so close to her slit. "Time." He dipped into her, teasing her entrance. "You." With his other hand, he held her open as he sought what he was looking for. "Come." At the last word, he thrust one finger in and gave one long lick up to her clit.

To her credit, she kept her arms to her sides, balling her hands into fists. But almost losing balance, she fell back hard against the wall as her knees buckled. "God."

He heard her breath rush out and had to refrain from making a comment about calling him God. Instead, he continued his onslaught, encircling her clit with the tip of his tongue as he moved his finger in and out, having almost a hard time with how much she was clenching around it.

The sounds she made drove him on, and with care, he worked another finger in as he alternated between licking along the length of her and focusing on her clit, until her body began tensing.

"Please. Please let me come," she mewled. The plea from her held an edge of desperation.

Good girl. She remembered. He made a small noise of approval and switched tactics, wrapping his lips around her clit, scraping his teeth against the sensitive nub. It was all the stimulation she needed as she came hard. "One," she screamed out.

He held his fingers inside and kept up with his tongue and mouth as best he could, moving his hand to grip her hips with a firm hold in an attempt to control the thrashing. As her first orgasm of the night tapered off, he eased back to let her catch her breath.

A whimper spilled from her lips as she tried to push away from the wall, but he pushed her back, keeping her pinned with both hands on her hips. His little pet must have thought he was done with her. *Far from it.* Without warning, he pressed back in. There was no buildup this time. He lashed his tongue against her sensitive clit with an almost sadistic cruelty.

"Two," she cried out again as another climax tore through her body. He didn't relent, drawing out her orgasm for as long as he could.

Her knees gave out, seeming unable to take any more. He pulled away, just in time to catch her and help her to the bed as she tried to draw in ragged breaths.

"That's good, sweetheart. That's it...deep breaths," he murmured in her ear as he stripped, moved onto the bed with her and positioned himself to sit with his back against the headboard before pulling her to him. He kept one hand on her chest, gauging her recovery by the speed of her heartbeat, waiting for it to slow. He throbbed with desire for her but he had no appetite to push her toward pain, given how sensitive she was.

She looked at him, her eyes still a little unfocused but with enough presence of a kind to give him a shy smile. He studied her as she paced through the grounding exercise he had given her and felt an absurd shot of pride.

He kissed her forehead with heartfelt tenderness and smiled. "Ready for round two?"

"Round...*two*?" A pause punctuated the two words, as if she was trying to process what he meant.

With a small chuckle, he eased her away from him and tore open the packet he'd taken out of his pocket earlier. It sent a thrill of excitement down his spine to see her more focused gaze on him as he rolled the condom on to his hard cock.

"Come here." He patted his lap.

To his delight, she responded right away to his command. His cock twitched as she crawled toward him. Once she was within reachable distance, he pulled her in once more and positioned her to straddle his lap, facing him.

"That's it." He murmured soft words of encouragement as she rubbed then began lowering herself onto him. It took all his control not to pull her hips toward him and sheathe himself in her with one hard thrust. There would be time for that later.

When he was buried in her to the hilt at last, he drew her hands back to crisscross her wrists at the small of her back. "Remember... Don't move. Keep those there."

She whimpered and started squirming. It drew a hard groan from him but he paused, remembering what he'd told her. *Damn me and my instructions.* Still, he would not have this end so quickly.

Instead, the position, his favorite, afforded him more opportunities to explore. With her shoulders drawn back, her breasts pushed themselves toward him and he took his time playing with them, holding the weight of them in his palms, kneading them. When he began rubbing her nipples back and forth with his thumbs, she spasmed around him.

"Beautiful."

"I need..." She trailed off into a moan as he rolled her nipples between his fingers

"What's that, little one?" He feigned innocence. It was not an easy task, considering how he was embedded deep inside her.

"Please, stop teasing me." The begging tone in her voice hardened him further, if such a thing were even possible.

"Hmm-m, but it's so much fun." He gave her nipples a tweak. "I love how you squirm." He trailed a hand along her stomach. "How responsive you are." Then he went lower still, seeking then finding what he was looking for. "All the little sounds you make." *Ah-ha.* He reached then pressed on her clit. "And how sexy you look when you lose control."

He circled and rubbed. Unable to help herself any longer, she began rocking back and forth.

"Yes, that's it, sweetheart. Ride me."

Her movement grew more frenzied as she pumped up and down, her body once more tensing at the telltale signs he had begun to recognize. He abandoned her clit and gripped her hips with both hands instead, then began pushing his hips back up and pulling her hard against him with each downward stroke, grinding her clit against his pelvis. It didn't take long before she threw her head back. "Three," she gasped out before she let out a long wail, tossing her head back as she came hard, her pussy convulsing around his cock.

Shoving hard with a last stroke and burying himself deep within her, he roared as he came, his own ass almost lifting off the bed as his seed poured into the condom.

They slumped back onto the bed together. He was grateful for the headboard that supported his back as she lay in his arms, sliding in and out of consciousness. Her arms hung at her sides but, given the circumstances, he figured that he could forgive her for that. He was still waiting for the world to stop spinning himself.

By and by, he recovered enough to nuzzle the top of her head. "Sweetheart, we can't stay like this forever."

"Can too," she muttered, not bothering to lift her face from his chest just yet.

He chuckled and placed a light kiss on top of her head. "Let me go get cleaned up then sleep and cuddles, okay?"

With a faint nod, she rolled off him and lay on the bed, splaying her limbs and her eyes already closing. Watching her tempted him to take her again but they both had work the next day and someone had to be the responsible one.

Jacob made his way to the washroom, cleaned himself and returned with a warm washcloth and a glass of water, only to find Luna already fast asleep. With a soft chuckle, unable to help but beam with pride, he cleaned her before crawling into bed and scooping her into his arms. With her warm body pressed against his, he too fell asleep.

Chapter Twenty-Four

Luna was not looking forward to tonight's meetup with Dylan. She was pretty sure he saw it as a date but she refused to call it such in her mind. In truth, the dread she had for the night was the only reason she hadn't been glowing all day.

When she opened the door to the coffee shop, a Starbucks rather than the cafe or bakery she liked to frequent, she glimpsed Dylan sitting in the corner. Under her breath, she cursed, wondering why he had to be such a gentleman. If only he had some flaw, something she could nitpick on so her guilt would stop eating away at her.

It wasn't that she was committing to Jacob. Not yet. She wasn't even sure if Jacob would be interested. But after the last few days with the Dom, she realized that the chemistry with Dylan was not there, and it wouldn't be fair to string him along. It would have ended like her other relationships, with her trying to make her partner into something he was not. Calling it off now was the right thing to do.

Still, that fact didn't make it any easier.

"Hi," she greeted and cursed again in her head, this time at her own breathlessness. It made her sound excited to see him rather than displaying the nerves she felt. The last thing she wanted was to lead him on.

"Hi." Dylan grinned, and they stared at each other for a second before he shook his head. "Want a drink? I can grab it for you."

When Luna shook her head and sat instead, Dylan's face fell, as if, for the first time, realizing that all was not well. She had to get it over with quick, rip the proverbial bandage off.

"Dylan—"

"It's not working out, is it?"

Luna winced, both at the bluntness of his words and at the disappointment in his voice. She shook her head and sighed, casting her gaze downward, so she didn't have to meet his eyes. It was getting to be more and more like she was kicking a puppy.

"I guess on some level I already knew, and that's why I didn't want to meet earlier."

Stabbity-stab guilt.

"I'm sorry," Luna murmured beneath her breath.

"Is there someone else? I mean, we were just starting out, and we weren't exclusive—but I need to know."

Luna's gaze snapped back upward, alarmed. Dylan was looking off to one side, slumped in his chair. His shoulders were sagged in defeat.

"Dylan, please, don't torture yourself like that. It's…. It's not like that."

"Like what?" When he turned once more toward her, his expression twisted his features with a mix of sadness and something else she didn't quite recognize. "Are you going to feed me some crap about the problem being you and not me?" He gave a small, bitter laugh. "Because I find that to be the most dishonest lie."

His words struck a nerve and Luna sat up a little straighter. He had no right to accuse her of lying. Fine, if he needed an honest reason for closure, she'd give him one. "There's someone—but that's not the reason. There are some things I need to figure out for myself." Torn for a moment between needing to keep her kinks a secret and hoping he would understand, Luna inhaled once and took the plunge. "I'm finding out that I need someone more dominant as a partner."

The last thing she expected was the laughter that shook Dylan. "Oh, so you're one of those girls," he commented once he'd calmed. "You've read too much *Fifty Shades of Grey*? Come on, Luna. I thought you were smarter than that. Guys like that are basically abusive."

She should have known by their previous conversation how he would have reacted and kicked herself for not putting two and two together. Something in her curled into a ball, as if trying to shield herself from the obvious derision he held, but another part of her recognized the situation was getting out of hand and she needed to leave. At least, somehow, his reaction made it easier.

She straightened, her body stiff as a rod as she tilted her chin up with a challenge in her eyes. "Whatever you may think, I respected you enough to give you what you asked for—a real reason. It doesn't mean that you get to judge or ridicule me for my life choices. I'm sorry it didn't work out. Good luck finding someone out there." She rose from her chair, her fists clenched. He was lucky she didn't punch him right there. And it would hurt. She didn't do slapping.

Now it was his turn to turn red, but he tried to lean back as if to play it off with casual indifference. With an amused grin, Dylan waved at her. "Sure... Good luck finding your Christian Grey."

Rather than stay and argue more, Luna walked out with all the dignity she was able to muster, while inside, she railed at the judgment she felt hanging over her. Even taken as comments from a jilted lover, it still stung. She was never telling anyone outside the scene about her involvement in the lifestyle ever again. From that moment on, she resolved to keep the two worlds as separate as possible. She only hoped he didn't go blabbing back to Brandon or Ted. At least, for better or worse, she'd done it.

When she got home, the anger evaporated, and she slumped onto the couch, her head reeling from all that had happened in the last few days. A small voice nagged at her. Was she really looking for abuse? Was control inherently abusive? Luna checked herself. No, none of it felt that way. Jacob treated her with respect. He was a man who would value her submission. She would know if it was abusive, right? She had done enough reading on D/s to last a lifetime. Half of it, Jacob had sent to her. Not a sign of an abusive partner.

With a groan, she grabbed a pillow and buried her face against it. Bed...and perhaps tomorrow, she would consider all this with a clearer head.

* * * *

Things in the morning didn't clarify themselves any more than the previous night, but Luna did her best to classify that piece of judgment as precisely that—judgment from someone that didn't understand the lifestyle. She still hated, though, how much she cared about what others like Dylan thought.

It wasn't until noon that her mood improved with a text from Jacob.

How's it going, sweetheart?

She liked him calling her that.

Okay. Work's been a slog.

Poor Luna. Wish I could help.

You already have.

Well, good. You free tonight?

Heat pooled to her center as her imagination ran rampant.

Yeah. Do you want to come over?

Yes. Actually, I'd like to talk.

Luna felt a tinge of disappointment but a sudden dread overshadowed it, settling in the pit of her stomach. Things were going well, right? Or what if they weren't in his eyes? Was karma being a bitch?

Okay.

It took about a full minute before the next text came in.

Good. I'd like to discuss the possibility of continuing to explore with each other beyond our sessions so far. Give it some thought.

Words. They were just words but her dread dissipated in an instant, replaced by a thrum of excitement. Her cubicle felt too small, and all she wanted to do was get up and pace. Response, right, he was waiting for a reply.

That sounds wonderful.

Good. Text me when you're home. I'll see you tonight.

She could almost see that smirk behind his text, all the way across town. He was pleased — or so she would imagine.

See you tonight.

Why can't it be tonight already?

A casual glance at the time on her computer, though, had her springing into action. Grabbing her wallet, she rose from her desk.

"Hey, lunch?" Ted called out from the cubicle over.

"Not today, meeting up with a friend. Tomorrow?"

"Sure."

With a wave, she was off, making her way to the same brunch place as last time. The summer sun was beating down hard, and by the time she entered the restaurant, she sighed in relief at the blast of air conditioning — one of the best inventions of all time, as far as she was concerned.

There was no sight of Lani yet so she grabbed a table, all the time scanning the restaurant while chewing her lower lip. She had run into Dylan here before and the last thing she wanted was to do so again, given the previous night's conversation. So intent was she on looking for him that she jumped at a light tap on her shoulder.

"Hey, earth to Luna." Lani giggled as she took a seat in front of her.

"Oh, hello," Luna breathed, hand to her chest to calm her pounding heart.

"Is everything okay?"

She nodded but swept her gaze across the restaurant one last time. "I just wanted to make sure we didn't run into someone." *Again.*

"You mean that boy from last time?"

Luna made a face, bringing her attention back toward her lunch buddy. "I gave him the it's-not-working-out talk last night."

"Ah-h."

At that moment, their waiter dropped by and took their drink orders — tea for both of them.

"Well, that's understandable." Lani studied her menu but peeked up. "Does that mean you and Jacob are a thing?"

Luna had to work to not drop her jaw, though she felt a flush beginning to blossom. "No... I mean, I don't know. I'm not sure yet." The uncertainty sounded lame to her own ears.

Lani closed the menu and, leaving it on the table, folded her arms on top of it. "Do I need to give the dear boy a slap upside the head for being unclear with you?"

"No, no, no! He's coming over for a talk tonight."

The Domme nodded. "Excellent. That means I don't have to go stab him with one of my heels yet."

The image made her giggle, and she had to cover her mouth as the waiter returned with their tea and took their lunch orders. When he stepped away once more, she lowered her voice. "Please don't stab Jacob. I'd like very much for him to be intact."

Lani let out an almost theatrical sigh and nodded. "Very well. But just give me the word." She grinned again and Luna found she couldn't hold back the question.

"So, are you still working on that contract?"

Lani blinked at her and Luna grinned at how, for once, she'd pulled the rug from underneath her friend. It was nice to not be the most clueless and teased person in the conversation. Before Lani could utter another word, Luna spoke up again. "I'm glad it's happening. I'm happy for you two."

"Thank you," Lani murmured in return, her gaze softening. Jacob was right. There was that spacey dreamy look on her face.

Curious, Luna leaned a little closer when Lani said no more. "What made you decide to take August as yours?" Perhaps it would help her understand if there was even a possibility for her and Jacob.

The food arrived, thick brioche French toast topped with slices of poached pear with eggs and bacon for Luna, a more subdued breakfast quesadilla for Lani. Silence fell between them as they both dug into their first bites.

"I think it was the way he served me." Lani's first words were soft, almost wondering. "August is incredibly attentive, and his confidence in his submission is very attractive." Her friend took another bite, as if it gave her time to process her thoughts. "Maybe it's the way he's quiet and composed but utterly passionate beneath. Maybe it's how thoughtful he is. Or perhaps it's the way he doesn't compromise his masculinity." Lani's shoulders rose and fell in a small shrug, a small wistful smile tugging at her lips. "If hard-pressed, though, I would say that it's been a long time since I've encountered any sub half as compatible with my style and my own kinks. And when something that rare happens, I'd be stupid to turn away from the chance to see if we can work."

Lani surprised Luna with the frank answer, enough that she didn't reply right away. She supposed she shouldn't be taken aback, though. As a counselor, Lani would be comfortable and in touch with herself enough to discuss these things, but her reasons gave Luna much to consider. August had also mentioned compatibility. She knew enough now to recognize that her first Dom had never been compatible with her.

Everyone paled compared to Jacob. She enjoyed hanging out with him, whether it was watching movies, cooking or just chatting. She found his explanations of power exchange easy to follow and agreeable. And the bedroom... *Wait! That all means that we're compatible, right? Does he feel the same way?*

Luna took another bite of her French toast with a slight nod, still wondering what would be the appropriate response to Lani. Instead, her friend took away the need.

"What about Jacob?"

She wouldn't blush, not again. Luna found it hard to swallow the bit of food in her mouth, though, and it took another moment or so as Lani watched.

"I've never been with anyone like him," she admitted at last. "But we're still in the exploring stage. I'm not sure yet if we're ready for commitment." Slow and cautious.

"But you're considering it." There was a twinkle of challenge in Lani's eyes

She could lie and say no. She could shrug it off. She could make up some excuse. But all that would be dishonest. "I'm thinking about it." Luna winced. "Sorry... It's too soon and I know I come off clingy or intense sometimes."

Lani sighed and set down her fork and knife. "Luna, lovely, there's nothing wrong with thinking about it. It's natural to consider things like commitment, even early on." She picked up her fork and waved it once. "Besides, it's probably on Jacob's mind, too."

Now the flush came. Luna's jaw dropped a little.

Giggles spilled from Lani's lips and she almost purred. "I've known Jacob for a long time, and he and I are very similar as Dominants. I've never seen him spend this much time with someone he's not interested in taking on." At Luna's still-bewildered look, she placed her free hand on top of Luna's. "See what he says tonight."

Tonight couldn't come soon enough.

Chapter Twenty-Five

The heavy rain hammered against the window as Luna alternated between staring outside and at her phone, even as she chewed her lower lip. A sudden summer storm had swept in, darkening the skies only moments before drenching the streets, and Jacob was much later than he should be.

When her phone rang at last, she jumped to pick up. "Luna?"

"Come on up." She hit the button on the dial pad to unlock the front door to the building.

"Thanks." Hearing the sound that indicated he had passed inside, she crossed her apartment to open the door, sighing in relief only when he'd arrived.

"Well, that was a thing."

Luna couldn't stop staring. His dark locks fell over his eyes and his simple black T-shirt clung to every curve of his body. Simply put, he was drenched. It was almost like when he had stepped out of the shower all over again, except this time, her memory, rather than her imagination, filled in the gaps.

"Want to let me in, sweetheart?" There was that smirk on his face, as if he was well aware of her appraisal of him.

Caught. "Oh! Sorry." Luna stepped aside, her cheeks burning, and forced her gaze away. "Let me get you a towel."

"Thanks."

When she returned, Jacob had already taken off his socks and shoes and he flashed her a grateful smile as he took the towel from her, proceeding to dry himself. "It's like everyone forgets how to drive in the rain," he muttered under his breath. Without warning, he sneezed hard.

"Let me make you some tea." She was already moving to the kitchen. She had readied the hot water earlier and now it was just a matter of steeping the tea. "You should get out of those wet clothes. They can't be comfortable. I can stick them in the dryer."

As she bustled about the kitchen, she paused, catching his eye with an amused smirk.

"Is that your way of trying to get me naked?" he asked, grinning.

"No!" Luna protested right away, though her cheeks were threatening to catch fire. She sniffed, trying to emulate Lani's reaction when she pretended to be affronted by something. As she returned from the kitchen, she pressed a mug into his hand. "I'm just trying to take care of you."

"Okay, okay!" Jacob gave a small laugh as he set the tea down on the kitchen counter and tugged off his T-shirt and pants. Luna looked to the side, trying to give him some privacy, and found a particularly interesting spot on the wall.

"You can look, sweetheart. It's nothing you haven't seen already."

Drawn back by his words, Luna swallowed as she beheld the sight of him standing before her, the contours of his body on display. There was a slight bulge in his boxers and she forced her gaze back up. *Nope, nope, nope...* He was not going to distract her.

With the smirk still lingering on his lips, he handed her his clothing and followed as she made her way to the small laundry closet where she deposited them and started the machine.

"Now, let's sit on the couch so we can have our chat."

The talk. Never had Luna felt such a mix of curiosity and worry. It must have shown on her face as he took her hand and held it to his lips. "Relax. Come on."

That was easy for him to say. He wasn't staring at an almost naked her. Maybe she should strip too, to even the playing field. No, this talk was too important. Luna shook her head to clear it. She was not going to act like some sex-starved, distracted nympho. She steeled her mind with thoughts of the talk instead and followed his lead to settle on the couch, taking comfort in the warmth of his hand around hers.

Gratitude welled in her when Jacob went straight to the point. "I want to do a check on where we're at and set some expectations."

Luna blinked and nodded.

"We've scened twice. I know I'm interested in exploring further, and if I've read things right, so are you." There was a seriousness in his eyes.

Luna straightened, shifting to face him. The question wasn't coming from a place of flirting or foreplay and, despite the hammering in her chest, she nodded, swallowing a few times to find her voice. "Yeah, I am."

"How far do you want to go?" Jacob asked.

Wasn't that one of the main questions she had tossed around in her head? She closed her eyes and sucked in a breath before exhaling. "I'm not sure," she admitted. "I'm interested in going beyond the bedroom, but I don't know how far that means." The words started slow but they tumbled from her lips faster and faster. "I'm torn. I know I want to retain my independence, but I also want to serve someone, to put their needs above mine and to follow their lead. But I don't know where that balance is yet. I'm sorry if it's not a very good answer."

"Shh-h…" Jacob smiled and let go of her hand, only to cup her cheek. "It's a perfectly good answer. And do you know why?"

Luna shook her head but could not help but lean into his warm palm, taking comfort in his small gestures of affection.

"Because it's an honest one. In any relationship — but especially in a D/s one — even as play partners, we need to be honest with each other. Now, tell me why. I know you know this one."

His words echoed much of the reading he had sent her and now Luna smiled, some of her confidence returning. "Because we're dealing with power inequalities that may lead to both emotional and physical safety concerns. Because if not treated with proper respect, D/s relationships can lead to abuse — intentional or unintentional."

"Good girl." He stroked her cheek before returning to hold her hand.

The gesture, outside of a scene, should have had her spitting mad. From anyone else, it would appear condescending. But Luna straightened under Jacob's warm, approving gaze instead.

"Why don't we play it by ear, like we have been until now. No pressure — but I'll keep pushing until it's too far for you, and you can tell me when. We can explore and test your boundaries and you can tell me no or to stop."

"Like a contract?" The last word came out as a squeak. She wasn't sure why she felt a twinge of disappointment when Jacob shook his head.

"Not quite. A contract would dictate very specific terms. Personally, I'd only draw one up if I am taking on a sub to train — and the term is three years." He curved his lips into a crooked grin. "Think of this as a trial period, for both of us. If you're interested in formal training as a sub, then we can talk more."

"What's in it for you?" Luna blurted out.

Jacob chuckled and shrugged a little. "I suppose you can say I have a good feeling about this…about you. And, in the meantime, I get a wonderfully responsive sub to play with."

The temperature in the room rose. Luna's cheeks flushed and her breathing grew a little more shallow.

In response, Jacob leaned forward, brushing his lips against her ear. "See what I mean?" Without waiting for a reply, he nipped at the ridge of her ear, sending delightful shivers down her spine before shifting to line small kisses along her jawline.

She moaned and tilted her head to one side, exposing more of her skin for him, half-closing her eyes with pleasure. Every nerve in her body was coming alive. "Bed?"

"Hmm-m not yet. I haven't had you on this couch yet." He reached her neck and began alternating between nibbles and kisses, even as he gave a gentle push to guide her to lie down on her back.

"Wait." She placed her hands-on his shoulders and grinned a little. "I have a surprise for you." Inspired by one of his answers in the truth or dare game, she had done a little online shopping after he'd left the past Sunday. Hurray for Amazon two-day shipping.

She served. She wanted to show him what it meant in the bedroom, given the chance. And now was that chance.

'Confidence is sexy.'

Lani's words echoed in her mind. She wanted to be confident for him.

Jacob raised his brow and eased himself back while offering a hand to help her sit back up. With a mischievous grin, Luna stood from the couch then spun around to give him a light peck on the lips. "Be right back. Promise."

She started as soon as she got to her room and half-ripped the packaging off in haste. Without another moment of hesitation, she stripped while recalling his words.

'Weirdest fantasy? Well, once I kissed this girl who had this vanilla lip balm on and ever since, I've gotten this weird idea of sampling someone and being surprised by what flavor they might taste like.'

She remembered how they'd all gotten a little flustered by the idea, enough that there was a bit of silence following his answer. Ever since, Luna had been hellbent on figuring out how to fulfill that fantasy of his — and she'd found the answer in edible massage oil.

Opening the first bottle in the variety five-pack, she dabbed the oil on and spread it across her neck down to her shoulders then using another bottle with a different flavor on her breasts. She continued to do so, working as fast as possible until she'd coated herself all over in a thin layer of oil. As the last step, she put on a touch of vanilla lip balm. Once completed, she wrapped a short black kimono-style robe around herself and made her way back into her living room.

Jacob had sat back on the couch. When she stepped into view, he tilted his head to one side in curiosity.

Bold. She would be bold. Theirs was a dance of give and take, and he had already given so much. It was her turn. As she stood in front of him, she unbelted her robe then let the silk-like material slide off her body until she was nude and glistening before him. Despite her self-consciousness, she offered a hand toward him. "Please."

His chest rose as he drew in a deep breath but he did not hesitate to take her hand, rising from the couch. In return, she rose to kiss him.

A small growl emerged from the back of his throat as his tongue darted across her lips. "Vanilla," he whispered as he pulled back, his eyes narrowing. "That's not your usual taste. Just what're you up to, Luna?"

"Please," she whispered once more and kissed him again. Then, with a gentle nudge, she attempted to guide his head lower. The muscles of his neck strained against her touch in resistance, his dominance chafing against her hand's mild pressure. "Let me please you," she pleaded.

He relented and dropped his head to place lazy kisses along the column of soft skin. When he darted his tongue out to lick the salted caramel off her skin, he let out a long groan. "You little minx, what have you done?"

"I wanted to thank you for the weekend and to return the favor. You had mentioned..."

He cut her off with a kiss then licked down her body, reaching to hold her wrists, pulling them back behind her. As he reached her breasts, he blew heavy breaths across her nipples and she bit back a moan.

"Hold still," he ordered.

With a maddening, leisurely pace, he sampled the flavor of her breasts, inch by inch, circling close to her hardening nipples. He would taste coconut, she remembered, but she was losing track of everything herself. Maybe it had started out as his fantasy, but she was growing more and more aroused with each sweep of his tongue.

"More," she whimpered as he grazed one nipple with the tip of his tongue, causing her to jump.

He said nothing as he wrapped his lips around it, sucking hard. Something shifted as his administrations grew rougher, his grip on her wrists tightening, though never painful enough to hurt. He swirled his tongue around and she quivered, soaked enough that a trickle of her moisture trailed along her inner thigh.

He paused, as if sensing she was on edge, before switching to the other side. She cried out then, arching her back, her lips parting. "Jacob, I'm going to—"

"Not yet." His voice was hoarse but full of command. Showing mercy, he left her nipples, licking his way down her stomach. Her body clenched as he licked the pineapple oil off her skin. She giggled, finding it almost ticklish, and she squirmed in his grasp.

He snapped his head back, something darker moving in his eyes.

"Fuck, I'll taste you more later."

She'd rarely heard him swear at all and that was the only warning she got as he threw her onto the couch then positioned her to lie along its length. As she lay there, wide-eyed, he wasted no time pulling his boxers off his hips. He dug out and rip off the packaging of a condom, rolling it onto his cock with now-hurried movements. When she tried to sit up to watch him, he pressed a hand to the base of her throat, not quite choking her but applying enough pressure to keep her down. Before she could register what had just happened, he was on top of her, his hard cock pressing against her burning core.

"So wet." The timber in his voice had taken on an almost primal quality. He spread her legs farther apart with his knee and positioned himself. Then with one long, hard stroke, he buried his cock in her.

Almost coming from that alone, she clung to his shoulders as he began to move. There was no easing into it as he set a hard and fast pace right away, grinding his pelvis into her clit with every thrust. Just as eager, she moved with him, her body soon tightening at the telltale signs of a hard climax.

"I'm going to—" she gasped out. It only made him drive into her harder, until her world narrowed to just his cock between her legs. With another hard thrust, he tipped her over the edge as he slammed into her, and she came, screaming his name, her body exploding from the intense pleasure of a hard climax.

With a long groan, he gave one final powerful thrust. He swelled inside her and he clamped his teeth down on where her neck joined her shoulder, marking her as he came.

They were both trying to draw air in with heavy pants and Jacob rested his sweat-soaked forehead on her shoulder. Neither of them spoke until Jacob lifted his head. Luna didn't understand the sudden near-panic she saw in his eyes.

"Shit, are you okay? I didn't hurt you, did I?" He lifted his hand as he studied where he had kept her pinned.

Luna blinked and shook her head. When Jacob didn't look up, she lifted her hands to cup his cheeks. "Jacob, I'm okay." It had been a little rougher than the last few times but still so very pleasurable. The only pain she felt was from the bite and even that throbbed with a pleasant achiness.

He let out a sigh of relief and lowered his head back on to her shoulders. "The things you do to me, sweetheart." He groaned.

"What...did I do?" she asked, worry in her voice.

Jacob lifted his head once more and gave her a weary smile. "My control hasn't snapped like that in a long time."

"Oh." His admission made her speechless. She had thought to just give him something he would enjoy. Little did she know what that meant. "That's a good thing? I pleased you?"

He chuckled and placed a tender kiss on her forehead. "Yes, little one. You've pleased me greatly." He began to withdraw from her, inch by inch until he stood once more then scooped her up in his arms.

"Now, let me take care of you. How about a nice warm shower together?"

She smiled at that and wrapped her arms around his neck. "That sounds absolutely wonderful."

Chapter Twenty-Six

"Hey, is everything okay?" Ted asked as they sat side by side on a park bench two days later, each with a hefty sandwich in hand. The shade of a large tree kept the burning afternoon sun from beating down on them, but it was still getting warm.

Caught mid-bite, Luna turned toward her friend, her cheeks puffed up still from the food in her mouth. Despite a substantial breakfast, she was still starving. Perhaps it was because breakfast had been rather distracting and she'd been getting a lot more exercise recently. *Sorta.* Unable to speak yet, she tilted her head to one side instead in question.

Ted rubbed the back of his head. "Well, I heard you broke things off with Dylan."

Ugh. Gossip was strong with Ted. She tensed as she swallowed the bite then winced when she had to choke it down. "Did Dylan mention anything else?" Wariness made her choose her words with deliberate care.

"No, not really." As if embarrassed now, Ted turned back to his own food.

Relief flooded her. Despite him making fun of her unconventional preferences, maybe Dylan had enough integrity to not discuss it with others. She would be less angry with him, though she doubted she would ever see him again.

Her friend, however, appeared a little too embarrassed from her lack of an answer. Luna placed a hand on Ted's arm and gave him a smile. "Hey, I'm okay, I promise. I appreciate you looking out for me."

"Of course." Ted recovered a little and gave her a thumbs-up sign then dropped his hand once more. "So, why did you do it?"

There was a moment of hesitation. She and Ted had been friends for a long time, and she was the first one he'd come out of the closet to. Part of her wanted to spill the beans, to celebrate her newfound confidence in her sexuality, but then Dylan's jeering words echoed in her head. No, she couldn't risk her friendship or her career.

So, instead, Luna gave a small shrug. "The chemistry wasn't there." That wasn't a lie, just vague. *Good.* It seemed that Ted bought it as he nodded.

"And this other guy who drove you to work the other day?"

Her reaction was instantaneous. Her cheeks heated and, to buy herself time, she crammed another bite into her mouth. She pretended to answer, but her words came out more of a garble, as she'd intended.

Ted laughed and shook his head. "Fine. I'm just bugging you. I'm sure you'll tell me when you're ready."

Luna cast a sideways glance at him then groaned and rolled her eyes. She knew Ted enough to recognize his retreat for what it was—a temporary reprieve. Sooner or later, she would have to confess, but she hoped, by then, she could come up with enough of a cover story. Already her mind was spinning.

Practice that night at the dojo was, if she were honest with herself, a disaster. Distracted, trying to gauge Brandon's reaction to her dumping Dylan, Luna's execution of the classic Judo moves was rather sloppy. As luck would have it, it was a full class that night and her sensei was a little too busy with the newbies to pay much attention to her

"Come on, Luna. Focus," she muttered under her breath as she bowed to her opponent in the last sparring session of the class. Up against her senpai, one of the more senior students in the dojo, she needed every ounce of concentration that she could muster.

When Brandon gave the signal, they came together and grappled, holding each other's lapels. Another shout from their sensei and they began tugging at one another, testing each other's balance. Luna grunted, sweat beading on her forehead. Her eyes widened as she sensed an opening and went for it.

She should have known it was a fake-out. Since her move already put Luna off balance, her senpai slid a hip underneath hers. In the blink of an eye, she flipped Luna over onto her back and Luna winced as she landed wrong—on her tailbone and lower back rather than the side of her hip. Luna had no one to blame but herself. She had been practicing long enough to know what a proper landing should be. Still, she couldn't help but grimace.

"Ow."

"That looked like it hurt." Her senpai offered a hand and helped Luna to her feet.

Luna nodded, rubbing her sore rear, and winced again as she felt how tender her backside was. It was not what she would call the good kind of pain.

However, it wasn't until the end of class when she was changing out of her *dogi* back to normal clothing that Luna recognized the full extent of her injury. Putting on pants had never felt more painful, and she cringed at the prospect of walking back home. Well, there was no use whining about it. It was time to tough it out.

As she stepped out into the warm air, she waved goodbye to the others. Her phone buzzed with an incoming call as she walked and she dug into her pocket to fish it out.

"How was class?"

Jacob. Her pain became a distant memory.

"Not the best," she admitted, resuming her walking. "I landed wrong and may have bruised my tailbone."

"Poor Luna. Want me to come over and take a look?"

The image of her holding her rear up high for him to inspect blossomed in her head and she had to shake it to clear her mind. She wasn't sure how she felt about it. Perhaps an awkward mix of embarrassment and arousal would be a good description.

It was that hint of embarrassment that made her shake her head, only to remember that he couldn't see the motion over the phone. "No, it's okay. This happens from time to time and isn't a big deal. I'll just sit on a bag of frozen peas or something," she replied with haste.

"All right. But, in all seriousness, if you need help, call me. That's part of submission too, letting someone take care of you, not just within a scene."

She contemplated his words. Luna had been on her own for so long, since college, that she hadn't even the foggiest idea about what depending on someone else meant. But, she nodded to herself. "Okay, I'll try to remember that."

"Okay."

There was reluctance in his voice, as if he still didn't want to let it go, and she began to waver, but before she changed her mind, Jacob spoke once more.

"Anyhow, I was calling to see if you'd like to accompany me to The Playgrounds tomorrow night. I thought it'd be a good idea for us to explore our dynamics in a more public setting. But, with your injury, I'm not sure it's a good idea to be up and about."

"I'm really okay. I promise." Then the implications of what he was saying hit her. Did that mean he was asking for them to make a public appearance as... Together? Was she ready for that? She had been honest with Lani and August about Jacob, but that was different. This would be in front of everyone. Then again, they had gotten pretty cuddly at Lani's birthday party too. So maybe it wouldn't be as big a deal as her mild panic was making it out to be.

"Well, if you're up for it, I think August and Lani will be there tomorrow too. It could be fun all hanging out again."

He had to dangle that carrot. She wanted to see the two of them together. After all, she was a fan of that ship. "Okay, yeah, I'll come."

"Excellent. I'll pick you up at eight."

Luna took the rest of the next day to shop, combing through the places Lani had taken her to all those weeks ago to find the right outfit. While she always enjoyed dressing up for The Playgrounds, tonight was different. For the first time, she was part of the community, with friends to meet on purpose.

By the time Jacob rang her buzzer, she was a bundle of nerves. It didn't help that her tailbone and pelvis still ached, making walking a bit of an awkward exercise. She smoothed her hand over her goth dress, a black Lolita-burlesque blended number with a corset-like, low-cut laced top that billowed out into a few layers of fabric, lace and tulle, without being too bulky. She paired the outfit with thigh-high lace stockings and a little top hat fascinator in her hair. It was a fun costume, and she liked the esthetics. She chalked up part of her nerves as uncertainty about how Jacob would feel about such an outfit.

She had her answer soon enough when she opened the door and saw Jacob's eyes darken at the sight of her. As she stepped back to let him in, the corners of her lips tugged into a shy smile before turning around. "Let me grab my bag."

"Actually." Jacob cleared his throat as he stepped through and grabbed her wrist to pull her back. When she stood, head tilting to one side in question, he let go and dug into his pocket, bringing something out. Balled in his fist at first, Luna couldn't quite make out what it was until he held it up, dangling a feather charm on a silver chain from his hand. "I'd like you to wear this for me tonight."

She blinked, speechless. It wasn't a collar, but it was still something—and unexpected.

"The raven is one of my favorite birds," he explained. When she made no reply, he waved a hand in front of her. "Luna?"

Had she zoned out? She blinked again to try to focus. "Um…hi?"

The necklace still dangled from his hand and she followed its path as it swung back and forth. It was hypnotizing, and a remote part of her recognized that her thoughts were getting hazy again.

As if realizing what was happening, Jacob set the necklace down on the kitchen counter and placed both hands on her shoulders. "Focus, Luna. Breathe."

The command cut through the fog and she began to focus on his face. She rubbed her eyes as her mind cleared. He had offered her something of his to wear. Even though it was just for tonight, she didn't miss the symbolism behind it.

"Better?"

When she nodded, he gave her a sheepish smile. "I should have realized. Sorry."

"No, I'm okay." Then, growing more confident, she gave him a wider smile. "And I'd be honored to wear it."

The way his eyes shone was more than enough for her. He grabbed the necklace and helped her put it on. The silver feather hung low on the long chain and still felt warm to touch.

"It matches your outfit."

Luna grinned at the pride she heard in his voice before realizing that he was staring at the feather nestled between her breasts. She reached to touch the charm, brushing her fingertips against the tip of the feather. Jacob cleared his throat again.

"Let's get out of here or we'll never leave."

The drive to the club was considerably shorter than Luna expected—or perhaps it was because it was full of conversation, ranging from the latest movies to her filling him in on August and Lani's new relationship. The time passed by quickly enough that it startled Luna when they pulled into the parking lot next to the warehouse building.

As they stepped into The Playgrounds, they found Lani chatting with Darryl at the bar, August at her side. Luna took a step back, attempting to position herself behind Jacob, like she had seen Dominique before with Erica.

However, Jacob turned and, with a hand at the small of her back, guided her to walk in front of him, bending forward to speak in her ear. "Every Dom has a different style and preferences. Read your cues from me. Copying how other subs are with their Doms won't necessarily work. If you have questions, ask me instead."

It was a good lesson to learn. She needed to be more observant of him.

When she nodded, they resumed making their way through the crowd, Jacob hovering behind but also holding his arms out, lest Luna's smaller figure get crushed.

"Luna, sweetie!" Lani drew her in for a hug as soon as they arrived at the bar. Darryl had stepped away to serve someone drinks at the other end. From behind, August smiled in greeting and Luna grinned back. He was sporting a new necklace—chain mail woven with a strip of black leather, a small Trinity knot charm dangling from it. The masculine necklace was short enough that it could double as a collar. Luna did not miss its significance.

"Hello, pest," Jacob called from behind.

"Brat." Lani released Luna and Jacob wasted no time in drawing her back into his arms. "Possessive brat."

"Only for tonight."

"Uh-huh."

Her heart skipped a beat when Jacob only rolled his eyes and tightened his arms around her.

"Hello, Master Jacob, Luna," August greeted from behind.

"Hi, August. I heard the news. Congrats, man."

Luna had to stifle a giggle as August blushed then dipped his head. "Thank you, Master Jacob."

"All right, all right, enough about that!" Luna wasn't sure if Lani was trying to divert attention away in an attempt to save her sub. "Now, Jacob, I demand that you share. I want to go dancing with Luna." Lani pouted and crossed her arms.

If not for her injury, she would be all for it, but her body reminded her of her still-tender bottom. Luna cursed herself for her earlier carelessness.

Jacob must have sensed her stiffening. "Not tonight, Lani. Luna's hurt."

She looked back and opened her mouth, about to retort that she could answer for herself, but caught sight of the warning in his eyes. "You're injured, Luna. I see it in the way you've been walking all night. Don't push yourself."

She snapped her mouth closed and ducked her head a little, chastised.

"What happened?" Lani's gaze cast downward toward her hips, dancing forgotten. Behind her, August leaned in with a frown.

"I landed wrong in the dojo last night. It happens from time to time but it takes a few days to recover."

"Have you been icing it?" Darryl chimed in, returning to socialize, now that he'd finished serving the other patrons.

"Yeah. I'll be okay, really. It happens all the time."

"Well, take it easy, Luna." August's frown eased just a little.

Never had so many people all expressed concern over her. In that single moment, she realized she hadn't just found a community of like-minded souls or a potential Dom. She had found a family.

Chapter Twenty-Seven

"You okay up the stairs?" Jacob asked for the third time as they made their way to the third floor of the club. He was bordering on nagging but he wasn't familiar with the injury Luna had sustained and, unable to identify with it, he needed to err on the side of caution.

"Yes." There was a sigh of mild exasperation accompanying Luna's reply, despite the way she hopped up the stairs. That, he recognized. She was trying to minimize the height to which she had to lift each leg.

Lani's teasing earlier echoed in his head. She had accused him of fussing over Luna like a mother hen.

He was not fussing.

"Luna." There was a hint of warning in his voice. She was a tough one, but he also needed to know that she wasn't pushing her physical limits too hard, in particular to please him. If she weren't in such pain, he would haul her in his lap and give her a good spanking for her attitude.

"I'm going slow. I promise."

Jacob sighed and pushed his hair back. His original plan was to show Luna the private rooms, since she'd never quite had a full tour of The Playgrounds, then run her through a simple positioning exercise, giving her a taste of what training with him would be like. But with her current state, the positions would exacerbate her injury, so he would have to content himself with only the first portion of the plan.

When they arrived on the third floor, he heard a small gasp and allowed himself a chuckle as they gazed down the long hall, doors lined on each side. "Each of these is a private playroom. The themed ones are closer toward the end of the hall, along with staff offices. But these..." He took her hand and led her toward one with an open door. "These are more general."

Aware that the sight of it would shock her, he kept his hand over hers, ready to ground her as he studied her reactions. Luna's eyes widened into saucers and her chest rose and fell in more shallow breaths as she beheld the room.

It was tasteful in its decor, much like most of The Playgrounds. Cherry red wood panels lined the walls, equipment and toys of sorts lined against one side. A harness dangled from a hook on the ceiling and another padded bench sat along the other side, looking much more innocent than it had any right to be.

"Are you okay?"

"Yeah, I think so." She sounded breathy and her grip had tightened around his.

It was time to intervene. He led her over to a panel of controls by the door. "Each room has a security feed, both video and audio. It ensures that safe play is happening, even in private. However, play partners can consent to turning video and-or audio off." As he explained, he gestured toward the well-labeled controls.

Luna studied the panel and he could almost see that big brain of hers turning, considering the possibilities. *Good.* He wanted her to imagine what could happen, to entertain thoughts of future time with him. Her imagination pleased him like it had the other night.

"I'd like to use one of these rooms for some light training. Not tonight, though. I don't want to make your injury worse,"

She swallowed and he felt a sudden urge to kiss down that throat. Perhaps he should just close that door now, tie her up and...

What's the matter with me?

"What kind of training?" She had tensed and there was wariness in her eyes. Jacob reached out to rub her shoulders, soothing her nerves.

"Have you ever had positioning training?"

When Luna shook her head, he wondered for a moment just what kind of experience she'd had. Well, they all had a past. She hadn't asked about his.

"There are various positions a Dom may ask their sub to assume, either during or before a scene — or when we're in a kink-specific setting like this place. They vary from kneeling or standing to sitting."

Her lips formed a small O. Had she realized that she had spread her legs apart and bent her legs at his description? Perhaps it was part of her martial arts training.

"Another night. I don't want to push it." For emphasis, he drew her aside and led her out of the room.

"I prefer private play and play in these rooms is acceptable. You may request it and I'll take it into consideration. If a piece of equipment strikes your fancy, let me know." He promised nothing but he would have her communicate her desires.

Luna nodded, quiet as she chewed her lower lip.

"Luna," he chided and tugged at it, tracing it with his finger. "One day you'll chew yourself raw. Then how am I going to kiss you?"

"Sorry."

"Please take better care of yourself—or I will really show you what punishment can be like."

Luna's entire body grew rigid, and she glanced back toward the room where the open door still showed whips and floggers hanging from the wall.

"Luna." Jacob's gaze followed hers. Then taking her chin by thumb and forefinger, he tilted her face back toward him. "I know anything beyond mild pain is a hard limit for you. There are other forms of punishment and we'll explore those too, if we have to."

She relaxed but looked up at him, still in surprise. "How did you—?"

"I've seen your responses to those implements, or the sight of someone being flogged, enough times to surmise that you have no interest in those kinks yourself." He smiled and leaned forward to kiss her forehead. "That's fine. They're not my cup of tea either."

Behind them, the door to another private room opened and a familiar-looking woman with a cascade of coiffured blonde curls emerged, clad in a slinky black latex dress and five-inch stilettos. Even from a distance, Jacob noticed her eyes widening as she caught sight of them.

"Oh my God, is that you, Jacob?" With a squeal, she closed the distance and tackled him.

He gave a yelp of surprise as he almost lost his balance, catching the over-enthusiastic girl in his arms. "Hi, Selina. What're you doing in these parts?" He chuckled as she kissed him on each cheek before stepping back. She had always been affectionate

"Ah, just in town for a quick visit with some friends," she replied. "You look amazing."

Selina was always energetic too. He remembered that much about her. How she had exhausted him in the year he'd trained her, even by the simple act of talking his ears off alone.

"Thank you. You too." Ah, Luna was staying silent, standing farther back behind him, as if giving him room. But her posture spoke of awkwardness and hesitation, as if she were curling into herself. That would not do. He reached over, wrapped an arm around Luna and pulled her close. "Selina, may I introduce you to Luna. Luna, meet Selina."

The wan smile Luna gave was not much of an improvement. But it didn't seem to deflate Selina's enthusiasm as she squealed, taking Luna's hand in both of hers. "Luna, oh my... Are you one of Jacob's new pets?"

Watching her cheeks flush, Jacob tried to keep the smugness out of his responding smile and gave Luna's shoulder a gentle squeeze. "For tonight anyway. Though I'm hoping she may agree to longer."

Selina leaned in toward Luna and, with a conspiratorial look, stage-whispered to her. "Isn't he always such a charmer? You should totally go for it. You'd be in for a treat. Trust me. I would know." She winked and giggled.

"Well, thank you for the raving review." Jacob rolled his eyes but noticed that Luna had not spoken, reverting to the little mouse he'd first thought of her as. Something was wrong. Perhaps she was feeling overwhelmed. Despite being a sub, Selina had a rather larger-than-life personality.

From behind them, the door opened again, and they all heard a growl. "Selina, you brat, where did you go?" An older man with just a light silvering in his hair came out of the same room, adjusting his shirt collar. He, too, turned in surprise when he caught sight of them. Jacob grinned. *Good.* Selina was still with the Dom he had matched her with. They had moved away together a few years back, if he remembered right.

"Piers, how are you?" Jacob extended his hand in greeting, even as Selina giggled, half skipping back toward the man's side.

"Jacob, fancy seeing you here." They grasped each other's arm and shook. He turned then toward Luna. "And this lovely lady is?"

"Luna, Sir." His mouse spoke at last.

"Pleased to meet you, Luna. Has Selina been bothering you? She can be a handful."

At that, Selina pouted and Jacob had to wonder how he'd survived her for as long as he had. *That's right...*They'd never done a formal contract, and after a year, he'd already been eager to find someone for her. Piers had been a pure stroke of luck.

"Not at all." Luna's voice was small but she remained polite.

Selina beamed at the answer Luna gave. "See! I'm behaving. Now I think you promised me a drink."

Piers sighed and placed a hand on top of Selina's head. "Okay, okay." He turned back toward Jacob.

"We're just heading down to the bar. Would you and Luna like to join us?"

Jacob spared another glance toward Luna then turned toward Piers. "Maybe soon. I was just giving Luna a tour."

"Very well. I hope we'll see you later." Piers was too polite in his comment, but Jacob glimpsed that slight smirk lurking on his face. He must have thought they were about to pick a room to play in. *If only.*

"Bye, Jacob. Bye, Luna. Have fun!"

Piers guided Selina out, who waved back with a last giggle.

They watched as the other pair left, but Jacob didn't break the silence until the couple was down the stairs and out of sight.

"What's wrong, Luna?"

There was wariness in her eyes as she turned toward him and he decided that he didn't like the look one bit. Other emotions flitted across her face but they were too quick for him to parse.

Luna opened her mouth and closed it again before taking a deep breath. Her chest rose and fell and the charm he gave her glittered against the black lace. She wouldn't have realized it but it was a rare gesture for him. Something in him had propelled him to give her something of his—and he always trusted his gut.

"I want to say nothing but, to be honest, I'm not sure yet." Her gaze remained on the stairs.

"Selina was someone I trained informally a few years back. She came to me, adamant that she was a sub." He rubbed the back of his neck. "To be honest, I probably bit off more than I could chew with her. But I gave her enough that she was ready by the time Piers came along, and I was happy to match them."

"How many subs have you trained?"

It wasn't the place where he wanted to discuss this, but he didn't dare take Luna back into a private room where their power dynamics might make her hesitant to ask what she needed to know. So, he stayed rooted.

"Over the years, around twenty." He had nothing to hide. His past was his past. It wasn't as if Luna didn't already know that he was a trainer.

"I see." A pause. "Selina called me one of…"

He shrugged. "Sometimes I took on two at a time."

"And now?"

Jacob raised a brow. The last question gave him some hint where her head was at. It was one thing to hear the stories about his experience as a trainer, and quite another to be shown it with actual names and faces.

"That was when I was younger and had more energy." He observed her, not wanting to make himself out to be someone he wasn't. If she wanted him, there were truths she had to accept. "I take on a sub and train them three years at a time. After that, I make sure they settle with a Dom who is not only compatible and someone they're interested in but also someone I know who will treat them right."

"I see." The same answer again. Jacob wished he could read her mind. She had schooled her face to a neutral expression.

He sighed and placed a hand on the small of her back to guide her toward the stairs. "Do you want to head home and take some time to process?"

She nodded once.

"Come on. I'll drive you home."

Well, there goes the evening.

Chapter Twenty-Eight

It had been three days. Luna still hadn't been able to bring herself to call or text Jacob since that night and he had let her be, giving her the space she needed.

Why does he have to be so damn nice?

Her fingers wandered to her lips, remembering the last tender kiss he had given her that left her very much wanting more. Jacob had told her to take however much time she needed and to call when she was ready to talk. She didn't want to leave him hanging, but wasn't sure what she wanted yet.

Who was she kidding? She wanted him. She just wasn't sure he was good for her.

As she sat at her small writing desk at her home, Luna stared at her silent phone then at the page in her journal, as blank as her mind. She didn't care about his past with other subs, but she wasn't sure about what lay ahead. Did she want to get involved with someone who had a three-year limit? Was that something she could live with? Would they be exclusive? Was that something she even wanted? Those questions circled like annoying flies but she still had no answer.

Why had she sat down again? Oh yeah, she'd thought while she'd showered that she had some inkling of decisions made at last. But nope, whatever conclusions she'd thought she had come up with had all scurried away. With a heavy sigh, she closed her journal and eased herself out of the chair. She had better get going or she was going to be late.

A short bus ride took her to a burger diner. For a brief minute, she forgot her confusion about Jacob as she looked forward to both the decadent strawberry milkshake and the company. It would be the first time she would get to hang out with both Lani and August at once by herself and she couldn't wait to tease the new couple.

When she pushed the door open, a blast of air conditioning and a cacophony of noises greeted her. The place was busy for a Tuesday night—always a good sign.

There they were, chatting, engrossed with each other, and Luna hesitated, wondering if she should intrude at all. After all, she would be third-wheeling.

Before more doubts could assail her, Lani waved from where they sat side by side. Luna waved back and made her way toward them.

As she slipped into the booth, their server swung by, smiling in greeting. "Hi. My name is Denise. How's everyone doing tonight?"

Lani returned the smile. "We're fantastic."

"Excellent. Is there anything I can get you to drink?"

"Strawberry milkshake!" Luna's hand shot up like she was in class again, her earlier doubts forgotten.

"Make that two."

"Make mine chocolate." The last was from August, much more subdued than her or Lani.

"Coming right up."

"So, how are you two doing?" Luna cut in right away before they had a chance to question her as Denise left. She knew why they had scheduled dinner with her. They had both texted with concern when she and Jacob had left on Saturday without a goodbye.

Luna had the pleasure of seeing August pinken and Lani grinned, patting him on the arm. "We're fine," he answered, pushing his glasses up the ridge of his nose.

"We're doing *great*." Lani emphasized the last word and gave her a wink. "We've been very busy."

Both girls burst out into giggles and August shook his head. "Jacob warned me once that the two of you together was trouble."

The statement only made both of them laugh harder until Denise returned with their milkshakes and took their food orders before striding off again with purpose in her steps. Silence fell as they all took their first sips. Luna's eyes rolled back in her head. The mounds of whipped cream on top made the drink all that more heavenly.

"So, how are you and Jacob?"

Luna's eyes snapped back to focus on the two before her. Although it was Lani who had asked, August studied her, his eyes intent.

"I'm not sure." Luna pushed her milkshake away a little and stared at an interesting speck on the table. The silence that returned to settle there seemed at odds with the rest of the diner and Luna squirmed before she looked at both of them again.

"We ran into Selina the other night." Luna pulled the milkshake back toward her and took a long sip, wishing that it contained alcohol. Then it hit her. She sounded like some insane possessive bitch.

"No, I mean, I don't care about that. We each have our own past," she explained with haste, her words tumbling out in a rush of near-incoherence.

She could see both August and Lani relax. "I'm not jealous of his past. He's a trainer, so that logically means he's had other subs in the past. I guess I'm just worried about the present and the future."

"You know," August murmured, "if I remember right, it's been at least two years since Jacob even contemplated taking on a sub and I don't know if I've seen him with anyone, even casually."

Lani nodded. "That's pretty accurate. He comes out to help other Doms sometimes, but it's been a long time since he's been interested in someone. To be honest, half of us thought he was semi-retired."

"Oh." Luna gaped at them both, unsure how to respond to that revelation. As luck would have it, she didn't have to, as their burgers and fries arrived. *Saved by food once more.*

"Enough about me, though," Luna declared at some point, while making headway with her own meal. She felt guilty for always using the two for them as free therapy. They were friends. They deserved better. "So, a long weekend coming up. Any plans?"

"Actually"—now Lani leaned in closer—"we're planning a longer trip away. Thinking of using this weekend to plan."

"Oh my God! Where to?" Excitement filled Luna's voice. If she weren't still holding her burger, she would clap her hands together. As she was, she bounced in her seat.

August cleared his throat and dabbed the corners of his lips with a napkin. Sometimes she swore he would eat his burger and fries with a fork and knife if he could.

"We were thinking Florida. Hit up Disney World and Harry Potter World at the same time."

Never had Luna seen someone talk about a kid place with such a neutral tone. She wondered if August was just indulging Lani, until she leaned across and stage-whispered. "Don't let him fool you. August's the biggest Harry Potter fan. He has every line in the book memorized and told me the first thing he wants to do is go get his wand."

Luna's eyes widened in disbelief while August only sniffed. "I am merely interested in how they accomplish those special effects that I've heard so much about. Apparently they try to emulate the movie, as the wand chooses the wizard."

Lani held her hand out flat, as if to present August and mouthed a silent word. "See?"

It was true. Luna did not miss the way August was trying to hide his excitement behind that calm and collected façade. It was in the way his brow twitched and the way he held himself rigid, as if to prevent himself from fidgeting.

Just then, August's phone screen lit up and he grabbed it before typing back. Both girls looked up, curiosity driving them to lean toward him.

"It's Cass. We haven't hung out in a while and she wants to catch up."

"You mean to catch up on the gossip about you and Lani." Luna grinned, enjoying the teasing.

"Oh look, the pot is calling the kettle black." If August wasn't August, Luna could see him sticking his tongue out at her. Instead, she stuck hers out at him in reply but grinned after.

"Now, now, children," Lani chided.

The rest of the evening was filled with just as much mirth, and Luna wondered why she'd ever had doubts that she would be uncomfortable, even if she was third-wheeling.

All too soon, it was time to go. As they stepped out back into the summer heat, Luna cringed at the thought of the bus ride home, however short it might be.

"Come on, Luna. We can give you a ride home." August motioned for her and she followed until they were all piling into his car. As August pulled out of the parking spot, she took out her phone. Maybe it was time to text Jacob back, even if it was to tell him that she still wasn't sure yet. Perhaps they could keep exploring until she was. They meant something to each other. For now, that would be enough.

They stopped at an intersection and Lani turned to glance toward Luna sitting behind her. "You okay, sweetie?"

"Yeah. I'm just thinking of giving Jacob a call."

"Good." Lani beamed and, from the rearview mirror, Luna saw August give a small smile too.

Their light turned green and August rolled out into the intersection.

"Hey, Luna, what do you think about making dinner, like tonight, a regular thing?" Lani suggested.

Luna never had a chance to reply. Without warning, the car lurched toward the passenger side. Her seatbelt yanked her back, cutting into her thin tank top as her head whipped toward the window. She reached out with both hands to brace herself, to keep her head away from the glass, only to hear a sickening crack as pain blossomed over her right wrist. Someone screamed, then she realized it was her.

The world slowed. The car came to a skidding stop. Her sight was blurry and unfocused as she shook her head, trying to clear her vision.

"August? August!" Somewhere in front, Lani's frantic voice broke through the silence in the car. She reached to unbuckle her seatbelt then cried out in pain. Afraid to look, she used her other hand instead and felt panic surge as it remained stuck. *The door*. If she got the door open, she could call for help. She reached out but she was too pinned to her seat. Her heart thudded in her ears as she struggled to no avail.

"Lani?" she called out but Lani only kept screaming out August's name. That was when Luna realized that she hadn't heard a sound from him. As her sight began to clear, she ventured a look to the driver's side.

Blood. There was blood and glass everywhere. She couldn't tell much from her angle, but she glimpsed August's hand hanging limp next to his seat. Bile rose in her throat. From beyond the broken window, she discerned the shape of another car, the front of it mashed into theirs. *T-bone*. The word came unbidden. Her mind was restarting as she began to process what had happened. They had been in a car accident. She was hurt. Lani was conscious, though she wasn't sure what state she was in. But August was badly injured.

The sound of sirens pierced the silence, growing closer. Jacob's voice came to mind and she tried to breathe, to ground herself, to use those techniques to keep the horror of the situation from overwhelming her. Next, a face in fireman's gear peered into the window next to her. "Stay calm, ma'am. We're getting you out. You're okay."

I'm okay. I'm okay. She clung to those words like a lifeline. She was okay. The emergency crew was here. Everyone would be okay. Everyone had to be.

Chapter Twenty-Nine

Luna sat in her own temporary area in the ER, listening to the beep of machines in the other rooms. Initial triage had determined that she had a mild concussion, whiplash and a broken wrist accompanying minor cuts. The concussion was enough to warrant at least an overnight stay at the hospital. At least the nurses had given her some acetaminophen and the pain had now receded to a dull pulsing.

"Please, can you let me know the condition of August Kane and Luna Weir? They brought me in here with them."

Recognizing Lani's voice, Luna scrambled off the bed and shuffled in her hospital gown, pulling back the curtain. There she was, the mass of red curls on top of the small figure. "Lani?"

"Oh, thank God." Lani's relief was palpable as she reached to pull Luna into a hug, only to see her hand in a splint.

There was a gash on Lani's forehead, already stitched, and several other smaller cuts along her arms. Luna breathed out. "Are you okay?"

The weak smile was the least vibrant she had ever seen from Lani, but it was more than understandable. "Yeah, I'm fine."

Lani looked less than fine with how pale she was, worry creasing her brows. Luna touched her friend's back, guiding her back to the nurse's station.

"I'm Luna Weir. Please, can you tell us anything about our friend August's condition?"

She could see the nurse struggle for a neutral but friendly face but the pity in her eyes was unmistakable. Luna's stomach dropped and she swallowed hard.

The nurse didn't even have to look at her log. Another bad sign. "Ah, I believe he's still in the operating room."

"Excuse me. Are you Lani McMillan?" an older woman in simple jeans and hoodie called out from behind them. With light brown hair piled in a messy bun and glasses framing large eyes, there was no doubt that she was related to August.

When Lani nodded, she stepped toward them and held out her hand. "I'm Madelyn Kane, August's sister."

Lani took her hand, shaking it, a little wary but Madelyn dove right in. "You're August's new Dominant, correct?"

Lani paused as shock registered on her face, while Luna's eyes widened into saucers. How did August's sister know? Did August tell her? Were the two close? Was August's sister also in the lifestyle? A thousand questions sprang to Luna's mind.

"It's okay." Madelyn's voice softened. "I'm well aware of my little brother's preferences. We've always been open with each other, and I accept his choices, even if I don't understand them. I'm just glad he's found someone."

Despite the calm demeanor, Madelyn's voice cracked and her eyes behind her glasses were red and puffy.

"Thank you," Lani whispered. "How's August?"

"They're still operating on him. Can you leave here? I wouldn't mind some company waiting. Our parents are out of town, so I'm alone."

"We'd be happy to come sit with you."

Madelyn turned and Luna venture a small smile of greeting. "I'm Luna. Luna Weir."

"Ah-h. I'm glad to meet you, though I wish it were under better circumstances."

They all glanced back at the nurse, who nodded toward the three of them. The sympathy in the nurse's smile was the hardest to bear and Luna braced herself. In her mind, a mantra began to play as she followed Madelyn's lead. *He's okay. He'll be okay. He's okay. He'll be okay.*

Just as they were almost stepping into the elevator, a strangled cry pierced the air, followed by heavy footsteps rushing toward them.

"Luna!"

There he was, his mop of dark locks a ruffled mess, panic showing in his chocolate eyes. Jacob stood, panting, before closing the distance to draw her into his arms, the last few seconds slowing down, careful of her injuries. "Oh thank fucking God." The words were muffled as he half buried his face against her hair.

"Jacob, I'm okay. Please." She was not going to burst into tears, not when one of her closest friend's fate was still unknown. "Please," she emphasized again until Jacob stepped back enough to give her some space.

"Lani?" He was looking past her now, as if remembering himself. Luna shuffled back a little more, one arm holding her injured wrist, and she nodded up at him. He took a step forward toward his long-time friend.

"I'm okay. But August…" Lani trailed off, managing by some miracle to hold back a sob.

He drew her into a hug and Luna moved closer to rub Lani's back. For a moment, they took comfort in each other's presence before Lani came to and, disentangling herself, half-turned. "Jacob, this is Madelyn, August's sister."

Madelyn gave a nod of acknowledgment. "We're just heading back upstairs to wait for him to come out of surgery."

"Sorry," Jacob mumbled as he let go of Lani and reached for Luna's uninjured hand. Though his grip didn't hurt, it was firm as if it brooked no argument. There was a desperation in the way he held her hand, smoothing his thumb over and over the back of it, as if reassuring himself that she was still there — or so Luna imagined.

"No apologies necessary." Madelyn stepped into the open elevator and they all shuffled in. In the back of her mind, Luna wondered at how the siblings even talked alike.

When they reached the operating room waiting area, the light was still on, showing that surgery was still in progress. They took seats and Lani wrapped an arm around Madelyn. They waited in the stillness with bated breath, none of them wanting to be more than five steps away from the door.

Minutes turned to hours. At some point, Lani and Luna were both informed of their new rooms for overnight stays but both refused to leave their vigil. They took turns sitting, pacing, standing, trying to work out the restless energy building from waiting until, at last, the operating light turned off.

It hit Luna before the doctor spoke even a single word. The careful neutral face, the sympathy in his eyes all spoke volumes. He asked for the next of kin and Madelyn rose, shoulders already trembling. Deep down, they all knew.

Luna reached for Lani's hand and felt her friend's slender fingers wrapped around hers in a vise-like grip. They couldn't hear the low whispering of the doctor to Madelyn but when she let out a single plaintive sob, Lani let go of Luna's hand and rushed over to pull August's sister into her arms. Lani's own tears fell unhindered but she did not utter a sound.

August was gone.

One minute he'd been there laughing, joking with them, making plans about the future, then the next, he was gone.

"Luna?"

She heard Jacob's voice as if from a distance but she couldn't focus enough to register what he was saying. It wasn't happening. It was just a bad nightmare. If she tried hard enough, she would wake up and August would be one phone call, one text away.

"Luna!" Jacob grasped her shoulders and shook her until she stared into his eyes.

"August..." she whispered. And the tears came.

"I know, sweetheart." His warmth enveloped her as he wrapped his arms around her. The more he held her, the more she cried, great heaving sobs racking her body as she clung to him like a lifeline. She closed her eyes, afraid to even make eye contact with anyone else as she struggled to come to terms with the loss.

Images of the evening replayed in her head. *Dinner. The sibling-like bickering. August's offer to drive me home.* If he hadn't had to drive her, would he have taken the same route?

Oh God. Lani. Poor Lani. If it was her fault in some way, how was she ever going to face Lani?

The rest of the night passed in a daze and her memory of it afterward never became more than a jumbled mess. At some point, nurses had come to escort her to her room. Jacob had asked whether she wanted him to stay but she only shook her head, everything still numb. She wanted to find Lani but, like a coward, she hid in the room instead, pulling one of the hospital blankets over her head to block the world out. Tossing and turning all night, she alternated between staring into space and weeping until her eyes ached.

The next day, the hospital discharged her. Without telling anyone, she snuck home in a cab. As soon as she let herself into the apartment, she emailed her boss at work to explain her absence and to request the rest of the week off. Then she shut off her computer and her phone and curled up on her couch. Even the bed felt too far away.

August had never visited her apartment. Why had she never invited him over? Cooked him a nice meal to show her appreciation? Maybe she'd thought there was time.

There wasn't.

Time ticked away as she lay there. At some point, hunger drove her to get up and she wandered into the kitchen in search of something to satisfy the hollowness inside. Anything involving turning on the stove or oven was too much effort. In the end, she found a bag of chips, half-forgotten in the back of the pantry, and fortified with cans of beer, she returned to her couch. With her splinted wrist in a sling, she'd had to make several trips.

Luna opened the bag and popped a chip into her mouth. In her mind, she could almost hear August's disapproving voice, see that frown of his as he chided her for not making healthier choices. Fueled by sudden anger, she began jamming handfuls into her mouth. Who was he to be lecturing her? He didn't even have the grace to be here anymore. He didn't deserve the power to make her feel so shitty.

As quick as the anger came, it fled just as fast, leaving her numb and exhausted. It wasn't as if August chose not to be there. No, that had been taken away from him. A drunk driver, they had told her, speeding and running a red light.

She stared at the can of beer in disgust, picked it up and threw it hard in no particular direction. It made a crunch on the floor then began leaking its contents all over.

"Shit, shit, shit." Luna scrambled to action, retrieving the can and running it to the kitchen then grabbing paper towels to clean the mess. It felt good to be doing something, anything to combat her sense of helplessness.

What started as cleaning the puddle on the floor became a full-fledged house cleaning. It took twice as long, given her injuries, as she had to both do most things one-handed and take frequent breaks. But she cleaned for the rest of the day, falling into deep dreamless sleep when she grew too tired, only to wake up and do it all over again.

Several times, she stared at her phone, willing herself to pick it up, turn it on and call Lani. But the longer she remained isolated, the more guilt gnawed at her. She should have been there at the start, helped her friend grieve. If the loss cut so sharply for Luna, she couldn't even imagine how Lani would feel, so new in love with August. The longer she remained out of contact, the harder it became for her to start.

Then there was Jacob.

Luna owed him an answer, but she couldn't bring herself to even think about her own tangled ball of emotions regarding that man. As she recalled his panicked face and his reluctance to leave her at the hospital, she was aware that she owed him at least a text to reassure him she was okay. But she had been afraid to even turn on her phone.

The only thing that felt good was the beautiful ache in her body from all the cleaning. Combined with the tightness of her healing wounds, the blend of pain felt perversely satisfying, proof that her self-inflicted punishment had salved off the worst of her guilt. It made sense to her in a world that no longer did. The pain was proof that she had control, that she was not helpless in her grief.

The sound of her landline ringing jolted her out of her morbid daze and she looked up, startled. She ignored the ringing, only for it to start again. The only thing that damn cordless phone was hooked up to was the buzzer downstairs, which meant someone was down there — and they were not leaving.

With a groan, she rose to her knees where she'd knelt, scrubbing the kitchen floor, then she made her way to the phone. She reached to pick it up with a shaky hand, bringing it to her ear.

"Luna, let me up."

Jacob.

Chapter Thirty

Two days. He had lasted two days before he'd come slinking around like some stalker to a girl's apartment, ringing her apartment buzzer nonstop as soon as he'd gotten off work. But after checking that no one else had heard from her either, Jacob had to make sure she was okay. Even as a friend, he would do no less.

When he heard her timid voice over the speakerphone, Jacob let out a sigh of relief. She was alive, conscious. At least there was that.

The second bout of relief came when he heard the ring and the latch from the front door, releasing to let him into the building. He struggled to keep his stride even as he made his way to her floor and across the hall until he reached her unit.

Luna cracked the door open at his approach.

She looked like hell.

"Ah, sweetheart," he murmured under his breath but was afraid to touch her. Luna cut such a fragile figure in her grief that he wasn't sure she wouldn't break under his touch, emotionally or physically. With dark rings circling her eyes and ugly bruises already blossoming on her arms, legs and shoulders—even one on the side of her cheek—she looked battered and broken. When she saw him, she turned around, leaving the door wide open as she shuffled away, her arms wrapped around herself as she hunched over in her oversized T-shirt PJs. Jacob felt something akin to his heart breaking.

"Have you rested at all?" One look around the apartment gave him the answer. It was spotless, shining to the point where he could almost make out his own reflection on the hardwood floor.

The woman was insane.

He closed the door behind him and followed Luna deeper into her home. By the way her body moved, he knew she was very much in pain, so why wouldn't she rest? A wave of almost unreasonable rage washed over him. The primal part of him screamed. Someone was hurting what was his, except the culprit was also that same person. He closed his eyes and breathed, steadying himself, taking a moment for his temper to calm.

"Luna." Catching up, he placed a hand on her shoulder, even as he forced a little more command into the word.

"I'm sorry," she whispered, her back still toward him.

"For what, sweetheart?"

"For not letting you know that I'm okay. For not giving you an answer. For… For not being in touch." Her voice trembled, but if she was crying, she wouldn't let him see the tears.

And so, he stepped up to her instead and wrapped his arms around her from behind, over her shoulders without resting his weight on them. With only light nudges, he guided her until she leaned back against his chest. As if obliging her wish, he did not look down, so she could cry in comfort without him seeing. "Don't worry about it, Luna."

"I keep thinking, that if…if…he…" Luna paused, as if struggling to say August's name then failing. "If August didn't give me a ride home, then maybe we wouldn't have been on that route and met that other — " She choked back a sob and covered her face with her good hand.

Jacob's eyes widened in horror. Was that why she'd left the hospital by herself and hidden the last few days? Did she think everyone blamed her the way she did herself? Was that the reason she was punishing her own still-healing body?

He should have come earlier. He had wanted to respect her space, knowing she was still undecided about him, had wanted to make sure she didn't feel influenced or taken advantage of in a moment of vulnerability. He was an idiot. Lesson learned.

Well, it's not too late to correct that mistake.

"Luna." He turned her around and tugged her hand away until he could see her tear-stained face. He waited until her gaze rose to meet his. "The only person at fault here is that bastard of a drunk driver — not you, not anyone else." He would try one command. "I need you to understand that and to stop punishing yourself. Here." He tapped her temple with his forefinger. "And eventually here too." His finger moved to her chest where her heart lay.

When she nodded, he felt another knot of tension in him release. It was the one order he wouldn't feel guilty about giving. If it meant exploiting her submissive nature to make sure she let herself heal, he would give the command in a heartbeat any time.

"I-I just don't know what to do with all this sadness. I can't think straight."

Now wariness filled him. Everything in him wanted to take over, to guide and give her the structure she needed right now to see her way out of the grief. But it was not his place, not yet. He didn't want to create a dependence when he wasn't sure she could accept the three-year term.

He growled at himself. The wishy-washiness was not like him. Lani's advice came unbidden in his mind. Luna was a big girl with her own mind. He would push until she pushed back. He had to trust her for that.

"Let me." Jacob kept his tone soft. "This is part of what a Dom is for. Let me take care of you."

Luna snapped her head back, her eyes growing round like saucers, the whites showing. She reminded him of a wild mare, bucking under control.

"I..." He could see the conflict of emotion across her face. The slight blush brought the first brush of color back to her complexion. Her lips parted, her chest rising and falling with quickening breaths. But her eyes... Those startling blues held hesitation and grief only. When she shook her head, it confirmed his suspicions.

"I want to say yes but I'm not ready yet. I don't know if..." She trailed off again but they both knew. If she was ready for him as a trainer, ready for the three-year term.

"It doesn't have to be a commitment." He needed her to understand that his offer came with no strings attached.

"I know. But I'm afraid that after a taste, I wouldn't be able to turn back. And it wouldn't be fair to you. I wouldn't be very good at serving right now."

The last was a flimsy excuse but he let it go. Instead, he inclined his head in acceptance and drew her into a full hug. When she leaned into him, he pressed a kiss on the top of her head. "Okay. But when you're ready, we can talk again."

"Okay." The answer was enough to soothe his aching heart and he wondered why her reply had hit him so hard.

"I'm a bit of a mess, aren't I?" A shaky laugh broke through her quivering voice.

"Life is messy, sweetheart. And it's always harder for those left behind."

He could feel her tears coming as her shoulders shook and his shirt began to grow wet. He rubbed unhurried wide circles across her back, letting her take whatever comfort she needed, because he would be here for her.

She leaned back and rubbed her cheeks. With more tenderness than she showed herself, he pulled her hand away, cupped her face and rubbed away the tears with the pads of his thumbs, using a much lighter touch.

Out of nowhere, her stomach growled and they both looked down.

"When was the last time you ate?"

Luna glanced sideways, refusing to meet his eyes. "I'm not sure. I had some chips."

Now Jacob growled under his breath. "Sit down. I'm making you food before I leave."

"But!"

"Sit."

He nodded his approval when Luna slid into a seat by the kitchen island. Familiar with her kitchen already, he opened the fridge and surveyed what he had to work with. In short order, he placed a plate of eggs and toast in front of her and pushed a fork into her hand. Simple, fast but it would fill her.

Leaning over the counter, he watched the first forkful enter her mouth. She sped up with the next bite, the first taste of food spurring her appetite such that she devoured the rest in no time. Satisfied, he turned to clean what he'd used to cook. The simple act of feeding her settled the Dom in him a little, enough to recognize that if he stayed longer, he would issue more commands, despite her saying she wasn't ready. And she would obey. Such was the natural dynamic between them. But there was one more thing.

"Did you want me to pick you up for August's funeral on Saturday? I'm driving Lani already."

Alarm and relief mingled in her expression as she shot right up then winced at the way the sudden motion sent shooting pains through her body's wounds. "Shit," she swore and grabbed her phone that had been tossed, half-forgotten, on the counter. She turned it on. And she was gone, absorbed by the incessant buzzing that started.

"Luna?"

She looked up once more and swallowed hard. "Sorry. I haven't checked my phone. I should have realized."

Ah-h. She had no idea the funeral was just two days away. He let her absorb the news and held his tongue.

"No. I think I should go alone," she replied, her voice growing smaller. "Please."

He wanted to ask more but her plea made him back off. Exhaling, he pushed his hair back. "All right. But promise me that you'll take better care of yourself in the meantime. Regular meals and sleep. No more pushing your body." At that, he waved at the spotless place.

Luna ducked her head as if she was a child being scolded after she'd gotten caught doing something she shouldn't. It was endearing but also close to reality. "Okay. I promise."

"Good." He walked the few steps that took him to the foyer and put on his shoes. Luna slid off her chair and followed.

When he turned, Luna's one arm hug caught him by surprise. She held him tight, burying her face against his chest so that he almost couldn't make out her words.

"Thank you for checking up on me."

"You're welcome, sweetheart. Good night." He brushed his lips across the top of her head once more.

"Good night, Jacob."

Chapter Thirty-One

'Did you see the proofs Eli sent over via email?' August had been drinking his tea, as nonchalant as usual.

'Yeah, did you reply to his question?' The photos, most in black and white with just a splash of color of the foliage to frame the subject, were tasteful and gorgeous. She almost hadn't recognized her own body.

'I did. I told him I was okay with everyone getting a complete set, if it was going to be easier on him. I believe Cassie said the same thing.'

'Me too. I'm looking forward to the prints.'

'Luna, I was thinking of gifting my set to Lani, just the ones of me, but I know we did a few composites together. Would you be okay if Lani had those too?'

She hadn't wanted to squeal and make August more uncomfortable than he'd already looked. His eyes hadn't met hers as he scratched his cheeks, so he hadn't quite seen her obviously silly grin. It had been a good thing, too. It would have made him even more uncomfortable.

'Of course, I don't mind. I think it's a great idea.'

The bright sun felt at odds with the heavy sorrow in her heart. Fingers of light cast patterns over the matte prints scattered across her coffee table. Taking advantage of the fact that she'd gotten dressed for the first time in days, Luna had gone downstairs to retrieve her mail and now she stared at the contents of the manila envelope, struggling to not start crying all over again. Later, she would sort out her feelings and what to do with the prints. She rubbed her eyes and rose from her couch. It would not do to be late.

As Luna arrived at the funeral home, she paused, hovering near the door as she watched the sedated crowd mill around in the reception area, a low rise and fall of murmurs filling the room. Whispers of condolences—"Oh, isn't it a shame. He was so young"—and other empty words set her teeth to grind. A flash of anger shot through her as she wondered how many of them truly knew August before she took her time to exhale, letting the emotions go.

She spied Jacob and Lani standing together, huddled in a corner, sipping warm beverages despite the rising heat. She held herself apart, even as Madelyn approached and gave each of them a hug. Luna chose a spot on the opposite side of the room to stand, not wanting to intrude, not ready yet to face them. *Some friend I am.*

The door opened once more and Cassie stepped through. *That's right.* August would have been hanging out with her today if not for what happened. Luna bit her lower lip hard to keep her emotions in check. She dug deep within herself for courage and walked toward her.

What she didn't expect were the cold eyes that narrowed at her approach.

"Cassie?"

"What do you want, Luna?"

Luna took a step back, surprised by the venom in her voice. "I-I..." She stuttered in surprise, unprepared for that reaction.

"Look... I don't want to cause a scene here." Something in Cassie softened just a little as she spoke.

Perhaps there was a chance. "Please, talk to me, Cassie." It was the wrong thing to say.

Cassie's entire posture stiffened. "Oh, so *now* you want to talk? Fine. August was my friend too. My *best* friend. And he was supposed to be hanging out with me that day but he postponed because he got worried about you. Then when he...he... You didn't even have the guts to tell me. Instead I had to hear it from Darryl, who wasn't even close to August. What kind of friend are you?" Cassie spat out the last words, her shoulders shaking with anger.

Under such intense rage directed at her, Luna wilted. Cassie was right. What kind of friend was she? A terrible one, that was what. She hung her head. "I'm sorry," she whispered.

"Just stay away from me, Luna." Cassie stomped off, leaving her standing, still rooted to the spot.

She would not cry, she would not cry.

"Hello, Luna."

She spun around. Madelyn stood before her with a grave nod in greeting. August's sister looked tired and worn, grief dulling her face. Despite an attempt with makeup, Luna saw the dark circles around her eyes and was pretty sure she herself didn't look so different.

"Hello, Madelyn." She had googled all the things to say at a funeral ceremony the night before but she couldn't remember a damn suggestion right now. "How are you doing?" In her head, she kicked herself.

"Holding up, I suppose. The parents flew back as soon as I got in touch with them and that's been both a blessing and a curse." Madelyn shook her head then before looking down. Luna followed her gaze to see a small leather-bound notebook in her hands.

"I think August would have wanted you to have this. I understand he was a bit of a mentor to you in the lifestyle." Madelyn extended the book to her.

With a shaky hand, Luna accepted it and bowed her head.

"Madelyn!" From a small distance an older woman called out and both of them turned toward the sound at the same time.

"I'd better go. Mother's been in perfectionist mode." Madelyn reached out to touch Luna's arm. "Take care of yourself."

"Thanks. You too."

As soon as Madelyn stepped away, Luna found a seat, placed the book in her lap and opened it then sucked in a breath. Pages and pages of notes, anecdotes and stories filled the pages, all in August's neat handwriting. She picked a random page and began reading.

Last night I ran into Luna at The Playgrounds. Like I wrote before, I think she's a kindred soul but I think she's still trying to find her way. She asked how I came to terms with my submissive nature and the question took me way back. I remembered how confused I was, how I didn't understand why anyone would desire the things that I did. I remembered thinking something was fundamentally wrong with me. To this day, I regret that period of repression I went through. All I can hope is that I can give Luna enough guidance that she doesn't have to go through what I did. It can be such a lonely journey.

A tear fell on the page and Luna rubbed her eyes. "Damn it." She blew at the page, relieved to see that the drop hadn't landed on any writing and smudged it. With infinite gentleness, she closed the journal, one finger stroking the well-worn leather cover.

August had once mentioned that he wrote to help understand himself as a sub. The journal must be the sum of his thoughts given form. Even in his death, August was still trying to help her. She clutched the journal to her chest. He was still here — in these words, in her heart, in all their memories.

"Please, miss, if you'd step this way. We're about to start the service."

Luna looked up and rubbed her eyes once more. A portly man held a hand out, gesturing toward the door, and he smiled. There was an open kindness that spoke of comfort. He must be one of the funeral home staff.

"Ah, thank you."

The rest of the service was lovely but Luna felt disjointed, as if she were seeing August in a context she was inexperienced with. He was much more than a sub of course — a son, a brother, a coworker, a friend. But to her, he was a mentor and, like his journal said, a kindred soul.

In the distance, she saw Lani sitting in her chair, her back straight as a board, her face raw with pain, and Luna wished she was sitting right next to her with Jacob. From the other side of the room, she glimpsed

Cassie sitting alone. Three chairs down, Darryl sat, casting glances over at Cassie from time to time. Had Cassie pushed Darryl away too? Her mind traveled back to Lani's birthday, not so long ago, and not for the first time, she wished she could rewind life back to that perfect moment — like Hermione with her time-turner in the Harry Potter books and movies. August would have liked that.

Then, it was the end of the ceremony. The director announced a last opportunity for viewing while the family prepared for the march to the burial site. Luna took a deep breath to brace herself and stepped forward as others made to exit the room. Journal still clutched in her good arm, she stepped up to the casket, determination driving every step.

There he was. He could almost be asleep. Luna remembered her last sight of him being his bloody hand and had to shake her head clear. "I'll miss you," she whispered.

"We all will."

Luna looked up as Jacob drew near. On her other side, Lani placed a hand on her shoulder and gave it a light pat. She gave a weak smile in return, tears beginning to once more stream down her cheeks and she found her mirror in Lani's face. For a brief moment, she forgot her guilt as they shared the single moment of heartache.

"Come on. Let's send August on his way." Jacob spoke with a gentleness that mirrored his touch on the small of her back.

"Yeah."

They followed on foot in the funeral procession that led them up the hill to the burial site, hole already dug, gravestone already erected. More words were said as they stood there but Luna let them wash over her without registering them, as all she could do was stare at the scene unfolding before her. When they began to lower the casket, Luna heard sobs break out and began trembling herself until Jacob took her free hand and held it tight. It was the only thing that kept her anchored.

Then, it was time. She stared at the casket, a rose in her hand. There was so much left unsaid. Later, she promised herself. Later, she would sit here alone and words would come.

"Goodbye, August. Thank you...for everything." With that, she let the rose fall.

* * * *

That night, she sat on her couch, staring at the photos, the journal sitting next to them. Luna took her time, studying each print, committing them to memory while also letting each image help her recall that corresponding moment during the shoot. Her mind roamed.

There, August was smiling at her in encouragement. There, he had stepped out, comfortable with his own nudity. Luna remembered admiring that.

Ah-h and there was Cassie. Poor Cassie. The heated words today were a lash-out in pain and Luna tried her best to not take it personally. Yet, she could not help but wish she had done better for her friend. Now she wasn't sure where to start — or if there was any path forward toward healing that rift. For August's sake, though, she would try.

Luna's lips parted into an O at the last shot in the pile. It wasn't one included in the proof package Eli had sent earlier electronically. Instead, it was a candid shot of the three of them in their robes, a close-up of their faces as they laughed. Luna racked her brain, trying to recall just what were they laughing over.

On the lower corner was a small title, written in simple handwriting. *Three muses.*

She was tired of crying but, nonetheless, she wept once more. Unlike earlier, though, these weren't racking sobs that left her heart raw in pain. Instead, the tears came slower as she examined each bright memory she held close in her heart and remembered that she was lucky in having known him at all. She leaned back with care so as to not get the photos wet and held her mug of tea in one hand, taking a sip from time to time. She did promise Jacob that she would take care of herself and that meant keeping hydrated.

Well, there was more she could do to honor August's memory.

She set her tea down and picked up her phone. Texting was a challenge one-handed.

Hey, you awake? Can I call?

The answer came back almost right away

Sure.

Luna hit the dial pad then lifted it to her ear. Lani picked up almost right away.

"Hey, sweetie, what're you doing up so late?"

"I can ask you the same thing."

"Touché. What's up?"

"I was wondering if we can meet up some time soon?" Luna would be back at work the day after tomorrow. She just hoped she could handle it, but some semblance of routine might help her get back on track.

"Sure. I'm not taking any clients yet but I'll be in the office catching up on paperwork on Monday. Want to come over for lunch? Do you know where my office is?"

Luna was hoping she could get Lani out somewhere for lunch but she could understand not being ready yet

"Yeah, I think so."

"Great. I'll see you Monday then. Now, go get some sleep."

"Okay, goodnight, Lani."

"Night, Luna."

She hung up and put the phone down then began gathering the photos. It would be the least she could do for a man who had given her so much.

Chapter Thirty-Two

"Lani?" Luna called out as she stepped into the empty office. The receptionist desk was empty, everything neatly stacked in its place. As she crossed the small waiting area, determination propelled her toward the only other door in the office.

When she heard the sound of papers shuffling, Luna knocked on the door, paused then opened it a crack. She peered inside and sighed in relief when she caught a glimpse of red hair.

"Ah-h. Come in."

Luna pushed the door farther out before her eyes widened. Lani sat on the floor, her back braced against her desk, her knees bent. Her one arm rested against one knee, and she was clutching at some papers she must have been reading. She rubbed her face, which was red from crying. The entire posture was so at odds with how Lani usually held herself that it caught Luna off guard and halted her steps.

"Sorry for the mess," Lani mumbled.

"Don't be." Before her friend could get up, Luna closed the distance and passed her a paper bag of the sandwiches she'd gotten them for lunch. As Lani accepted it with a soft thank you, Luna joined her on the floor and took off her messenger bag.

When Lani stared off into the distance, the paper bag already forgotten, Luna reached over and took the bag from her, taking out and pushing a sandwich into her friend's hand. "You need to eat."

"Right. Of course." With a brief smile, Lani unwrapped her sandwich and bit into it. Luna wondered, though, whether she tasted anything.

"It's a common misconception that grief dulls with time. It doesn't, not at first, not for a long time. Instead, it hovers in the background. You think you're doing better today, that perhaps it's starting to get manageable, then some innocuous thing triggers a memory and the pain comes right back like a fresh, open wound." Lani set aside the sandwich and Luna noticed that she hadn't even put a dent in it. Jacob should worry about Lani more. Then again, she was sure he already was.

Lani went on. "You learn these things when you're getting certified for counseling. But it still comes as a surprise, like the rational brain is disconnected from the rest of you." She raised a hand to tuck her hair behind her ear. "It's not that I haven't lost someone, but I don't think I've ever lost with this much regret before."

The anguish in Lani's voice washed over Luna and left her unsure how to respond. Luna could understand Lani's feelings. Hadn't she felt the same, to a lesser degree? But what could she say that wouldn't sound trite?

Nothing.

So, instead, she put down her own sandwich and took Lani's hand, giving it a gentle squeeze. The universal gesture, letting Lani know that she was there for her, seemed enough that Lani relaxed her shoulders. Lani's squeeze back and her small smile, no matter how sad, eased Luna's guilt a smidgen.

Luna's mind raced, however, trying to figure out the right time and the right words to lead into what she'd come to do today. But there was never going to be a right time, was there? She drew a deep breath and plunged ahead. Luna let go of Lani's hand to pull the prepared manila envelope from her bag. "I have something for you."

A spark of curiosity flickered in Lani's eyes as she took what Luna offered. While Luna felt encouraged by her friend's reaction, she also braced herself as Lani opened it and began to tug out the contents.

Beside her, Lani drew a sharp breath. "Oh, Luna."

"August wanted you to have these. He wanted to make it a surprise."

Lani nodded but said nothing in return as she examined each photo. From time to time, Lani would take one finger and trace August's outline, as if in memory. A stillness descended on them as Lani gazed upon the images of the one she'd lost, a bittersweet smile tugging on her lips.

"You know" — Lani's voice cracked and she cleared her throat — "bondage was high on August's list, but I've never been great at it. Jacob was going to start me on lessons this week."

Without another word, Luna wrapped her good arm around Lani and tugged her close. Her friend buried her face in her shoulder and it wasn't until that moment that the tears came, for both of them.

"I wish I'd had more time—even a day more. I'd have given him time from my life in exchange, if I could've." The words came through muffled, punctuated by sobs.

"I know, Lani. I know," Luna whispered.

"It was supposed to be my job to take care of him. I'd never gotten someone to take care of before—not this way."

Lani finally gave her raw pain form as she spoke her regrets. Luna listened, rubbing Lani's back as Jacob often did for her—to soothe her, bearing witness to the mourning. It was the least she could do to honor her friends—both of them.

By and by, there was nothing more to say but they remained that way for longer, taking comfort in each other's presence. When Lani leaned back, Luna let her go, if only so she could clean her own face. Having only one usable hand was damn inconvenient.

"Thank you," Lani mouthed without a sound and gazed at the photo, brushing her fingers along the curve of August's back in a light caress.

"Luna…" Lani's tone grew a little stronger, sounding more like her usual self. "I know you still have doubts about Jacob, but don't make my mistake. Don't let your fear of getting hurt stop you from what could be the most amazing experience of your life. I'm positive you and Jacob are good for each other. The future's unknown. The risk is worth it."

Lani flipped to another photo, arriving at one of August staring into the camera. Luna remembered that shot, in particular with how Eli had captured the intensity of his gaze. Was August thinking of Lani when he was posing for that?

"There're a lot of things I wish I'd done differently, but having August, even for the short time we had? That's the one thing I would never regret. It was worth it. *He* was worth it."

* * * *

Hours later, sitting at work, Lani's words still echoed in Luna's head.

Hadn't she been thinking along the same lines as she'd pored over August's journal on Sunday? After the funeral, Luna had felt as if she had gained some clarity of mind, able to see a little beyond her grief. There had still been some crying, but it was no longer a haze of pain. She still wasn't sure if she would be okay with the limit when the time came, but three years was a long time away. Lani was right. She couldn't let the possible-future-Luna impede the present-Luna. The only thing she had to be careful of was to not appear as though she was trying to change his mind on the matter. It would not be fair to him.

As a thought experiment, she tried to imagine what would happen if she was in Lani's shoes and Jacob was the one who had passed away. The thought was unbearable.

"Hey, Luna, are you okay?"

Ted's question jolted her out of her thoughts. It was about the tenth time he had asked her that day, but she recognized the worry on his face. It mirrored the number of texts he had sent her during her time off.

"I'll be fine. I promise."

Ted slung his backpack over his shoulders. It was leaving time, but Luna was still trying to play catchup after her time off.

"Okay. If you need anything, anything at all, you speak up."

Her time with Lani had taught her something. Isolating herself didn't help and she wanted to value every moment she had with everyone. "Lunch tomorrow?"

The hope in Ted's eyes lifted her spirits. "You bet," he replied. "Hey, actually, Brandon was wondering if you wanted to come over for dinner some time this week? He's in one of those perfecting-a-new-recipe streaks again and wants your opinion." Ted put his hands together in a pleading gesture. "Save me. I swear if I have to eat his miso salmon one more time with him alone…"

Luna laughed at his expression. It felt good to laugh. A small voice whispered that perhaps she should be ridden with guilt for doing so, but she shoved that demon away into a deep dark hole.

"Dinner sounds great, and hey, if you don't want to eat it anymore, that just means more for me! How about Thursday? I'm pretty sure Brandon's not teaching that night."

"Sounds good. I'll check with him, but let's say Thursday for now." Ted's face softened. "I'm glad you're okay, Luna."

"Thanks, Ted. Now get out of here before they find more work for you."

He gave a laugh and a wave. "'K. Call me if you need anything."

"Yes, Dad!" She waved him off.

The office was quiet, most people having left for the day. Luna inhaled, even as her eyes fell on her phone.

There was one more person to talk to, one more answer she had to give. She picked up her phone, beginning to compose a text, but she paused. She missed him. It seemed like a trivial matter, what three years later would look like. What she was certain of, in this single point in time, was that she missed him and wanted to be with him. The rest, they could figure out together. She trusted him enough for that

She switched to the dial pad and called him instead. "Luna?"

"Hello, Jacob. How are you? Is this a good time?" *Pause. Take it slow. Don't babble.*

"Sure, is everything okay?"

"Yeah. Do you have time tonight to meet up and talk?"

There was a slight pause. "Sure. Want me to come over?" She recognized the careful neutral tone in his voice and realized how ominous she sounded. No, she wouldn't put him through that, even for an hour. That would make her a pretty bad sub, wouldn't it?

"Yeah. Give me about an hour? Have you had food? I'll pick up something up for dinner on the way home." She was about to say more but Jacob cut in with an exasperated sigh.

"Luna, you're still injured. If you want food, I can pick some up on the way over."

"I want you."

There was silence on the other end. Luna's face grew hot as the seconds ticked by. There were a gazillion better ways to tell him, so why had she blurted it out like that?

A small chuckle, however, warmed her heart. "Sweetheart, you still need food. I need food. But yes, you can have me too."

How the hell was she going to respond to that?

"Still there?" he asked.

She cleared her throat, hearing the teasing smile in his voice, and sank deeper into her chair. "Yeah, yeah I am." Despite how flustered she was, Luna knew it was the right thing to do. August would have wanted this for her, but she was also doing it for herself.

"All right. I'll see you in an hour."

"See you."

Luna hung up, stared at her computer screen and rolled her eyes. Work catchup could wait. She rose from her chair with renewed vigor and stretched, mindful of her healing cuts and wrist. With one last glance at the clock, she grabbed her bag, slinging it over her shoulder, even as she checked inside.

These days, she never left her home without August's journal. It might seem odd to others but to her, it was like carrying a piece of her friend with her — a way to remind herself that, though he was gone, he lived on in their memories. He had changed her life and she would never let herself forget what he had done for her.

As she settled into a seat on the bus, Luna retrieved the journal and opened it. She and August had been even more alike than she had first guessed and her favorite passages were those where he theorized about power dynamics and why they even existed. Some days, he thought it was a tie-over from biological survival instincts. Other days, he would note heavy cultural upbringings that would influence someone's preferences. His musings went beyond the bedroom, enough to speculating dominance and submission as a sliding scale that all people fell on, regardless of whether they were in the lifestyle.

She was still reading when she got off the bus and walked the short distance home. It took a lot of effort to tear herself from August's fascinating thoughts but she needed to get ready.

It was going to be one of the most important talks of her life.

Chapter Thirty-Three

The concept of a contract between two individuals in a power dynamic is a fascinating construct. We all know that there is no way for such a document to be legally binding, and yet it has become one of the most significant symbols of commitment within the community. It holds a strange power. To sign an agreement and later break it is not only to risk one's reputation and earn social stigma but also to have one's trustworthiness and integrity come into question. In other words, despite not being enforceable by legal means, the words in the contract bind the Dom and the sub together inexorably, nonetheless.

The phone rang. This was it. Jacob was a short elevator ride away.

Luna jumped from the couch and winced as the movement still jostled her broken wrist. As she crossed the room, she picked up the phone and smiled as she let him into the building. Eager to see him, she flung her apartment door wide open and stood, fiddling with her necklace. It was the one he had given her before the night at The Playgrounds. Wearing it felt right.

As soon as the elevator doors parted, she couldn't wait any longer. Her first few steps were hesitant, but soon she broke into a sprint, barreling down the hall and tackling Jacob in a hug as he stepped out.

"Oof." Jacob took a half-step back but wrapped one arm around her as she buried her face against his chest. He smelled of apples and cinnamon.

"Hello, sweetheart. I missed you too." He brushed by the top of her head with his lips and smiled, even as moisture gathered in her eyes. When had she become such a crybaby?

"Let's head inside." He nudged her back and leaned over to place light kisses on each side below each eye where she refused to let the tears fall. It was then that she noticed the large bag he held with one hand.

"Whoops, sorry." She released him with a step back then led him back to the apartment.

"Let's eat first." From the moment they entered her apartment, Jacob took over and began herding her. First, after making sure she sat, he proceeded to withdraw the contents from the bag. Fortunately, she'd had the foresight earlier to set the table so that she had already neatly placed the plates and utensils.

"I was off early today and too much takeout is not a good idea." Two large Tupperware containers came out before he brought out a third one. He opened the first two, one containing rice, the other a chicken stir-fry.

Jacob had cooked a meal for her? Luna tried not to swoon. *Wait!* What was in that third container? She tried to take a peek.

"It's a surprise for later." With a smirk, he set it aside and began dishing out the food, heaping a generous portion onto her plate.

When he pushed the plates across the counter toward her, Jacob paused, tilting his head to one side to make out the journal Luna had left in the open. "What's this?"

"Oh." Luna touched the edge of the leather cover. "I was reading a little before you got here." To distract herself from jitters, but she would never admit that out loud. "It's August's journal as a sub. Madelyn gave it to me at the funeral and said August would have wanted me to have it." Her smile was wistful. "I suppose August's still helping me, even when he's not here anymore."

"That's a good way of looking at it. I'm glad you have something of his." Jacob kissed her on the temple as he came around and took a seat next to her. "Now eat."

She didn't hesitate. The first bite was lovely, with just the right amount of teriyaki sauce and not too overwhelmingly sweet. Her body was craving the fuel she needed to heal and, in no time, she was done, even ahead of Jacob.

"Good girl." Jacob set down his own fork and slid off his seat. "Now, for the treat." He returned with two smaller dishes and the last Tupperware box. He opened it without ceremony.

Two flaky golden-brown pastries sat inside. Despite all the food she'd packed away, Luna salivated and she let out a small whimper.

In response, Jacob chuckled as he placed one on each dish. "Apple pocket pies. Homemade versions of the turnovers you like so much."

Why did she ever think being with Jacob was a bad idea again? She would gladly do whatever the man wanted if it meant he kept feeding her. She might have trouble still reconciling how much she desired more of that mind-blowing sex she had with him but she had no problems owning up to the fact that he had her by the stomach and sweet tooth.

"Silly pet," he murmured and held a forkful to her mouth. It was only then that she realized she was spacing. With a sheepish smile, she parted her lips to accept the first bite and moaned, her eyes closing to savor the taste. *Heaven.*

"Maybe I should have waited until later to feed you dessert," Jacob muttered. When her eyes fluttered open, she saw his darken and felt heat coil across her core. With a soft sigh that sounded a lot like reluctance, he held out her fork to her.

Luna took it and began to dig in herself, taking the time to relish each bite. She tried her best to not make any more noises but the occasional *mm-m* still escaped. The pastry was just right and she couldn't help but scrape her fork over it at least once to hear that crusty sound, a technique she'd learned from watching Gordon Ramsay in action.

Soon, they both pushed their dishes away. As Luna moved to clean up, Jacob shook his head. "Leave them for now. I'll help you clean up later. Come to the couch with me."

Once settled, Jacob reached out to take her hand in his. "Tell me, Luna. What's on your mind? What do you want?"

She had prepared what she was going to say beforehand. She really had. Wasn't that why she'd called him over? But one look into his warm brown eyes, so soft with tenderness, and all semblance of coherence fled.

He waited as she tried to reassemble her brain. At last, she closed her eyes and dug deep until she found the right words. "I want to be with you—not just exploring." She opened and her cheeks warmed. "I mean, I get that we still have a lot to learn about each other. That, in some ways, we'll never stop exploring but..." She was babbling and not making much sense again. Luna inhaled once more to steady herself and tried again. "I want to serve you on a more formal basis. I want to learn...if you will have me."

"Are you sure you want me to take you on formally?" Jacob's voice was gentle. "I don't doubt your willingness, but have we addressed all your earlier concerns?"

"Do you mean am I letting what happened with August warp my judgment?" There was no bite to her words. It was a valid question. "I can't say that it hasn't affected my decision. The truth is, I don't know what I'll think in three years, but I know what I feel now. It doesn't mean I don't accept those terms, but it does mean that I don't want to lose sight of the now—and I'm willing to take the risk." She smiled. "That's the best I can do."

Jacob nodded. "That's fair. And I can promise you this. In three years' time, whatever happens, I'll be there. We'll deal with it together. I won't just drop or abandon you, okay?" He gave her hand a squeeze and, in return, she nodded.

"Okay."

He let go of her hand and rose from his place to walk to his bag by the counter. Luna sat there, following his path as she once more toyed with the feather charm, the movement becoming a habit. She found that it brought her comfort.

As he returned with an envelope in hand, Jacob smiled, dipping his head toward her hand in acknowledgment of the fact that she was wearing his gift. When he resettled on the couch, he held it out to her. "I had a feeling."

She steadied herself before taking it in hand, flipping the flap up. It was obvious what it was but it didn't lessen her anxiety any less. With a trembling hand, she tugged it out.

She inhaled again as she unfolded each sheet of paper. There it was. The contract consisted of standard wording, similar to templates she had seen online, but the clauses were specific. It listed general ones that applied to both parties first—commitments to trust, respect and take care of each other, prioritizing a healthy lifestyle, including eating and exercising right. There was a specific statement on open communication and respect of hard boundaries. For the Dominant, there was a promise to lead, to protect and to cherish and to train and teach with patience. For the submissive, to follow and ask when there were questions and to seek permission before certain actions such as play with others. Most was common sense.

"Do you have questions?"

If Luna didn't know better, she would have thought he was nervous, with the way he smoothed his hands over his jeans, up and down, and how he studied her expressions as if he was trying to discern her thoughts.

"No… It's just that I thought the contract would be more specific?" The last word held an uptick in tone as she cocked her head to one side.

"Ah, that could end up making the contract a book thick," Jacob replied with a chuckle. "We'll discuss the details as we go along. Like you said, we'll keep exploring and figure out the right level of submission for you, especially since you've mentioned that you're interested in submitting outside of the bedroom."

Luna dipped her head in acknowledgment before she continued to read. At seeing Jacob's signature on the line for the Dominant already, her stomach did a funny flip. Without looking, she groped for a pen on the coffee table. "What about you? Would you be interested in being served outside of the bedroom?"

"I don't want a fifties housewife, if that's what you mean."

Luna snapped up her head in horror and Jacob chuckled. "Yeah, I didn't think you were interested in that either."

She dropped her shoulders with relief and shook her head with a wrinkle of her nose.

Jacob spoke. "Submission comes in many forms and sometimes it's subtle. Every relationship, every contract is different. We'll settle into our own rhythm and it'll be a good opportunity for both of us to learn."

Her gaze drifted back downward. They were just words on a page. Nonetheless, there was a power to them, something that had nothing to do with social constructs or expectations. By the sheer act of signing, the symbolic commitment would bind her to him. And, at last, she was ready.

The line above the submissive called to her and, with a last small intake of breath, she scribed her name on it with a wobbly flourish. When Luna tilted her head back, the smile she found on Jacob's face warmed her down to her toes. With slow, deliberate movements, she folded the paper and tucked all the pages back into the envelope. "Now what?" For some unfathomable reason, the signing did little to calm her racing pulse.

Jacob leaned forward, taking the envelope from her hand and setting it aside without ever breaking away. He was so close that his lips brushed by hers as he spoke. "And now, I get to take care of what is mine." With that, he pressed forward, sealing her lips with his in the most tender kiss.

A kiss that promised the beginning of everything.

Epilogue

"Part your legs a little farther for me, little one."

Luna struggled to keep another moan from escaping from her lips, even as she followed his instruction, her skirt already hiked up to her waist. Jacob's new black Jeep with tinted windows situated them high above the other cars, ensuring that no others on the road would see her compromising position, but she blushed still with a heightened sense of vulnerability that only seemed to send her arousal into overdrive.

Jacob had balled up her panties and stuffed them into one of his pockets. A souvenir, he'd called them. She was going to have to buy more, the way he'd been collecting them over the last three months. They had come a long way, growing more intimate in their play. She had even gotten an IUD put in at her doctor's office the previous month.

He rested a hand on her knee, stroking up to her inner thigh, but he made no further move to touch her. He glanced at her as she'd complied but had turned back to the road. In the darkness, it would be hard for him to discern much, but by now, he already knew her body enough for his mind to fill in the gaps. That man was one of the most imaginative she had ever known in bed.

"Good girl."

Luna locked her fingers together over her stomach in an attempt to not touch herself. "Where are we going?" She hardly recognized her own voice, breathless with need.

"You'll see. It's a surprise."

A brief light from an opposite car passing by illuminated the carriage and Luna caught a quick glimpse of Jacob. Only the white knuckles on the steering wheel and the set jaw betrayed the effect she was having on him. She deepened her breathing to steady herself.

He moved his hand up, brushing featherlight touches against her slit. In response, her hips pushed upward to increase and prolong the contact, only for her to whimper as he withdrew with a chuckle. "So wet already." He paused as he made a turn then merged onto a highway. "Not long now. But keep yourself ready. Play for me."

She swallowed hard. Wasn't that what she wanted? But still she found it hard to unlace her fingers, her natural shyness still inhibiting her, even after so long. It took another thirty seconds before she crept her hand down to cup her own mound. Unable to hold back any longer, she let out the low moan that had threatened to escape earlier.

"That's my girl," Jacob murmured, approval in his voice. "I want you to take your middle finger and slide it back and forth. Keep your touch light. Don't penetrate just yet."

Oh dear God. He was going to talk her through it. Her wetness dripped down her thighs. She was going to leave a puddle in his car soon

"That's it, sweetheart, back and forth. Just imagine if it was my cock, pressed hard against you. That's right, a little harder now. Press in just a bit."

She closed her eyes. It wasn't until she noticed her seatbelt strap tightening over her shoulder that she realized that she had begun to rotate her hips in little movements.

"Stop."

She did, holding herself still, but she whimpered again in protest.

"Mm-m, take both hands now, and I want you to part yourself. Circle a finger around that tight entrance of yours."

His commands had already set her body aflame. His control over her, the words he uttered, set her mind on a path straight to insanity. She parted her lips, a steady stream of small moans filling the air. When they hit a patch of bumpiness on the highway, designed to help keep drivers awake, the shaking in the car caused a new vibration that made her gasp.

"You make the sexiest little sounds."

Her stomach clenched. She had drenched her fingers.

"Drag your finger up now. I remember those nails. Scrape one upward until it's on your clit."

She was not going to last. When she reached the hardened nub, she bucked, pinned down only by the seatbelt.

"I'm… I can't," she gasped out.

"Faster now. Circle and rub your clit. Put a finger inside. I want to hear you." His hand returned to her bare leg, running light scratches along her inner thigh. It was one of the many things she'd discovered she loved in the short time they'd been together so far.

Her mind raced. He hadn't given her permission to come and yet he was instructing her to drive herself to the brink. Her moans grew louder, even as she grew so wet that she could hear a small slick squelching when she paused her groans to suck in more air through her mouth. Her face reddened in pure embarrassment and she slowed to tiny perceptible motions, trying to hold back her body's enthusiasm.

"Pet…" There was a warning growl in his voice. His stroking stopped and he squeezed her knee in warning, just once. "Don't stop. Let everything go."

She began to move a little faster, hesitant. It got easier as he made a turn off the highway. Roads changed in no time to trails, and all semblance of civilization fell away. In the darkness that enveloped them, she began to lose her inhibitions and soon, she was riding her own hand with abandon, pleas to be allowed to climax spilling like a litany from her lips.

He remained silent, as if deaf to her begging. There was no permission for release, nor was there mercy in letting her ease her pace. She bit her lower lip hard, trying to use pain to keep the orgasm at bay. She would not fail him.

"Sweetheart, look at me."

She snapped her eyes open. The car had stopped. Soft, dim light filled the car, sourced from a single light by the rearview mirror. Outside was only blackness. But she refocused as his face filled her vision, his eyes darkened with lust. He cupped her hand, his lips a hair's breadth away.

"So close." His voice was thick with desire. "Come for me, sweetheart." With that, he pressed his hand harder against hers, tightening the friction against her clit as he slipped a finger inside, next to hers.

She exploded against their hands, letting out a long cry of pure ecstasy. He covered her lips with his, drinking in the sound as he held both of them still, letting her ride her climax out until she slumped into the seat, sweat coating her forehead.

"Good girl." He stroked her hair, smoothing it back even as he withdrew his other hand, her wetness coating his finger. When she began to focus, he held his finger up and darted his tongue out to lick his finger clean. "So sweet."

She swallowed hard and sank deeper in her seat, conscious of her thighs still coated with her own orgasm. But everything felt too floaty for her to move.

From somewhere, he produced a water bottle and helped her take a sip before pushing a dark square of something past her lips. Bitter sweetness flooded her senses and she moaned for a different reason. *Dark chocolate.*

"We have to keep your energy up for the rest of the night."

When her vision began to clear once more, she pushed herself up. "Where are we?"

His smile was enigmatic as he reached back to grab a heavy-duty flashlight, switching it on, then he turned off the car light overhead. He opened his door and slipped out then made his way to her side, opening the door and holding a hand to her. "Come find out."

Luna placed her hand in his and, with wobbly legs, stepped out of the car.

"Watch your step. The terrain is rough out here."

The autumn air sent goosebumps across her exposed skin. As if sensing the chill, Jacob wrapped a blanket around her and made sure it was secure around her shoulders before he led her off what felt like gravel and dirt to a more grassy area, but then he tightened his grip, indicating for her to stop. Over the course of the last three months, she had learned his subtle signals, especially as the noise on the first floor of The Playgrounds was sometimes too loud for speech.

She stopped, even as her eyes began to adjust to the dark beyond the few feet of visibility that the flashlight allowed. There was a stillness but she could make out little sounds of night critters awakening and a faint breeze rustling the trees above. They were in the middle of a forest and no woods were ever that quiet.

Jacob switched the light off. At the same time, he leaned over and whispered in her ear. "Look up."

A million stars scattered across the sky. The view was nothing like she had ever seen, not in person, having been a city girl all her life. She tightened her grip around his hand, drawing the blanket close as she pulled the fresh night air deep into her lungs.

"Thank you." She could not tear her eyes away.

"A reward, for how well you've done and how far you've come." He positioned her until he could wrap both arms around her, her back against the warmth of his chest, even with the blanket between them. "I'm so proud of you, Luna."

His words made her tremble, as deep yet-to-be-named emotions washed over her. Rather than over-analyzing them, she let them come, let them rock her back to lean further against the man who would take care of her, would hold her safe.

They stood for a little while longer, gazing upward at the stars. At some point, Luna tilted her head back, her gaze turning toward her Dominant instead. Yes, she could call him that now. The word still tasted wonderfully strange, even in her head.

"So, was it yours or my fantasy that we try sex under the stars?" He wasn't the only one that could tease.

She felt as much as heard his laugh rumbling in his chest. "Yours. But mine is to have you on the car hood, so I think we can check both off the bucket list in one go."

Luna was grateful that, in the dark, her flush would not be as visible. But the shiver that shot through her body was enough for Jacob to give her a light squeeze.

"I think someone likes that idea."

"I can't help it if we like the same things," she muttered and shook her head. Then practicality took over. "Besides, only if we're sure no one else is around."

"I'm sure. Look." Jacob switched on the flashlight again, aiming toward the car.

He had driven the car into a small clearing, off even the dirt road that had led them here. A circle of old growth shielded the clearing from prying eyes while the Jeep blocked any other vehicle from entering, with its hood angled inward.

Grasping her shoulders in both hands, he spun her around. He cupped her cheek, stroking her cheekbone with the pad of his thumb. "Beautiful."

"The stars?" She understood what he'd meant but she wanted to keep the moment light.

He growled in return. "Don't play innocent." He nipped at her lower lip with a playful grin then began trailing kisses down her jaw to her neck.

There were no more words as he began to stoke the fire in her once more. He traced the curve of her hips before circling to grasp her rear, kneading, drawing her closer to him. "Mine." With that single word, he bit down harder to mark her once more, drawing her cry.

Distracted, she almost didn't notice as he maneuvered them back toward the car until she felt its front bumper at her back.

Jacob leaned away and took the blanket from her, folding it before handing it to her. "Go lay that on the hood."

What she didn't realize as she did as he'd told her was that it exposed her backside to him. He pressed his hand to the small of her back, keeping her leaned over. It was only then that she understood his wisdom, as the blanket created just enough of a cushion that no car parts would dig into her uncomfortably.

"Still wet," he whispered as he sneaked his hand up to her too-accessible pussy. She shivered as he explored before flipping her skirt up.

Without a word, he left her once more. She could not help but squirm as she stood bent over the hood of the car, exposed.

She felt him. There was no prelude, no teasing. He attacked her core with his mouth, displaying the ravenous hunger of a man who had gone without for days. She gave a yelp of surprise before it dissolved into long, low sounds of pleasure. As he circled and prodded her clit with his tongue, her legs began tremble until she thought she would slide right off the Jeep.

As if sensing her nearness, he redoubled his efforts and slipped one finger inside. He probed within her then crooked his finger until he found her G-spot.

"Come. Please let me come." She gasped the words out, clenching her hands into fists. "Please." There was no hesitation as her desperation for permission drove any semblance of shyness away.

He rose, pulling away all stimulation. The sudden absence of his mouth and fingers left her empty and cold, enough to pull her back from the edge.

That was until she felt his hard cock nestling against her slit. Rather than entering her right away, he rubbed himself along her, coating his member in her wetness. Just the anticipation of his hard, pulsing length so close to entering her brought her climbing back toward her second orgasm.

She squirmed, grinding back against him, attempting to entice. It evoked a growl as he grabbed her hips. With one smooth stroke, he entered her, pushing almost to the hilt. Normally he would take it slow, but she was so wet, so aroused that she had no problem accommodating him.

"Oh God. Yes," she whispered under her breath, reveling in being filled and stretched by him. She pushed back, only for him to tighten his grip around her hip, holding her still.

"Not yet, little one." She heard the words through his gritted teeth. They stood still, filling the surrounding silence with heavy panting.

He moved, dragging himself out ever so slowly one inch at a time, drawing out groans from both of them until only the tip of him remained inside her. Then he pulled her back, sinking himself into her once more. He leaned over, letting go of her hip with one hand.

He began to thrust at a steady pace. Her entire body rocked back and forth, forcing her hardened, sensitive nipples to rub against the material of her lace bra. Soon her body quivered nonstop once more, racing back to that edge where she could dive headlong into pleasure.

He trailed his hand downward and, without warning, he held himself still once more, deep inside, as he found her clit. She stiffened.

"You may come, as much as you want," he whispered in her ear and, with those words, pinched her sensitive nub between his thumb and forefinger

Overloaded, she came, screaming his name, the sound echoing through the woods. Her inner muscles clenched around his cock, drawing a long growl from him. She flew apart as he kept going with his attention on her clit, rolling it between her fingers, drawing out her orgasm until, wrung out, she was reduced to no more than a quivering mess.

She was still trying to catch her breath when he took hold of her hips once more. "My turn."

There was no more finesse to his movements. He thrust in and out with a renewed urgency. She moaned as he moved inside her, stimulating already over-stimulated nerves such that her body shook with mini orgasms, aftershocks that caused her to keep spasming against him.

"Ah, fuck." His strokes grew shorter and shorter until, with one last deep push, he buried himself as deep as possible, coming hard inside her. Her muscles clenched one last time, milking him within her.

Spent, he rested against her, both of them waiting for the world to stop spinning. Luna attempted to swallow to clear her dry throat, but she gave up, drawing deep breaths into her lungs instead as she rested her face against the coolness of the car hood. Her brain felt empty as she basked in the afterglow of their play.

A cold breeze swept low, enough for goosebumps to rise on her skin. "Come on, Jacob," she whispered.

He growled and wrapped an arm around her hips instead. "Mine."

When another breeze whipped by and Luna shivered, despite his body heat, he gave a reluctant sigh and withdrew from her. She felt their combined juices flowing down her thighs.

"Leave it."

When she tilted her head back, she could see the crooked, cocky grin on Jacob's lips. As he helped her straighten, he grabbed the blanket, wrapped it around her and pulled her close.

"Mine," he whispered once more, pressing a kiss on top of her head.

Deep contentment settled in her. Whatever may come in three years' time, in this moment, in this now, there was no other place she would rather be. Unfettered by doubts and fears, she smiled and looked up at him, cupping his face until their eyes met, his chocolate browns to her startling blues. And with the stars as her witness, she finally gave shape to the two little words she'd held back until now.

"All yours."

And she was.

Want to see more like this?
Here's a taster for you to enjoy!

Diomhair: Secrets Shared
Raven McAllan

Excerpt

"What do you mean this won't do?" Jess looked down at her light gray silk racer back top and dark gray skinnies. They worked well with her pale skin and ginger hair. A typical Celt, she had to be careful of her color coordination. In her mind, her clothes were perfect for a night's clubbing. "We're going clubbing. Last time we went to a club I wore these and you said they were perfect."

Kath rolled her eyes. "There's clubs, hon, and there's *clubs*. A French Connection concoction, gorgeous as it is, won't exactly hack it where we're going. Not to mention you always wear those wherever we go. No, tonight you need to wear something like this." She smoothed her hands over an almost-there mini skirt and a tiny bustier. Jess reckoned it would either cut off Kath's circulation or pop her boobs out of the material like a jack in the box.

"And here's yours. A dress instead, though, as you seem to have an aversion to my tops." With a smirk Kath handed over a tiny scrap of bright pink material.

It was a beautiful clash with Jess's hair and Jess winced.

"Go on get changed. We haven't much time." Kath held the material out to Jess, who ignored it. Kath stuffed the dress into Jess's hands, smirking as Jess took it and held onto it automatically. Jess looked on as Kath took a deep breath and her boobs almost spilled over the top of the leather bustier then shook her head in mock despair. Surely it was mere willpower that held it up?

"Kath, that top is almost indecent. What does my lovely twin say about you going out showing nearly your all?"

Kath giggled. "Jessie, love, he chose it. And he'll meet us at Diomhair later."

"Jeever?" Jess repeated, doing her best to copy Kath's accent. "What's that?" It wasn't a name she'd heard before, and she'd bet her new handbag it wasn't spelled how it was pronounced.

Kath sighed and Jess got a strange feeling deep in her stomach. Scary, like the time Kath had persuaded her to bungee jump from the Finnieston Crane, or when they'd sky dived. In her opinion, Kath was sneaky. Jess replayed Kath's words in her mind.

"Hold on, you say Jeff's meeting us?"

Kath nodded.

"Well I might as well not come then. He's worse than our mum. If a guy even smiles at me he wants his life history. Heaven help me if one asks me to dance. Especially not dressed in a scrap of almost nothing."

Kath giggled. "Er, Jessie love, I maybe need to tell you exactly where we're going. Before the car gets here."

Oh ho. Jess's body clenched. She'd seen that particular look on her friend's face before.

"Go on." She did her best to keep the wariness out of her voice and was sure she hadn't. "And stop shoving that pelmet at me, no way am I going anywhere in that."

"Diomhair, it's Gaelic for—"

"I know what it's for." Why hadn't she made the connection earlier? "Secret. Oh shit, don't tell me it's some weird pop up place, and we're blindfolded to get in? Oh no, Kath, no, no, no, you're not dragging me into anything weird. Not again. That shop in town was bad enough." Jess blushed as she remembered the bondage shop Kath had dragged her into. She'd chosen to ignore the way her nipples had puckered when she'd seen clamps and chains designed for that part of the body, and her juices had gushed looking at a clit clamp and various jewelry to decorate it. Once she'd worked out what it was meant for, that was. She might have the idea she was fairly street wise, but Jess knew now, that whatever she'd done she was a babe in arms compared to a lot of people—Kath probably being one.

Kath howled with laughter, then sobered. "Where do you think I got this from?" She ran her hands over the bustier. "Look, hon, you said you wanted to get out of your rut. Jeff and I decided this was the best way. Hell, I reckon if you'll let yourself, you'll not only enjoy the night, you'll be more than interested to indulge."

"In?"

"Whatever you fancy. Oh, Jess, don't look like you're going to watch an execution, you don't *have* to do anything. Hell, you can stop in the bar and drink orange juice if that's your preference, but you did say it was up to me to shake you up a bit."

"Hmm there's shaking, and there's *shaking*." Jess knew she sounded less than enthusiastic. "So, what exactly are we going to?" The way Kath looked at her made her heart pound and her stomach churn. She wasn't going to like the answer she was sure. "Fess up."

"BDSM play night."

She was correct, she didn't.

Jess just knew her mouth had dropped open and the heat that flooded her would show on her face. *Damn it, no. Not that. Are they crazy? They don't know, they do not know.*

"No, no way. Are you stupid or what? Not in a million years…and you're saying Jeff is okay with this? He knows what you're up to?"

Kath rolled her eyes. "Well, duh. Whose idea do you think it was anyway?"

Jess swayed, and her skin crawled as if someone was stroking her with a spider's web. She closed her eyes to shut out the images that flashed into her mind, and counted to ten. They had no idea what those letters conveyed to her. How could they? She swallowed as the contents of her stomach threatened to leave her, and the horrible sour taste in her mouth increased. Spots began to dance in front of her eyes, and a rushing noise, like the wind on a wild winter's day grew louder.

"Hey, don't look like that, there's no need to faint." Kath grabbed her friend's arm and held her steady. Gradually the roaring in Jess's ears faded, and she blinked rapidly.

"Er, that's a matter of opinion." Jess knew her voice was shaky. She probably sounded like an old woman. Shit, she felt like an old woman.

They don't know. I can't blame them. They don't know. No one does. Jess kept reciting those few words under her breath, like a mantra. She'd blocked all questions about that time of her life, and in the end, to her relief, Jeff and Kath had ceased asking. Now she wished that maybe they'd nagged her a bit more.

"Look, Kath, I honestly don't think this is a good idea. I'm not into stuff like that. I'm a teacher for God's sake, so I need to set a good example." *There, that sounds reasonable, surely?*

"Oh for heaven's sake, you're a university lecturer, not a corrupter of innocents."

Evidently not an acceptable answer then. Shit.

"I'm an accountant and Jeff is, well, Jeff. We're normal people who have a right to a healthy sex life. It doesn't matter what you do, I even know a vicar and a magistrate who have a healthy — watch my lips — healthy interest in the lifestyle."

It wasn't so much what Kath said, but how she said it that sent warning bells ringing, and a shiver down Jess's spine. She didn't care if the Prime Minister was interested, she wasn't

Liar, liar, pants on fire. She ignored the little voice that mocked her and concentrated on what Kath had said.

"Jeff is what?"

"Gorgeous." Kath giggled. "Oh come on, Jess, lighten up. Look I promise you, if you can't cope with what you see, you can leave, okay? There'll be a car waiting for you. Do I lie? Well okay," she added hastily. "I sort of did tonight, but do I over big and proper stuff? You know I don't. Seriously? You have to come."

"Why?" Not to anyone would Jess admit to the gut-churning shivers that filled her. "There's no have to about it. Weird stuff like that is so not my scene. Here take this back." She almost threw the Lycra dress Kath had given her back at her. "You go, en…enjoy yourself but count me out." She sat down on the bed behind her with a thump, trying not to cry. She'd been looking forward to a night out ever since she had told Kath she wanted to lighten up a bit. All work and no play had definitely made Jess a dull girl. But this? This was a step or twenty too far. She'd got the idea they'd go clubbing, dance until their feet hurt, grab a curry or a kebab and snigger about their evening's antics all the way home in a taxi.

"Actually, there is a must about it." The tone of Kath's voice was enough to make Jess cry. "Jeff said to tell you, if you don't come willingly, then he'll come and drag you. You need, in his words, to see where your money comes from."

Now she was in the twilight zone, surely? And there was a nest of serpents wriggling over her and nipping her skin. To say nothing of the spiders in her tummy. "How do you mean? Look, Kath, I'm seriously freaking here. My money comes from investing… Oh fuck. The sod, he said we'd move into new areas, and idiot that I am I didn't press the bugger too closely when he said he was preparing a report for me. You mean I part own the building or something?"

Kath raised her eyebrows, and the sympathy in her eyes was almost Jess' undoing.

"Or something." Kath shrugged her shoulders in an uneasy gesture. "Hey, I'm not supposed to tell you, and you can bet I'll suffer for it when I own up to spilling the beans, but you're part owner of the club." Her eyes cleared and twinkled. It was obvious the punishment didn't worry her unduly.

Jess shook her head to clear it. Her long red – no, not red – carroty hair spun around her face, and strands stuck to her cheek. She brushed them away impatiently. Had April Fool's Day been transported to February? Instead of Valentine's Day perhaps?

"Now come on, Kath, I might look like I've come up the Clyde on a Tourist Boat, and be sweet and naïve, don't you dare laugh." Kath was giggling. "That's a lie. I own the property business with Jeff, yeah, but do you think I'd not know if I was a partner in something like that? I've never heard of it before now."

"So you say, I know differently. But it's not for me to say."

A car horn blared outside. Jess shivered and wondered why it sounded ominous.

"C'mon that's for us. Are you sure you won't change?"

"Positive, in fact I might go and get a jumper." Jess turned to the wardrobe only to be pulled back from it and almost frog-marched to the bedroom door.

"Oh no you don't. You can take a coat to wear in the car." Kath pushed her along the corridor, and picked a coat up from the hooks on the wall. She patted one of the hooks as if it was her favorite piece of furniture. "Mmm, just a good height these. You got your door key in case you need it?"

Jess halted abruptly and stared at her friend. "You are screwy. Of course I'll need it, else I'll not get back in without pinching Jeff's. And what's a good height for what?"

"Oh, er, nothing, come on or we'll be late, and I'll be the one who gets the punishment. Your brother is getting a lot too creative these days." She put her hand in the small of Jess' back. The soft touch made Jess tingle. It was a long while since they'd agreed enough was enough, but she could still appreciate the warmth and love it projected.

"It's still there, isn't it?" Kath said softly. "You know we could…"

Jess shook her head and took a step back. "No, not now, you've got Jeff, and well…" And well Jess didn't know what to say. *And well, it would crucify me all over again?*

The car horn sounded again. Jess shrugged. "Someone's impatient. We'd better go, I guess."

"You do know Jeff knows we had a thing going, don't you, Jess? He's fine with it. He knows I was bi, and if you gave me the nod, I would be again." She shrugged. "My man has a capacity to understand more than I ever considered possible, and still love me and want me for who and what I am. He understands I'd never leave him, and that we both know he'd come first, but well…"

The smile on Kath's face was half-hearted and didn't chase the shadows from her eyes. Jess could have cried. It had been the right thing to do at the time. To break up and ensure neither of them had to give up their dreams. Now, on a long, cold, lonely night she wondered what if? Still, there was no going back.

"I know, but I can't, Kath, I'm sorry." She wished she could block out the memories of pain on Kath's face all those years ago. "Let's face it you're my twin's partner now, and whatever you say Jeff feels about us together, it would seem like incest or something. I'm fine, honestly." Jess knew Jeff and Kath worried about her, it had been one of the reasons she had agreed to go out with Kath that evening. Although she *had* thought it was to a regular nightclub. With hindsight, Jess wondered what had made her think that. Neither of them had ever been keen on nightclubs when they were younger, and now in their early thirties there was even less reason to want to spend hours in the midst of sweaty loud twenty-somethings.

"Ah well, if you ever can, I'm here. Now let's get a move on, before Jeff sends the cavalry to find us. Sure you won't change? You'll be positively over-dressed."

"So someone's gotta be. And there is no way I'm putting that on, so don't ask again."

Kath grimaced and shoved the so-called dress in her bag. Jess mistrusted the look on her companion's face but chose not to query it. She had a feeling she might not like the answer. Instead she followed her out of the house, and locked the door behind them.

The cab wasn't what she'd call a cab. It was a black limo with the rear windows dark. Standing by the door and holding it open was the most drop-dead hunk of a guy she'd seen in a long while. Her clit went into overdrive and sent messages pulsing through her body, and her juices out of her pussy to soak her knickers. If he was a chauffeur, his uniform was unusual to say the least. Indigo blue denims and a black silk shirt fit as if they had been sprayed onto him and there was a black leather jacket thrown carelessly on the seat next to him.

He stared at her with dark almost-black eyes, his face blank. All of a sudden, the arousal Jess had felt dried up faster than an oasis in the midst of a desert summer. She shook, not with arousal, but with worry. Something about him, and the way he watched her so closely, spelled trouble.

It seemed Kath had no such qualms as she waved to him as they approached the car. Jess had no chance to hang back because Kath held her as tight as a limpet clung to a rock.

"Thank you, Ma—David. This is Jessica."

Jess had no time to wonder what her companion had been going to say before the man bowed and smiled.

"Jessica, welcome."

She didn't think so. His voice rumbled through her, and set off a minor earthquake in her clit. She didn't welcome it. Cocoa, a good book and her yellow duck jammies had never seemed more of a good idea than then.

Home of Erotic Romance

Sign up for our newsletter and find out about all our romance book releases, eBook sales and promotions, sneak peeks and FREE romance books!

About the Author

P. Stormcrow has always been an avid reader across the fantasy and sci fi genres but early on, found herself always looking for the love story in each book. Coming to terms with her love for love later in life, she now writes steamy romances that examine social norms and challenge conventional tropes of the genre, usually on her phone. And yes, she has walked into walls and poles doing so.

When she's not reading or writing (or even when she is), she enjoys copious amounts of tea, way too much sugary treats, one too many sci fi / fantasy / paranormal TV shows (team Dean all the way) and every otome game she can possibly find.

P. Stormcrow loves to hear from readers. You can find her contact information, website details and author profile page at https://www.totallybound.com

CPSIA information can be obtained
at www.ICGtesting.com
Printed in the USA
JSHW020005110622
26965JS00001B/1

9 781839 438912